**S0-CAL-916**

PRAISE FOR *NEW YORK TIMES* BESTSELLING AUTHOR PHOEBE CONN!

MIDNIGHT BLUE

"*Midnight Blue* is a wonderfully endearing novel. Ms. Conn masterfully commandeers your attention and abducts your imagination to the high seas...a fast-paced and pleasing read. I recommend it to anyone looking for a real love story—it will make a lasting impression in your heart."

—Romance Reviews Today

"*Midnight Blue* entertains with stimulating dialogue between the hero and the heroine. I smiled all the way through the story, wondering which of the two would get the last word in. You might be surprised to know which one does."

—Fresh Fiction

WILD DESIRE

"A great Western romance...[that] will capture your heart. For a western with action, romance, and a little sensuality mixed in, this is a book fans and all readers will have to try."

—Romance Reviews Today

"Phoebe Conn has done it again with her novel, *Wild Desire*. This historical romance is a pure delight to read from cover to cover."

—Roundtable Reviews

"Ms. Conn packs quite a wallop with [*Wild Desire*]."
—*Midwest Book Review*

A Mother's Advice

"Awaken Michael's desire, but you must also practice all that I've taught you about men. Be contrite when he is angry. Be aloof when he lusts after you. Appear to be reluctant to service him...but then do so with such natural grace and abandon that he will gladly promise whatever you desire for more."

Françoise moved closer to emphasize her point. "You may become curious, which is as it should be, but do not offer up your virginity. Your whole future depends on it."

MANGO SUMMER

PHOEBE CONN

LEISURE BOOKS   NEW YORK CITY

A LEISURE BOOK ®

January 2008

Published by

Dorchester Publishing Co., Inc.
200 Madison Avenue
New York, NY 10016

ISBN 10: 0-8439-6009-4
ISBN 13: 978-0-8439-6009-9

The name "Leisure Books" and the stylized "L" with design are trademarks of Dorchester Publishing Co., Inc.

Printed in the United States of America.

10 9 8 7 6 5 4 3 2 1

Visit us on the web at www.dorchesterpub.com.

MANGO SUMMER

Chapter 1

Mango summer, steam
Stickiness between my breasts
Red Sun . . . here he comes

Jamaica, summer 1816

Françoise tightened her hold on the earl's black leather boots. "Watch his head," she warned in a frantic whisper.

Guy Barnett fought to suppress a strained grimace, but he had a firm grip on his best friend's shoulders. "He's lost weight since Amelia's death, or I swear we'd need another man to lift him."

The elegantly dressed pair struggled as they attempted to carry the man from his home without waking the servants. They had to pause and rest on the steps, but at last they reached Guy's open buggy.

His dapple-gray gelding snorted a greeting and took a restless step forward. Guy spoke softly to settle the horse, then backed up into the buggy and hauled the heavily drugged earl up beside him.

"Quickly," he urged his mistress, and Françoise provided the last shove.

She brushed off her kid gloves, and after a furtive glance over her shoulder, climbed up to join the men. "We must not let dawn catch us on the road."

Guy leaned across his sleeping friend to kiss her soundly. "Do not fret. We'll reach the boat within the hour. Just keep a steady hold on Michael so he does not slide off the seat."

Françoise placed her arm around the young man to cradle his head against her shoulder. She waited until they were on the dark trail to the cove before she spoke again. "If this bizarre scheme of yours backfires, you will die by my hand."

Unfazed, Guy dismissed her threat with a deep chuckle. "If a week with your lovely daughter fails to halt Michael's mad rush to the grave, then he is indeed doomed. I shall not begin preparing his eulogy just yet, however."

Fearing discovery, Françoise saw a menacing shape in every shadow. She shuddered and clutched the earl more tightly. "Delphine will pierce his melancholy with a single glance, but what assurance do we have that he will leave her a virgin?"

"Michael is, above all things, a man of honor, my pet. He will surely be furious with us for our part in this scheme, but he will abide by my terms."

Françoise smoothed the earl's thick, black hair off his forehead. "Do not underestimate Delphine's talents. She will not only restore Michael's soul, but steal his heart as well."

Guy shot her a sidelong glance. The moonlight revealed only a fraction of her exquisite beauty, but it was enough to make him ache with longing. "It is only a week, Françoise. I intend for Delphine to tempt him toward life, but I doubt she will enslave his heart as easily as you have mine."

"You are almost as charming a liar as I am, my lord," she said archly.

"Which is an effusive compliment indeed. Besides, there is no great danger. You have raised Delphine to be a rich man's mistress. Michael is the perfect choice in that regard."

"Indeed he is, but I want the bargain struck before she is fully his."

"You cannot seriously believe that other men would lose interest should Delphine no longer be a virgin."

The shadows hid her frown but intensified the hesitation preceding her response. "No, but the man who is her first lover will pay a steep price for that privilege."

"I was not your first," Guy chided, "and haven't I been exceedingly generous?"

Françoise lifted her hand from Michael's shoulder to caress Guy's cheek. He was not only generous, but also handsome and so devoted a lover she fully intended to keep him bound to her forever. "Indeed you have, but we negotiated first, did we not?"

"Frankly, I have forgotten everything but my endless passion for you."

Françoise smiled to herself. They were a finely matched pair, which Guy and his wife most definitely were not. The silly bitch preferred to remain in London to gossip with her vapid friends rather than spend the fragrant Jamaican nights in her husband's arms.

"You are my last lover and easily the best," she promised in a throaty whisper. "Let's hurry so that we may spend more than the dawn in my bed."

His mission of mercy all but forgotten, Guy clucked to his horse and hurried their pace toward the sea.

When the door of the small cottage swung open, Delphine leapt from the bed and darted out of the way as her mother and Guy carried the limp form of Michael Mallory over the threshold. As the pair wrestled him onto the bed, Delphine rounded the end to assist by removing his boots.

"I feared your plan had gone awry," Delphine greeted them.

"I dared not drug his brandy until after he had sent his servants to bed," Françoise replied. "I would have stripped him naked, but Guy insisted that we leave him his shirt and trousers."

Delphine dropped Michael's buttery smooth boots to the floor and tossed his socks atop them. She assumed he must own a magnificent wardrobe. He had surely been wearing a tail coat, waistcoat, and cravat earlier, but now he was dressed in only a fine linen shirt and well-tailored black woolen trousers.

She had caught a glimpse of the Earl of Clairbourne once from her mother's carriage. He had been standing on a Kingston street corner with Guy, and from his animated gestures, and Guy's laughter, it had been obvious they were arguing over something only Michael deemed important. That had been a couple of years ago, before his wife had died producing a stillborn son, and before Delphine was old enough to take a lover.

Françoise studied her only child's rapt expression and smiled knowingly. "He is as handsome a devil as I promised, is he not?"

Delphine shrugged slightly and her pale silk gown dipped low on her shoulders. "He is handsome for an Englishman," she conceded.

Anxious to leave, Françoise slipped her arm through Guy's. "You see how beautifully I have tutored her? She will drive your dear friend mad with desire while her heart skips nary a beat."

Guy leaned down to grip Michael's shoulder in a manly grasp. "I want him to recall life's pleasures this week, Delphine, so you must not simply tease him, but satisfy him as well."

"A small challenge," Delphine responded confidently. "Now you two best be gone before he wakes, or he's likely to seize your boat and strand you here with me."

"God forbid," Françoise whispered under her breath. "Give us a moment will you, my sweet?"

As Guy stepped away, he pulled a letter addressed to Michael from his coat pocket and laid it on the small bamboo table beside the iron bed. "I'll wait outside the door, but do not tarry."

"Of course not, we mustn't lose all of the night," Françoise remarked coyly, but she waited for Guy to close the door before she offered her daughter one last bit of advice.

"Guy means for you to awaken Michael's desire, but you must also practice all that I've taught you about men. Be contrite when he is angry. Be aloof when he lusts after you. Appear to be reluctant to service him with your hands and mouth, but then do so with such natural grace and abandon that he will gladly promise whatever you desire for more."

Françoise moved close to emphasize her point. "You may become curious, which is as it should be, but do not offer up your virginity without the signed agreement we've discussed. Your whole future depends upon it."

"Perhaps you should have left me a copy," Delphine replied dryly.

"Were I not wary of leaving a mark, I would slap you for that bit of insolence. It may well work to your

5

advantage with an earl accustomed to a woman's fawning attentions, but it will never be effective with me. Now I want your promise that you'll do nothing foolish in the coming week."

"I have never done anything foolish," Delphine admonished.

"Do not begin now." Françoise picked up her skirt. "Michael will probably not wake before noon, so have your fun. I almost feel sorry for the poor wretch," she sighed, and hurried out the door.

Guy quickly took her elbow. "Delphine is a beauty, but I fear she lacks your warmth."

"It is not warmth, but wanton temptation which is needed here." Despite her brief scolding, Françoise was very pleased with what her daughter had become. She had taught Delphine how to enslave men without ever caring a whit for them. The child was heartless, which was exactly how it should be for a woman forced to make her own way in the world with an all too fleeting beauty as her only asset.

" 'Tis a shame we've no boatman to take the helm," she offered slyly as Guy helped her into the sailboat they had left tied to the island's small dock. "Or I would make love to you as we sail back to the cove."

"I can manage the helm while you manage me," Guy insisted as soon as they were seated in the sleek craft. "Let's not waste another moment of this splendid moonlight."

Françoise laughed as she knelt between his knees. "I have always admired resourceful men." She removed her gloves to unfasten the buttons on his trousers to free his sex, and with a resourcefulness all her own, she gave him a most memorable voyage.

* * *

6

Delphine sat down on the edge of the bed to study her drugged captive more closely. Guy had sworn convincingly that his friend had been courting death since the passing of his wife and unborn child, but she saw no evidence of it. True, his ebony hair was a mite long, but it glowed in the lamp's light with a healthy sheen. His clothing, while understandably rumpled now, had obviously been neatly pressed earlier in the evening.

He was clean-shaven, sported a healthy tan rather than a sickly pallor, and smelled slightly of sandalwood. Even if he had lost interest in living, his valet's attentive care had kept him presentable.

In the morning, Michael's servants would find a note stating that he had left for a week of fishing. Because his staff would assume he had written the message after sipping more than a prudent amount of brandy, as had been his habit of late, the unsteadiness of the writing would arouse nary a suspicion that it might have been Guy who penned it.

"They'll believe you're with Guy, and no one will come looking for you," Delphine whispered softly. "For a week at least, you'll be mine alone, and my only challenge is to make certain that you enjoy it."

She began the task by removing his shirt. His broad chest was covered with thick black curls that narrowed to a slim trail over his flat belly. She leaned down to lick a dark nipple, then sucked it between her teeth for a playful nip. When he failed to stir, she discarded all caution, and though it took some effort to lift his hips, she removed his trousers and soft cotton drawers.

None of her mother's lovers had known it, but she had observed them for years and knew there was a great difference between a man who was aroused and one who was not. She ran a fingernail across Michael's

7

scrotum and watched the furred sack tighten. Next she stretched out along his thigh and sniffed the dark curls encircling his sex. He had a musky scent that was as appealing as his dashing good looks, and she breathed it in deeply. He was still relaxed enough for her to draw a testicle into her mouth, and she rolled it gently over her tongue before caressing its twin.

Michael moaned slightly, and wary, she sat up to assure herself that he had not wakened. When his breathing remained deep and even, she used the palm of her hand to roll his cock against his belly. It grew hard almost instantly and took on a life of its own.

Delphine leaned close to whisper against his ear, "You appear to be most willing, my lord. What do you like, a firm hold, or a light one?"

Inspired to have so responsive a partner, albeit a sleeping one, she stood to remove her gown so that she might feel the warmth of his body against her own. She slid over his hair-roughened skin and rubbed against him as an affectionate cat would. Her mother had taught her how to take her own pleasure from a man, but for now, this closeness was enough.

Sitting back, she grasped his cock and pumped slowly. "Let's put an end to this morbid longing for your late wife," she suggested, and after adjusting her own position for comfort, she licked around the sensitive corona and then slowly sucked his cock into her mouth.

He moaned again, even raised a hand in a clumsy caress, but remained lost in drugged dreams. Now convinced he could not wake, Delphine traced the pattern of engorged veins beneath her fingers as though it were a treasure map of his soul. He was so hard, and yet his skin held a velvet softness.

She sucked him toward release, then drew back and waited for a silent count of ten before renewing her attentions. Awake, he would not have been able to stand much more of such provocative teasing, but asleep, he could only protest with muffled moans.

Delphine felt for the sensitive spot behind his scrotum, where her mother had taught her to press. She wanted to be able to feel the ejaculate flowing through his cock and hold it back a moment to make his need ride him even more fiercely. Certain he was almost ready now, she tilted her head to spill her hair in a silken veil across his belly and took him still deeper.

She pressed down, felt him buck slightly as he fought for the ecstasy she refused him, but she subjected him to no more than a few seconds of such divine torture. She sat up so that he would release on his belly and observed closely as his whole body tensed, and his cream spewed forth in rhythmic spasms. Spent, he lay beside her, as relaxed as a rain puddle.

Françoise claimed some men could make love only once a night while others had nearly insatiable appetites. Delphine could not help wondering into which category Michael Mallory might fall. She took the time to clean him up with his own shirt, and then washed it and hung it outside to dry in the gentle breeze. Believing he had had long enough to rest, she coaxed him toward another convulsive release, this time entirely with her hands.

She did not want to make him sore, if such a hazard even existed, but she was enjoying herself just as her mother had insisted she would. This time she used his drawers as a convenient cloth to cleanse him. She washed the undergarment, along with his socks, and hung them outside with his shirt.

Still nude, she strolled down to the shore and turned slowly in the moonlight. Men were obviously as easily manipulated as her mother had always claimed, and she was enjoying this newfound power.

When she returned to the cottage, she pushed Michael's long, muscular legs apart and snuggled down between them. It took her a moment to find a comfortable pose, but his cock was as responsive as it had been earlier and quickly hardened against her tongue. She raked her fingernails up his thighs each time she paused to rest. He twitched slightly, as though he would be terribly ticklish when awake.

Now eager to taste him, she kept him in her mouth as he climaxed, and let his cream spill down her throat. It was slightly salty, but not at all unpleasant. Then fearing he would awake too exhausted to think, let alone understand why he had been brought to the island, she decided her experimentations had provided him with enough pleasure for one night.

She bathed him as gently as she would a babe, then pulled her nightgown back over her head, and lay down beside him. The night was too warm for covers, and his body radiated too much heat to need them. She had never shared a bed, but she found it rather pleasant to press her breasts against his side as she fell asleep.

Awash in sensation, Michael fought to escape the silvery fog hiding his lover's face. Even without seeing her, he knew she would have the sweetest mouth, and her smile would lure him past all reason. He wanted to hold her, to suckle at the breasts pressed against his thigh, but his arms were too weak to grasp more than moonbeams.

Each time she left him, he cried out for her, but his

words rang hollow in his mind. Her absence was agony, but she always returned to him, an enchantress whose eager kisses coaxed forth the ultimate bliss. He sought to lock her in an inescapable embrace, but he captured only the ends of her shimmering hair as it raked across his chest. She was as elusive as smoke, but the pleasure she gave was so tantalizingly real he craved more, and still more, until the magic of her touch seared away all memory except that of her eager kiss.

When she abandoned him for the last time, he thought he might die from wanting her, but then he felt her presence, gentle now rather than insistent. He prayed that the morning might never come, but all too soon, he awakened to the brightness of a new day.

Michael blinked, then raised an arm to shut out the glare. The pounding in his head was even worse than usual, and he knew better than to sit up quickly. Instead, he lay still and listened for the songbirds that fluttered every morning through the hibiscus growing outside his bedroom window.

Today, all he heard was the ocean's low, keening roar. His estate was located some distance from the Caribbean Sea, and through the remnants of a drunken haze, he recalled being at home last night.

Then the painful sweetness of his erotic dreams flooded through him, and his cock stiffened with more than the need to relieve himself. He opened one eye, half expecting to find himself sprawled in his favorite chair in his study, but the walls here were covered in split bamboo rather than bookshelves laden with leather-bound volumes.

He had been warned heavy drinking would create gaps in memory, but he refused to believe he had reached such a sorry state when his dreams remained so sharply defined. Dreams did not transport the dreamer far from home, however, and he risked increasing the pain in his head to sit up.

Discovering that he was not alone in the bed shocked him as much as the surprising change in his surroundings, and for a long moment he simply stared at the blonde nestled by his side. Her long, silvery hair spilled over her shoulder and hid her face, but he knew exactly who she was, and recognition filled him with a cold fury.

He grabbed her shoulder and shook her. "My God! What have you done?"

Jarred awake, Delphine brushed her flowing hair aside and sat up. She smothered a wide yawn behind her hands and then regarded Michael with cool green eyes framed by long, dark lashes. "What have I done with what?" she asked politely.

"With my clothes for a start."

Delphine surveyed the striking blue eyes, beneath the decidedly hostile tilt of his dark brows. A quick downward glance revealed his cock did not share his feelings, and she could barely contain her smile.

"I folded your trousers and laid them across the chair in the corner. Your shirt, drawers, and socks have been freshly laundered and are hanging outside."

Her voice was soft and low, slightly husky, and he recognized it instantly from an amused comment in his dreams. He sprang from the bed to yank on his trousers, but blinded by a pain threatening to split his skull in two, he reeled against the wall. The blonde rolled off the bed and ran to his side, but he shoved her away and slid to the floor.

The pain rolled down Michael's body in waves. He

propped his elbows on his knees and cradled his head in his hands. "What have you done to me?"

Delphine knelt beside him. "I've not harmed you in any way, my lord. I never would."

Michael glared at her. Her loose-fitting nightgown had slipped off her left shoulder to reveal a smooth creamy breast whose pale pink tip was adorned with a small gold ring. Only one type of woman would pierce her nipples, but this lovely creature nearly glowed with innocence, confusing him all the more.

"If you didn't do this to me, then you know who did. Tell me the brigand's name this instant."

Instead, Delphine left him to fetch Guy's letter. "This letter explains everything. Would you like me to read it to you?"

"Yes, but cover yourself before you do."

Her nightgown was now in place and Delphine was uncertain what he meant. "It's too warm to wrap myself in a shawl. You'll simply have to avert your glance if you don't find me pleasing."

Michael responded with a rude snort. She was pleasing all right. Or at least she had been incredibly so until he had discovered she was real. "Just read."

After again kneeling at his side, Delphine removed the single sheet of monogrammed stationery from its envelope and smoothed it against her thigh. "Guy Barnett wishes you to know he regards you too highly to allow you to drink yourself to death, so he arranged for you to recuperate here at his fishing cottage. He promises to return for you in a week, and bids me to keep you entertained."

Michael ground his teeth to force back a curse. "Is that what you were doing last night?"

Delphine smiled sweetly. "I didn't realize that you'd recall our games."

"Well, I do, and in vivid detail. You must have failed to use enough of whatever drug you forced down my throat."

"I was not there," Delphine insisted. "You will have to direct your complaints to Guy when he arrives."

"You may be certain I will," Michael vowed darkly. He shut his eyes against the bright morning light, but it failed to ease his pain. "Get me a drink. Rum, whiskey, wine, anything will do."

"Did you not understand Guy's intention? We have no spirits here, only rainwater collected in the cistern."

Michael began to swear, but the sound of his own voice worsened his pain and forced him to bite off the vile words in mid-curse. "I will kill him for this."

Delphine reached out to sift his hair through her fingers. It was thick, but as silky as her own. "Go back to bed," she encouraged. "The next time you wake, you'll feel better."

Her voice was enticingly sweet, but Michael refused to lose focus. "How do you know Guy Barnett? He dotes on his mistress and keeps only one."

With a small shrug, Delphine allowed her nightgown to slip low over her breasts. "I am Françoise's daughter, Delphine."

Michael leaned back to tilt his head against the wall. "Are her nipples pierced too?"

"Only the left, like mine." Delphine cupped her breasts to raise them to his view.

Michael shut his eyes rather than watch her flaunt the two perfect rounds. The tips were as sweet as pink rosebuds, justifying her pride, but still, her total lack of modesty appalled him. "It must have hurt."

"Only a moment, but women endure all manner of tortures to be beautiful for men. Now every time you look at me, you'll think of the ring, and wish to suck it into your mouth."

"Never," Michael spit out through clenched teeth.

Delphine rose with an easy grace and dropped the letter. "In his last sentence, Guy forbids you to take my innocence, but apparently you'll not even be tempted."

"After last night, how can you expect me to believe that you are any more innocent than Françoise?" he argued.

"Believe whatever you wish. You really should go back to bed, my lord. I'll catch us some fish for our breakfast so there will be something for you to eat when next you wake."

Michael was incredulous. "You intend to fish?"

"There is nothing particularly difficult about tossing a line into the sea, but perhaps you would rather catch our breakfast."

"I cannot even stand."

Michael watched her leave the small cottage with a gentle sway that made him wonder if her bottom weren't as gorgeous as her bosom. Convinced it was, he dragged himself to his feet, and staggered outside to use the privy. As he took hold of his cock, it was her small, soft hands he felt, and her mouth he longed to fill.

Chapter 2

Oceanic rust
Cinnamon flavored sighs
Gray gulls brush the waves

When Michael awoke, the sunlight slanted low across the cottage floor. His head still ached, and he wanted a drink. That Guy would strand him with a lascivious virgin was one thing, but it was quite another to force him into sobriety. Certain there had to be spirits of some kind hidden in the one-room cottage, he shoved off the bed and began a thorough search.

Delphine's small trunk held silken nightgowns scented with lavender sachet, bottles of perfumed oil, a hairbrush, and a journal written in French. That the week might be reduced to a few lines in her diary infuriated him anew, and he tossed the book aside.

There were towels stacked on a shelf beside the washstand but there was nothing concealed in their folds. Beside the water pitcher and bowl, he had been left a small round mirror, new toothbrushes, shaving soap and a razor, which would make a very fine weapon upon Guy's return.

There were pewter plates, mugs, and sterling utensils on the table, along with ink and a pen. Fishing

16

poles and nets were heaped in the corner. There was a jug of oil for the lamp, and extra linens and blankets for the bed in a chest beneath the window, but even a search under the mattress failed to turn up a single drop to imbibe.

Michael stood for a moment with his hands on his hips, but he could devise nothing harsh enough to re-pay Guy's treachery in kind. That left him with but a single target for his fury. He grabbed his shirt and made his way down to the rocky point where Delphine stood fishing.

She was wearing a broad-brimmed straw hat, but under it, her hair floated free in the breeze and her cheeks held a bewitching blush. She had drawn the back hem of her nightgown up through her legs and knotted it at her waist to fashion a pair of pantaloons. Her bare legs were long, slender and lightly tanned. No decent woman would expose more than an ankle, but she greeted him with a smile as though she rou-tinely paraded about in such flimsy attire.

"Have you no other clothing?" he called as he ap-proached.

"I've a dozen gowns, all as pretty as this one. With the weather so warm, I'll not need anything more."

He had discovered as much, but scowled rather than admit he had searched her trunk. He gestured toward her line, which drifted slack in the sea. "You've not caught anything?"

"The bonito are plentiful here, and I caught a fine one for breakfast and an equally tasty one at mid-day. It's a pity you were too tired to join me for either meal. Now I'm looking for our supper, but why don't you bring out a line if you doubt I'll have any luck."

"I'm a horseman, and I'd rather ride than fish."

Delphine raised her hand to shade her eyes. "Well, I've not seen a horse near about, so you'll have to fish for a pastime."

"All I want is a drink. Haven't you a way to signal Guy? What if one of us fell ill or was injured? How would you summon him?"

"What do you expect, a signal fire?" They were surrounded by the azure sea, and she gestured toward the horizon. "When you can't see the coast of Jamaica, how do you expect them to notice a fire here?"

Confounded by that display of logic, Michael shook his head. "We might be able to signal a passing ship."

"We're not in the shipping lanes. That's why the fishing is excellent here. Have you never come here with Guy?"

"No, I told you I'd rather ride."

"Yes, you did, forgive me if I appear too curious."

Clearly disgusted, Michael raked his hands through his hair. "After the diabolical way you treated me last night, I'll forgive nothing."

"As you wish," Delphine assured him, hiding her concern. "But I must protest that this was Guy Barnett's plan rather than mine, and I would like to apologize for my part in what was obviously an ill-conceived plot against you. But when Guy told me he feared his best friend would not live out the year, naturally I wished to help him in whatever way I could."

"Why? I'm nothing to you."

Delphine regarded him with a slight smile. "But you mean a great deal to Guy, whom my mother adores, and I could not refuse him."

He stepped closer. When he had been stretched out on the bed last night, or collapsed against the wall this morning, she had not realized how tall he was, nor

18

how muscular. She took a cautious backward step.

"When did Guy begin counting the week—with last night, or today?" he asked.

"Today. I'll keep track of the days if you like."

"I can count," he nearly snarled, "but how am I to endure seven days with nothing but the sea and sun?"

He appeared revolted by the prospect, and insulted, Delphine tightened her hold on the bamboo pole. "Guy expected me to provide ample entertainment for you. Unfortunately, he appears to have been mistaken; had I known you were such a disagreeable sort, I'd have brought along a cask of brandy for you myself."

Michael set his dark gaze on the sea. "Do not patronize me. I was drugged and abducted. I should have Guy and your mother hanged for the crime and you along with them."

Delphine shook out her hair. "I do wish that you'd speak in a more moderate tone. I fear you're frightening the fish."

"But not you?"

His glance was harsh, darkly skeptical, and she forced her attention back to her line. "The day is far too lovely to waste mulling over something so dire."

Michael remained with her, but was silent a long while. "I'm going to search the island for wood to build a raft."

Delphine raised her chin slightly. She had not only walked around the island, but across it. The only wood of sufficient size to build a raft had been transported by boat to construct the cottage. She was not about to inform him of that, however. Her line jerked, and she was grateful for the catch.

"You'll need to eat before you go off exploring. I've already gathered driftwood for a cooking fire."

"How many days have you been here?"

"I came to the island a few hours ahead of you, but I've been here several times since I was a child. It's such a peaceful place, but then, I wasn't brought here against my will."

Michael reached out to take the pole and yanked the twitching bonito from the water. "I did not realize that Françoise would appreciate such an isolated retreat."

"You might be surprised by what my mother enjoys."

"After last night? I doubt it."

Delphine had to turn away to hide her smile. She picked up the knife she had laid upon the rocks. "Would you care to gut the fish, or shall I?"

"You'd trust me with a knife?"

"I trust Guy's judgment," Delphine insisted, and handed him the blade. "He would never have brought us together if he'd believed there was the slightest danger that you'd harm me."

Michael turned the knife slowly in his hand. It was small, but possessed a keen edge. "He was wrong about how I would regard you. He could have been equally mistaken about your safety."

"True, but when you think so little of me, why would you jeopardize your wealth and future by harming me? It would make no sense, and you've impressed me as a man devoted to reason."

"You impress too easily," Michael swore, but he bent down to clean the fish and then led the way back to the cottage. While Delphine sat down in the shade, he fanned the embers in the fire pit and added fresh wood from the pile she had stacked against the house.

"Why would peace appeal to a child?" he mused aloud.

Pleased he had remembered her comment, Delphine chose her words with care. "I am not my mother, and it was always a relief to escape the demands of her life."

Michael's eyes narrowed as he turned toward her. "Was it Françoise who was with me last night?"

"Guy holds you in high regard, but he would never be that generous with his mistress. I was the one who shared the bed. You have a magnificent body, my lord, and it was truly a pleasure to be with you."

Michael's hands balled into fists at his sides. "Have you no idea how easily I could kill you and dispose of your body? I could swear you fell from the rocks while fishing, and were swept away by a large wave before I could save you."

Delphine's gaze drifted slowly over his chest, caressed his narrow hips, and then slid down the length of his legs to his bare feet. Even his feet were well-formed. "A man of honor would never do such a terrible thing."

Michael responded with a bitter oath. He bent to flip the fish on the grill, then brushed off his hands. "Even honorable men can be driven mad. I'm not hungry. I'm going to take a look around the island."

"As you wish. I'll save part of the fish for your return."

"You needn't bother."

Delphine watched him walk the path to the shore with a long, confident stride. He picked up a stone and skipped it across the water. Despite his eagerness to explore, he remained there a long while. The waves crashed against the shore and sent foamy tongues speeding to his toes.

Though Delphine was loath to admit it, she was even more perplexed than he. Men had always pursued her mother, and Françoise had accepted only those affections she craved. She had dismissed the others as though they were as insignificant as shopkeepers whose wares displeased her. Delphine had expected her life to be equally blessed, but clearly that was not to be. She possessed her mother's remarkable fair beauty, but must somehow lack the essential element which drew men's love.

It was a distressing discovery, and she wondered if perhaps she was the one who ought to be seeking an escape from the island.

Focused on the restless splendor of the sea, Michael walked a long way before he cast a single glance toward the beach where he had hoped to find a serviceable boat washed ashore. All he found was driftwood cast along the rocks in tangled piles. Against his will, his thoughts turned to Delphine.

The young women in his circle had curtsied demurely, hidden their smiles behind fans, and muffled their giggles in their gloves whenever he had spoken their names. None had ever regarded him as boldly as Delphine continually did with an unflinching gaze that damned him without a blink.

He rounded a rocky point and sat down, desperately thirsty for the burn of fine whiskey or brandy's numbing warmth. He had slept last night, but only because he had been drugged. Tonight, there would be nothing to keep his ghosts at bay, save for a delectable virgin, who observed him with an insulting detachment. He could accept Guy's gift and pursue her, but that would simply be trading one nightmare for another.

Frustrated in his efforts to get off the island rather than succumb to a lovely nymph half his age, he shoved himself to his feet. All he needed was a drink, and then all temptation would fade. He had seen mangoes growing near the house and brandy could be made from any fruit, but he was uncertain how long it would take to ferment. Too long, he feared.

When he returned to the house, Delphine was still seated where he had left her. He sat down and reached for a hunk of the fish she had pushed to the edge of the grill.

"There is an abundance of foliage on this miserable isle, but not a single stick of sufficient size to serve as an oar, let alone a plank in a raft."

Delphine leaned forward. "I must admit to being relieved, because if you'd found the materials to construct a raft, I'd have felt obligated to accompany you."

"In your nightgown," Michael scoffed.

"I am a creature of the sea, and I would have brought you luck no matter what I wore."

Her sea-green gaze was as convincing as her words. Even seated in the shade, she shimmered all silver and gold, and he believed her odd pronouncement. He cocked his head.

"Why the sea?" he asked.

"My father was a ship's captain, a Dane, who was lost in a storm soon after I was born. Mother says I have his eyes. I've always felt closest to him at the shore. To me, visiting this isle is like coming home."

Touched by her wistful comment, Michael nodded thoughtfully. "I'm sorry."

Delphine shrugged off his sympathy, and her gown again dipped low off her shoulders. "Tell me about your horses. Do they comfort you?"

"No, nothing can." A troubled light filled his eyes as he gazed out toward the sea.

Delphine resisted the impulse to touch him. She certainly wanted to, but knowing how little he would welcome her embrace, she looped her arms around her bent knees. "We have so many hours to pass, and I'd like to hear about your stable."

Michael shook his head. "Do you know anything at all about horseflesh?"

Taken aback by the harshness of his tone, Delphine nevertheless quickly recovered. "Very little actually, but I can at least distinguish a stallion from a bull."

The unexpected barb forced a laugh from Michael before he could contain it. He could not recall the last time a woman had said something that amused him. It made it difficult to dislike her, which he was adamantly set on doing. He shoved himself to his feet.

"The walk made me hungry. I'll catch more fish." He grabbed her pole and started toward the shore.

"Good luck," Delphine called after him.

Michael refused to respond, but he feared the only luck he would encounter on this godforsaken isle would be bad. He climbed over the rocks, baited the hook with one of the mussels he had gathered earlier, and tossed his line into the sea. When he glanced over his shoulder, Delphine was watching him from the bluff behind the cottage.

There was no escaping her, but he turned back toward the sea and fought to shut her out of his mind. Then a few minutes later she appeared, not twenty feet away, and nude, walked into the sea. It was a shock not merely to his senses, but to his sense of propriety as well. She was tall and willowy, with gently flaring hips, a narrow waist, and as pretty a pair of breasts as he had ever seen.

He had caught only a glimpse as she strode past him, but he had grown hard the instant she came into view. He watched her swim and was filled with as desperate a yearning as a merchant seaman daydreaming of a mermaid.

Ashamed by how quickly his body betrayed him, he told himself it had simply been too long since he had lain with a woman. Then he recalled last night's debauchery and gave up that convenient lie.

Unable to turn away, he watched Delphine swim with long graceful strokes in the trough between the gently cresting waves. She swam with an easy rhythm, and apparently ignoring the dangers in the constantly shifting sea, appeared to be as at home as a child frolicking in a placid pond.

He felt a sudden tug on his line, but let the unfortunate fish thrash and flop unheeded. He could envision the whole week clearly: Delphine would show him no mercy in her quest to ensnare him in a web of passion and he was equally determined to resist her wiles. She would parade herself naked from dawn to dusk. He would admire the sight, but go no further.

The chit had not an inkling of what icy restraint he possessed. Let her dance around him clothed only in an enticing smile. He would merely welcome the breeze.

He ate the fish alone, but as he finished, Delphine rounded the house carrying a basketful of mangoes. Her hair was freshly washed, and she had donned a fresh nightgown. She smiled pleasantly, as though they were neighbors who frequently exchanged gifts of produce.

After going inside to fetch a plate, she joined him to slice the fruit. "I do hope you enjoy mangoes."

"Not really," he admitted, but he accepted a slice. Perhaps it was merely hunger, but the exotic fruit tasted especially good that day, and he took another slice and another.

"I won't share the bed tonight," he announced firmly.

Delphine licked the sweet juice from her fingers. "Do as you wish; I'll not insist upon it, but I doubt that you'll find the sand comfortable."

Dumbfounded, Michael stared at her a long moment. In the gathering dusk, she was even more lovely, and he had to force himself to look away. "I meant to take the bed."

"Really? You are merely a guest here, my lord, and though I've invited you into my bed, you've no right to ban me from it."

"No right?" Michael gasped.

"None," Delphine almost purred. "You could rig a hammock from a blanket, but if you're not used to sleeping in one, you might fall out frequently and pass a most uncomfortable night."

"Just how am I to hang a hammock without any trees?" Michael clenched his fists but the gesture failed to relieve the temptation to fit his hands around her neck.

"A small problem. I imagine you could construct two towers from rocks and secure the ends of the hammock from those."

"That's the worst idea I've ever heard."

Delphine favored him with a sweet smile. "It scarcely compares to stranding you here, does it?"

"No!" Michael exclaimed as he wondered how long it would take him to swim to Jamaica.

"Please forgive me if I've upset you again," Delphine murmured. "When you are so averse to accepting my attentions, I'll not force them upon you. We can share the bed without your needing to worry that I will compromise you in any way."

Michael spit out his reply through clenched teeth. "I have absolutely no intention of ever sharing a bed with you."

"Again," Delphine stressed. "You've already shared it one night, which I believe was immensely enjoyable. At least I enjoyed it."

"Have you no shame?"

Delphine leaned forward as she shrugged to make certain Michael caught a glimpse of the gold ring. "No, why should I? Men and women were created so that each could give the other abundant pleasure. To pretend otherwise is ridiculous."

"Are you calling me ridiculous?" he snapped.

"No, of course not, my lord. But to pretend that our bodies do not fit together perfectly is to ignore the truth. No one else will ever know what transpires between us, so why not allow yourself to revel in it?"

Unable to think of any coherent response, Michael stood and silently strode off into the night. He was hard and ached to strip off his trousers and shove her head into his lap, but to give in to her would be to welcome Guy's fiendish plot.

In preparation for bed, Delphine brushed her hair with distracted strokes. She had attempted a variety of her mother's favorite ploys, but none had proven to be effective with the mighty Lord Clairbourne. Perhaps he would warm to her as the week progressed, but what if he did not?

She had seen through her mother's insistence that

Delphine be the one to seduce Michael Mallory. Françoise would never admit to jealousy, but at nineteen, her daughter was more rival than pretty child; and it was time Delphine had a wealthy lover who would provide her with a luxurious apartment of her own.

Guy and Françoise might have considered Michael to be the perfect man for her—after all, he was not only rich, but handsome as well—but they had obviously failed to consider Michael's feelings. Perhaps he merely preferred petite brunettes, or voluptuous redheads, and never gave blondes a second glance.

But despite his perpetual frown, she rather liked him. He provided nothing in the way of encouragement, but still, she understood his dismay at having been taken from his home. The one time he laughed, she had glimpsed the charming man he once had been. Her mother never advised humor as the way to a man's heart, but perhaps it was an important avenue Françoise had simply overlooked.

Troubled by the day's failures Delphine could not fall asleep for a long while. She came awake when Michael pulled the door closed behind him. She waited for him to launch a new argument over the bed, but he leaned back against the door and remained silent.

There was nothing menacing in his relaxed stance, and she wondered if perhaps he was too proud to speak, or too tired. She moved over to create room for him and patted the feather mattress lightly.

"We can just sleep," she whispered.

After a lengthy hesitation in which he appeared to be debating the wisdom of such a move, Michael finally approached the bed and then stretched out with his back toward her.

Delphine waited for him to wish her good night, but

when he did not, she closed her eyes and promptly went back to sleep. When next she woke, Michael was coiled around her like a vine. His breathing was low and deep, but clearly he had wanted to be close to her in his dreams.

She was tempted to coax him awake with an intimate touch, but fearing such a ploy would infuriate him anew, she lay pliant in his arms. He smelled of the sea, and it frightened her to think he had gone swimming after sunset. He had a powerful build and was undoubtedly strong, but the Caribbean currents could be treacherous.

She sighed against his chest, but couldn't sleep. Instead, all too aware of her distracting companion, she awaited dawn. When at last the room began to lighten with the coming day, Michael shifted slightly, and she quickly slipped from his grasp. She rolled off the side of the bed, and hurriedly left the cottage to seek the tranquility that eluded her in Michael's arms.

Michael found Delphine seated on the sand near the rocks where they had fished. She was wearing her hat and writing in her journal. He knelt beside her.

"What have you written about me?" he asked.

His beard had formed an attractive shadow yesterday, but she was surprised that he had not bothered to shave that morning. His beard grew low on his cheeks to provide a handsome accent to his finely chiseled features, but no man who wished to impress a woman sported a new growth of beard. It was in her view, a deliberate insult.

She carefully replaced the lid on the bottle of ink and set it aside with her pen. She closed her journal but left it cradled in her lap.

"I do so hate to disappoint you again, my lord, but I'm gathering images for my poetry, not recording your every frown and sneer. But perhaps you can explain why my journal lay in a corner rather than in my trunk where I left it."

Michael ignored her pointed remark. "You write poetry?" he asked. "Pretty verses about the softness of bunnies or the sweet scent of a rose?"

Not surprised by his condescending tone, Delphine responded in kind. "No, today I'm describing the map of veins on your cock."

Michael nearly choked as his breath caught in his throat. Aghast at her taunt, he made a grab for her journal, intent upon hurling it into the waves, but she caught his shoulder and, off-balance, he went sprawling.

She leapt to her feet and with the book clasped tightly against her side, ran along the damp sand at the water's edge. He picked himself up and sprinted after her. He gained on her steadily, but when he finally succeeded in catching her arm and spinning her around to face him, she laughed, and all too willingly came into his arms.

Her hat knocked askew, she smiled up at him. "When you have such a magnificent cock, my lord, why would you object to my idolizing it in verse?"

Michael shut her mouth with his own, but she drank in his savage kiss, wrapped her free arm around his waist and pressed close. He had never kissed a woman with such brutal passion, and he returned it with an intensity that shocked him as much as her provocative words. Her taste was delicious, and he wanted more and still more, until disgusted by the lust she aroused, he took a firm grip on her arms and forced her a step away.

She glanced down at the front of his trousers, where his arousal stretched the fabric invitingly. "Surely you don't wish to stop now," she chided.

In truth, Michael did not, but as he struggled to regain his breath, what little remained of his self-respect reinforced his resolve. "You are not to write a single word about me, not one, or I'll tear your book into tiny pieces and toss them into the fire."

His anger was so convincing, Delphine thought better of pointing out that any verse consigned to the flames would still live in her memory to later be transcribed anew. Hoping to appear contrite, she licked her lips, which tasted of him.

"When you offer such a delightful distraction, I'll have no desire to pen poetry, my lord."

It was Michael who provided the shove this time, and he turned his back on her and walked back the way they had come. Delphine was sorry he had not been moved by her kiss, but encouraged that he had kissed her several times before he had recalled his anger and broken away.

Other men had kissed her cheek, but none had shown Michael's daring and invaded her mouth with a warm tongue. It might have been rage that had prompted the exchange, but his masterful kisses had been worth it. Convinced she would be able to learn many more intimate lessons before the week was out, she hummed softly to herself and continued on around the island.

Chapter 3

Pelican vespers
Hinged wings soar in creaking flight
Shadows on the sea

Michael was furious as he stripped and ran into the water. He swam not with Delphine's relaxed strokes, but with remarkable vigor until it dawned on him that she might hide or burn what few clothes he had. He strode toward the shore with water streaming off his shoulders and was relieved beyond measure to find his shirt and trousers still lying where he had thrown them.

He shook water droplets in all directions, yanked on his trousers, and was just donning his shirt when Delphine came wandering along the beach looking as though she had not a care in the world.

He refused to greet her on his way to the cottage for the fishing poles. He tossed her one and then smashed a mussel against the rocks for bait. His expression a clear indication of his dark mood, he flung his line into the sea.

Before following him out on the rocks, Delphine fetched her ink and pen from the sand, then went into the cottage to place them on the table and hide her journal in the rafters. When she returned to the beach, she shared Michael's bait, but took care to take up a position well out of his reach. When neither of them had a bite, she was the one to attempt conversation.

"I had hoped my first kiss would be far more romantic," she commented wistfully.

Michael responded with an exasperated sigh. "Have you forgotten where you kissed me night before last?"

"By where, may I assume that you are not referring merely to the cottage?"

"You may." This time Michael punctuated his remark with a derisive grunt.

"Well, yes, it is true that I kissed you, if what I did can be described as simply a kiss, but it was nothing like your kiss this morning. You kissed me as though you could barely control your passion."

Michael shook his head. "What you tasted was disgust."

"Now you have confused me. Why would a man go against his true emotion and kiss a woman who disgusted him?"

"Why indeed," Michael responded darkly. "Perhaps it was simply because a gentlemen does not strike a lady."

Delphine could not contain her smile. "Now I believe I understand. You were pushed to take action, so chose the only acceptable option."

Michael offered a reluctant nod. "You could say that."

"Good. Will you mind awfully if I push you again?"

Michael shifted his grip on the pole as though he meant to use it as a club. "No, you ought not to risk being so foolish."

"And you ought not to waste a beautiful day with

an obliging woman," Delphine countered. Her line dipped in the water, and she gave it a quick yank to suspend the bonito above the gentle waves lapping against the rocks. "It looks as though I've caught the first fish. Please join me for breakfast."

"I'll wait to catch another," Michael replied, but craving a challenge other than combating the delectable Delphine's seductive invitations, he used the knife she had left behind to carve the end of his fishing pole into a spear. It took him far longer than he had anticipated, but he was inordinately proud when he finally speared the largest bonito they had seen.

He carried it up the beach to their grill, but by that time Delphine had already finished her portion of the first fish and was eating a mango. "You'll have to try using a spear," he urged. "It makes fishing an adventure."

Delphine's appreciative glance raked him from head to toe. "My interest lies in an entirely different type of adventure, but if it will please you, I'll try it later."

Michael added another piece of driftwood to the fire, placed his catch on the grill and sat down opposite her. Unable to look away, he watched her lick the juice from her fingers and fought to ignore the memory of how skillfully she had used her tongue on him.

"I wish we had some apples, or oranges, or better yet a ham," he said.

"Yes, we really should have been left with more provisions." He had bruised her mouth, and it was all she could do to eat without wincing. "Although I made a passable chutney by chopping a mango and spreading it on my fish."

If annoyed him that she could enjoy herself when all

he longed to do was escape. He prodded the fire with another piece of driftwood. Then a brilliant idea came to him in a flash, and he stood and began to pace.

"Perhaps I was being too hasty when I ridiculed your suggestion that I build rock towers for a hammock. I still doubt that it would work, but I could certainly construct a small shelter so we needn't share the cottage."

He appeared enormously pleased with himself, but Delphine was utterly dismayed. "Where did you hope to build this shelter, my lord?"

"On the other side of the isle, of course. That way neither of us would be bothered by the other."

Delphine fought to hang on to her composure while he turned his fish. She was only partially successful. "You are no bother to me," she emphasized softly, her mind racing as she struggled to recall any of her mother's advice that might be of use in dissuading him.

Michael sat down again and braced his elbows on his knees. "But you are a great bother to me, Miss . . . do you even have a last name?"

"I am Delphine Antoine," she replied with a slight lift to her chin.

Michael frowned. "Antoine? That does not sound like a Danish name."

"No, it isn't, but I didn't say that my father and mother were wed."

There was no shame in her direct gaze, and Michael was the one to look away. "Miss Antoine, then," he began again, "it would make this ghastly week easier to bear if we were not forced to spend so much time together."

"Not for me," Delphine replied. "I was brought

here to be your companion, and if you refuse my company as well as my affection, then I'll have no purpose whatsoever here."

Michael now noticed the slight swell to her lower lip and felt sorry that his angry kisses had done her even the slightest harm. "I did not request your company or your affection," he reminded her.

Thinking this was too much, Delphine looked down at her hands. It would be pathetic to beg, she reminded herself. She had been raised to cater to men, but her first attempt to enchant one had failed miserably. It was a shattering blow to her feelings, and her eyes filled with tears.

Michael was fascinated by Delphine's downcast expression. Had not her every sly glance and pointed word shown her to be a tart, he would have believed that she actually cared. "I'm not abandoning you," he said more gently. "I can accept the fact that Guy meant well, but he misjudged my mood badly, and I've no need of you."

There, he had said it again, and the sting was just as sharp. "You'll have to explain your decision to him then," Delphine murmured. "I should not want him to blame me for failing to keep you entertained."

"You need have no fears in that regard. First, I intend to hit him hard enough to knock him flat; then I'll haul him to his feet and denounce this insane plot of his in exquisite detail. When I finish with him, he'll not even recall that you were here."

Delphine still felt as though she were at fault. She had been sweet. She had been brazen and tried several approaches in between. None had touched his heart. That meant she would have to find another man, perhaps a great many, before she encountered one who found her acceptable as his mistress. She could so easily imagine a whole string of handsomely dressed gentlemen shaking their heads regretfully and stating that she simply would not do.

"You must excuse me," she insisted in a desperate rush and hurried off toward the path to the bluff.

Michael had meant to protect himself, not to be cruel, but the tears in Delphine's eyes turned the taste of the prized fish to dust.

Michael scouted the island for the best location to construct a shelter. He wanted to build on high ground and, like the cottage, be unaffected by the tides. But he did not wish to have to carry every rock to the site either. Finally he found a gully where jagged stones had tumbled from the bluff to the sea. He walked a little farther, then finding no other such abundance of building materials, he chose the gentle slope bordering the gully.

He had led an active life and possessed a muscular build, but he had never worked as a laborer and soon tired of lifting the scattered rocks and arranging them in a semi-circle. Sweat dripped into his eyes, and it shocked him to realize how thirsty he was for a simple glass of water.

He sat down on the largest of his newly relocated boulders and tried to recall how he had felt when he had awakened that morning. To his amazement, all he remembered was his curiosity about Delphine's whereabouts. There had been no blinding headache, no terrible thirst for spirits, which was ample proof he was not the pitiful drunk Guy had feared him to be.

It was not a particularly comforting thought, however, when it still left him stranded there. The ring of stones was a start, but at his present rate, it would take him the rest of the day to create walls high enough to top with driftwood and sparse shrubbery. And despite the enormity of the effort, Delphine would still have all the fresh drinking water.

He carried his shirt around the isle and donned it as he approached the cottage. He rapped lightly at the partially open door, and Delphine appeared with her pen in hand.

"Yes?" she inquired sweetly.

"Is there a jug I might borrow to carry water?" he asked.

Delphine brushed a strand of hair from her eyes. "Only the porcelain one on the washstand. Would that do?"

"Yes, but then how would you carry water from the cistern into the house?"

Delphine relaxed against the doorjamb. "It appears we are at an impasse, my lord, but perhaps a squall will appear, and you'll be able to collect rainwater of your own."

"In what, my hands?"

He was annoyed with her again, but Delphine had had time to adjust to his stubborn need to avoid her. "It was your choice to go elsewhere, so you will just have to solve whatever problems your departure creates on your own. If not a pitcher, I can at least provide you with a pewter mug."

Michael took a step back and offered a mock bow. "Thank you, it will have to do."

He filled the mug from the cistern, poured the water down his throat and then refilled it. Still too hot, he showered water over his head and let it splash his shirt. The day was warm, and the linen would dry quickly. He sipped the next mugful slowly, but when he turned, he found Delphine at the side of the cottage observing him.

"I fear the sea provides only enough driftwood for one fire," she called to him. "You're welcome to use mine, unless of course, you've discovered some other means to cook your meals."

"No, and I thought there was sufficient wood laying about to fashion a roof."

Delphine remained where she stood, forcing him to approach her. The breeze ruffled her hair and teased the hem of her nightgown. "I'm afraid not, although I suppose you could sleep beneath your roof tonight, and if we run out of driftwood tomorrow, we'll just have to burn it."

"We must have more than a day's worth stacked by the cottage," he argued.

"We shall see," she offered agreeably. "I'm sorry there's no shovel so that you could dig a hole and put up your own privy."

Michael had completely overlooked the need for such a vital structure. His thirst gone, he had to force himself to drink the last of the water. "It appears that I'll have to make do with yours."

"Everything belongs to Guy," she reminded him. "But we are missing so much. I have already begun a list so that he might better provide for his next guests' comfort."

"How very thoughtful of you." Michael was fascinated by the puffiness of her lower lip. She kept flicking the tip of her tongue across it, and each swipe made him ache to taste that luscious tongue again.

"What about the mangoes?" he asked. "Does your generosity extend to them?" He moved so close their bare toes were nearly touching.

Delphine looked down, and then peered up at him through her thick sweep of lashes. "My generosity extends much further, but you've refused to accept my gifts."

"Gifts?" Michael repeated, but his voice had grown husky with desire, and he feared he had unwittingly revealed too much.

"How else would you describe my affection?" When he did not reply, she ran her fingertips down his arm. "Perhaps it would be easier if you pretended I were someone else, a woman you would have chosen to share this week."

Her voice was honey smooth. He could not even remember another woman when he was with her. The gold ring in her nipple came to mind, just as she had predicted it would, and he swallowed hard to dispel the taunting image.

"I'm no good at pretense," he swore darkly.

"Then just close your eyes," Delphine murmured. "Call me by another's name, remember her perfume, and the softness of her skin. You'll create her in your mind."

Michael closed his eyes, but rather than exercise his imagination, he recalled Delphine walking nude into the sea. She was the only woman he craved, but when she slid her hand down the front of his trousers, he grabbed hold of her wrist to push her away. It was too late, she had already felt him grow hard.

He flung the mug into her hands and walked passed her. "I came for water, nothing more."

Head down, his arms pumping, he reached the ring of stones without drawing a steady breath. He had never met a man, let alone a woman, with such fierce determination to have her own way, and he feared he was fast running out of excuses to avoid her.

He sat down and cradled his head in his hands. How could Guy have imagined that all he needed to become the man he had once been was time spent on an idyllic isle with a willing woman? That carefree man was lost forever, and not even a goddess like Delphine Antoine could bring him home.

Delphine waited for Michael to return to fish for supper, but there was no sign of him before nightfall. Too hurt to be hungry, she sat on the beach and watched the moonlight dance upon the lazy waves. She had truly thought an imaginary lover might appeal to him, and clearly his cock had welcomed the idea, but like all her earlier attempts, he had refused to pursue it.

She could still swim, fish, write poetry, and gather shells, but she had hoped to leave the isle with her future secure, and that was not to be. Overwhelmed with sorrow, she was unaware of Michael's approach until he sat down behind her.

He pulled her between his outstretched legs and against his chest. He slid his hands around her waist, and then up to squeeze the tender tips of her breasts. His fingers found the gold ring and gave it a tug.

"Don't say a word," he whispered against her ear. "Just do what you did when I couldn't object."

Delphine swallowed a cry of confused delight and, unsure what had prompted this abrupt change in attitude, rested a long moment in his arms. Then, secure in her ability to do at least one thing right, she rose and slowly pulled her nightgown off over her head.

Once nude, she walked around him and trailed her fingertips through his hair.

She stepped between his legs and bent down to remove his shirt. He tossed it aside and waited for her to unbutton his trousers, but she was in no hurry. She knelt between his knees and used the slight pressure of her nails to scrape the front of his trousers. He was already hard, and Delphine slid her hand under him to cup his testicles.

She felt his heat and raised her other hand to comb through the hair on his chest. She found a flat nipple and rolled it between her thumb and forefinger. His breath quickened, but she maintained a slow, steady touch to his groin while she teased his other nipple until it grew firm as a pebble. She leaned close to take it into her mouth, and he reached for her breasts again. Michael squeezed them in time with her gentle sucking, but swiftly broke free to stand and shuck off his trousers.

She rose up on her knees and ran her hands up his thighs. He was all muscle, lean and tough. She licked only the smooth tip of his cock, then sat back on her heels and used her tongue on the inside of his thigh. He laughed, and she was pleased to discover he really was as ticklish as she had supposed. She raised up again, gripped his buttocks for balance, and this time licked his balls. She rolled them against her tongue, then sucked them into her mouth.

He moaned deep in his throat, then wound his hands in her hair and pulled her down on the sand. Now flat on his back, he ordered gruffly, "Just do it."

Delphine swept her hair over his belly, then placed a kiss in his navel. Aching for her to aim lower, he pushed down on her shoulders, but she moved at her own luxurious pace. She licked him and teased him with her nails before she finally caressed the head of his cock with her lips. She felt his whole body jerk and knew he was close to coming.

She paused to run his cock over her breasts, circling the tips, then moved astride his thigh before sucking him deep into her mouth. She reached for the spot behind his balls and pressed down with her fingertips to contain his climax. Michael bucked beneath her and made a furious grab for her hair; but she ignored his insistent restraint as she milked him with her fingers and varied the swirling strokes of her tongue to send him climbing higher and higher. When she lifted her fingertip dam, his grateful moan echoed all around her, and with a fierce jolt, he exploded in her mouth.

She stayed with him, eagerly pumping, and drank his cream down to the final slippery drop. When the last blissful shudder rolled through him, she lay down, rested her head in the hollow of his hip, and waited for him to speak. She soon realized he was exhausted and unlikely to utter a sound before dawn. Even then, she told herself bitterly, he would probably call her by another woman's name. She eased away from him, slipped on her nightgown, and went back to the cottage to sleep alone.

The cool breeze off the sea teased Michael awake, but he still felt as though his body had melted like butter and fused with the sand. He reached for Delphine but caught only air. He propped himself up on his elbows to search for her, but found himself alone under the stars.

He lay back down to gather the strength she had

sucked right out of him and could not help but laugh. He had been with a variety of pretty women from obliging widows to bawdy country maids, but he had never encountered a woman who even approached Delphine's amazing talents. She had turned his blood to molten gold, and while he had considered himself a man of the world, he had not known her tricks were even possible.

It had been such sweet torture, but God help him, he wanted more. He hauled himself to his feet, yanked on his pants, and slung his shirt over his shoulder. The cottage door stood ajar, and he took it as an invitation. He was deeply disappointed to find Delphine already asleep.

He dropped his shirt to the floor, climbed into the bed, and pulled her into his arms. "This is all a dream," he murmured against her hair.

Delphine yawned and curled against him. Dreams were what men wanted from a mistress, the dream of youth and virility, or power, but Michael Mallory was young, virile, and rich, which meant he had no real need of her except for the most exquisite of pleasures.

The last time she had filled his dreams with ecstasy, he had awakened furiously angry. Now he sounded merely wistful, as though the truth were impossible to bear. She had known he was a widower, but not the depth of his despair. He might have surrendered to-night, but certain she had played the part of his late wife in his mind, it was a bittersweet victory.

She had wanted him to want her, not some ghostly memory. Tomorrow, she would be alluring and yet distant, enticing but elusive until it was her name he called in a hungry whisper.

* * *

Delphine woke before Michael and, encouraged that he had remained with her all night, she carried his spear down the beach to the shallow tide pools. She climbed up on the rocky ledge bordering the pools and, with her spear at the ready, watched the fish tossed into the pool on one wave, swim out with the next.

The sun was already high and the day warm. Hungry, she concentrated upon spearing their breakfast until Michael shouted her name. Delphine turned, but slipped on the uneven surface. She tried to catch herself, but stepped on the hem of her nightgown and fell into the pool.

Michael sprinted across the wet sand to help her. He feared she was hurt, and carried her only a few feet before he sat down in the sand to cradle her across his lap. "I shouldn't have startled you. You'd not have fallen otherwise."

Delphine felt more embarrassed than hurt until a gash in her elbow dripped blood onto her nightgown. She slapped her hand over the wound. "I'll be all right," she exclaimed. "I just hit the rocks rather hard."

Michael covered her hand with his own. "If I'd moved to the other side of the island, I'd not have known."

"If you'd been on the opposite shore, I'd not have fallen," Delphine countered. "But I've suffered no great injury, so let me up, and we can catch some breakfast."

The bow at her neckline had come undone offering Michael a enticing view of her pale breasts. He shifted his hold on her, lowered his head to capture the gold ring in his teeth, and sucked it into his mouth. Her skin was cool, salty, and delicious. Her nipple hardened as he nipped it, and he felt her hand move through his hair in a lazy caress.

He raised his head. "Is it too early for this?"

She welcomed the teasing light in his eyes and shook her head. "I'm all wet, sandy, and my elbow hurts, but no, of course not. It's never too early to indulge you. That's why I'm here."

"Let me see your arm." He pulled her hand away and found a long, ugly scrape. "I'm sorry. I'm afraid this might scar. I'll carry you up to the cottage, and we'll find something to use as a bandage."

Delphine could have walked the short distance on her own, but it was never wise to refuse a man the opportunity to be of service. She waited for him to help her to her feet, then looped her arms around his neck as he scooped her into his arms.

"I doubt many an earl is as strong as you. Is riding strenuous?" she asked with a fluttering sweep of her long lashes.

"It can be, if the horse objects."

"I can't imagine any creature objecting to you." She licked his ear, and he stopped several yards from the cottage.

"Did your mother teach you what to say no matter what the occasion?" he asked.

His question appeared sincere, so she answered truthfully. "She tried, but I fear I'm a very poor student and continually improvised my own versions of her practiced lies."

"Are you admitting to telling lies?"

"Not to you, my lord, but I still fear that you don't believe me."

Michael continued on into the cottage and lowered her very carefully into a chair at the table. "Can any beautiful woman be believed?" he asked. He went to the washstand for water and wet the end of a towel.

"Of course, but most men want flattery rather than the truth. Then again, you are not most men." She had pushed her sleeve up when she had first left the pool, but blood had already stained the lacy cuff. "This gown is ruined. Let's rip it up to make a bandage."

"It's not ruined at all," Michael argued. "I'll rinse out the bloodstains and it will be white again. We'll tear up one of the extra sheets to bandage your arm."

Delphine studied his face as he pressed the towel against the wound with gentle pats. She much preferred his present tender concern to yesterday's fiery rage. Of course, a great deal had passed between them since then.

"Whatever you wish," she said. "You would make a fine physician."

"No, I was destined from birth to be the Earl of Clairbourne; no other pursuits would have been allowed."

"Is it very taxing being an earl?"

"Terribly, that's why I have such need of you."

The teasing declaration caught Delphine by surprise, but she recognized it instantly for the playful lie it was. "How splendid, because it has been my destiny to fulfill your every desire."

"I hope the wait hasn't been too long. Would it shock you if I inquired as to your age?"

"Yes, but you're the only man I'll ever tell," she confided, "so you must guard my secret with care. I'm nineteen."

"Most girls are wed by your age," he observed.

"True, but most girls are not raised to be a mistress, and an extra year or two works to my advantage."

"In what way?" Satisfied her arm had ceased to bleed, Michael lay the towel on the table, went to the chest where the bedding was kept, and found a sheet. He ripped the hem with his teeth and tore off a long strip.

"Do you actually expect me to confide all my secrets?"

"Of course, how else are we to pass the time?"

"Well, before I was interrupted, I had hoped to learn how to fish with a spear. That will obviously take some practice to perfect. Occasionally a pretty shell washes up on the beach, and I enjoy collecting those. Walking around the isle is a pleasant diversion.

"Then there is swimming, which is also fun. I do believe I mentioned that I write poetry, or at least gather images with that intention. Then there is the challenge of finding new ways to combine mangoes and fish."

Delphine extended her arm, and he wound the strip around her elbow, split the end, and tied a knot. "You've forgotten the most appealing aspect of this tiny isle."

"What might that be, my lord?" she asked with forced innocence.

"We have no one to please but ourselves." Michael opened her trunk and removed a lacy white nightgown with blue ribbon trim. He handed it to her and turned his back to offer her the privacy to change.

It struck her as a quaint gesture when he had already seen her nude. She had not noticed the freckles on his shoulders, and once she had let the stained gown drop to the floor, she pressed her cheek and bare breasts against his back. She wrapped her arms around his waist and snuggled close.

"Have I mentioned how handsome you are?"

Michael laced his fingers in hers. "I don't recall."

Before Delphine could respond, her stomach growled, and laughing, she slipped from his grasp to pull on the new nightgown. "It appears I'm hungry for something other than you. May we please make another attempt to spear some fish?"

"Certainly, I don't want you to grow too faint from hunger to enjoy whatever the day might bring." He grabbed her nightgown from the floor and carried it over to the washstand. He poured water into the bowl, but as he began scrubbing soap into the stains, his posture stiffened.

"I have so many pretty gowns, I wish you wouldn't—"

"Be quiet, please." Clearly preoccupied, he added more water and soap.

Delphine would admit to perhaps talking more than she should, but they had been exchanging such teasing banter that she had not expected him to order her to be still. Hurt by the curt rebuff, she went outside and walked down to the sea.

He had not wanted her to talk last night either, and she needed only a moment to recall that his wife had died in childbirth. The poor woman must have been drenched in blood, far more than he could ever rinse from a silk nightgown.

It saddened her to think the simple act of washing a few stains from her gown might have brought back the horror of his wife's death. Now it was lodged in her mind as well. How he must have loved her, she thought sadly, and they could not have been married long.

She wished that she had kicked the soiled gown under the bed and made love to him again. She would use the perfumed oil next time and show him how delicious a slippery hand could be. With her fingers coiled around him tight or floating tempting as feathers, he would be most appreciative of her touch.

Her mother would be proud of her in that respect, but while she could give Michael brief tastes of rapture, she feared it would not be enough to bind him to her for more than a single magical week.

"I'll have to be more imaginative," she vowed.

When Michael joined her to fish, he found that she had fashioned a sarong from her nightgown and left her beautiful breasts bare.

Chapter 4

*Pale shells ground to bits
Days stretch to engulf the night
Tears fine as sand*

Michael's slow perusal of Delphine's sweetly puckered nipples was interrupted by the sight of a sail on
the horizon. He grabbed her arm roughly. "That's not
Guy's boat, and you told me this isle wasn't near the
shipping lanes."

"It isn't," Delphine assured him. She raised her
hand to shade her eyes. "They're coming this way.
What should we do?"

Michael slid his hand along the tender skin of her
inner arm before lacing his fingers in hers. "It's more
likely a stranger than a friend. Let's get off the beach
and clear what we can from the cottage."

He pulled Delphine alongside him as he ran, but
they parted to rush through the narrow doorway. He
sat down on the bed to yank on his boots. "Put your
nightgown on properly before anyone else has a
chance to take a look at you. Where's the knife?"

"Oh, damn, out on the rocks." Delphine threw her
fishing pole into the corner and hastily rearranged her
gown to provide what modesty it could. She then

reached up to remove her journal from the rafters.

"I'll grab the laundry. You put out the cooking fire."

"Done," Michael replied without arguing that he was the one giving the orders. He snatched the razor on his way out.

In less than a minute, they had scrambled up the bluff and were hidden behind the misshapen juniper clinging to the sandy soil. Lying flat, they stared at the rapidly approaching vessel.

"It has but a single mast," Michael observed, "and while it is larger than Barnett's, it's still a small pleasure craft. There can't be many aboard."

"Could they wish to bury treasure?"

Michael responded with a cynical chuckle. "That's far too small to be a pirate's boat. They must have come from Kingston. We'll keep hidden and watch what happens."

"We have a right to be here," she leaned close to confide. "Maybe Guy is sending the provisions he should have left stored here for us."

Michael's eyes narrowed as he glanced her way. "Not after he plotted to strand me for the week. I wish I had the knife, but all we had in the cottage was a razor."

"Surely you'll not have to defend us."

"Hush, they've reached the dock. Keep your head down, and I'll provide a running account of all that occurs."

Certain he would produce a highly censored version of what transpired, if that, she removed her hat and kept her glance level with his. She was relieved that he had not rushed out into the surf to greet the boat, but it was little consolation if they were in for trouble.

From where she lay, she had a clear view of the tall gangling man who leapt from the boat to the dock to secure a mooring line. He was followed by two stocky men who shoved and pushed a fourth whose slender build made him appear much younger than his hostile companions. The quartet made their way down to the beach, with the captive struggling the whole way.

"What can they mean to do?" Delphine asked.

Michael raised a finger to his lips. "Cover your eyes. They may intend only to frighten him, but it could come to much worse."

Delphine's eyes widened in alarm. "You mean they might kill him?"

Michael shook his head. "Had that been their plan, they would have slit his throat and tossed him overboard rather than bother to bring him here."

His words may have been meant to sooth her, but the muscles tensed along his jaw bespoke his deep concern. She pressed closer to his side. "Maybe they're unspeakably cruel and plan to torture the poor wretch for hours."

Michael rested his forehead on his outstretched arm. "Do not even think such an awful thing."

"How can you not?"

Michael raised up to glare at her. "They are armed with pistols. What would you have me do, run down the bluff brandishing the razor?" He wrapped his arm around her waist to hold her close. "They would shoot me dead before I came within twenty feet of them. Then they would find you."

She clung to his arm. "I don't want to see you hurt."

"Good, now do as I say and keep your head down."

The prisoner on the beach let out a long, piercing

scream, and Delphine released Michael to cover her ears. She cringed and waited for the pistol shot she feared would surely come. The wait grew excruciating, but just as she dared to draw in a breath, another high-pitched shriek carried on the breeze. She could not bear to look now.

"What are they doing to him?" she sobbed.

Michael whispered against her ear. "They're pushing him around between them. Whenever he stumbles and falls, they kick him and yank him to his feet."

"Why would they treat him so badly? What could they want?"

"I've no idea, but men usually fight over money or women," he added with a rueful smile.

"He looks young. Could they have caught him with another man's wife?"

"Could be."

The next scream ended in a watery gurgle, and Delphine held her breath until her lungs threatened to burst. She knew Michael was outnumbered and armed with only a razor against men with drawn pistols; but those excellent justifications for restraint failed to soften the heart-wrenching impact of the poor captive's pitiful cries.

She raised up slightly. "I could distract them, and you could disarm a man, and—"

"There would still be two left who would shoot us both. Now for the last time, hush."

Delphine felt sick. What if they had not spied the boat in time to escape notice? Michael would have had no choice but to fight, and the men on the beach might have silenced him with a single shot rather than allow a witness to their brutality to live. There was no need to speculate on what her fate would have been then. They'd have raped her until she was too bruised and bloodied to provide them any pleasure and then slit her throat.

"If they know of this isle," she whispered, "they must know Guy. Do you recognize any of them?"

"The rogues are dressed as gentlemen, as is their captive, but no, none of their faces is familiar."

"Would you recognize any if you saw them again?"

"The tall man perhaps, but not the others. I'll certainly not go looking for them."

"No, but you'd not wish to make their acquaintance by chance either, would you?"

Michael's expression was grim, his voice strained. "Of course not. Now, is it simply impossible for you to be still?"

Delphine briefly considered his question, but she could not voice an objection without confirming his sorry opinion of her self-restraint. The poor soul on the beach began to plead in high-pitched wails, and she was again forced to cover her ears. This was not proving to be the instructive week she and her mother had anticipated.

The tallest man grabbed the captive by the collar and whispered a suggestion in his ear that made him squeal like a terrified pig. Michael prayed it was an idle threat and pulled Delphine tight against his chest. He covered her hands with his own to muffle the poor bastard's pathetic cries.

He had observed enough to confirm his earlier suspicions of the captors. They merely sought to thoroughly humiliate their victim. Relieved to think the poor soul would survive burdened only by shame, he rocked Delphine gently until the captive's anguished cries ceased.

Michael waited several minutes before easing his lovely companion aside to risk a glance toward the beach. The three knaves were dragging their hapless captive back toward the dock. He offered no resistance; the toes of his boots gouged deep furrows in the sand. Upon reaching the boat, the trio of bullies shoved him aboard, and after passing around a jug of rum, they pushed away from the dock and set sail for Jamaica.

"They've gone," Michael said wearily, "and their prisoner was still alive."

Delphine's breath caught in her throat. She knew she should rejoice that the man had survived such a miserable ordeal and that they were no longer in danger, but her fright had run too deep. Badly shaken, she rose and, wanting only to escape into solitude, quickly donned her straw hat and made her way down the bluff.

Michael watched her go, her step sure, her grace undimmed by the limb-numbing pose she had been forced to hold. Except for her mishap on the rocks, the morning had gotten off to a promising start, but clearly she now wished to get as far away from him as possible.

Wasn't that precisely what he had originally craved? Indeed it was, or at least it had been, so why did her hurried departure carry such a sharp sting?

Delphine clutched her journal tightly to her breast. Tears stung her eyes as she recalled how enticing her mother had made a week of lazy seduction appear. Michael was not so easily seduced, but she had definitely made progress in that regard. What worried her was the knowledge that if one band of brigands had landed there, even more blood-thirsty rogues could swiftly follow.

Despite Michael's comforting strength, she had seen ample evidence of how little opportunity he would have to use it. Alarmed to be so vulnerable, she stepped out onto the wet sand and welcomed a foamy rush across her toes. She had naively assumed Michael would be her only challenge on the island, but now it appeared dangerous complications might easily overwhelm them.

"We should have been better prepared," she murmured darkly. But Guy and her mother had abandoned them with a pitifully small store of weapons. She prayed that lack of foresight would not prove tragic.

Delphine could scarcely share her fright with Michael when he had been brought there against his will. Glancing in the direction of the cottage, she hoped he was giving equal thought to becoming better prepared, for surely there was something they could do to enhance their defenses before the next threat appeared.

Michael rinsed out Delphine's gown and hung it up to dry. He then traced a restless figure eight in front of the cottage and cursed Delphine with every step. Clearly she thought him a coward, and he could not fathom why her poor opinion should pain him after she had played such a despicable part in stranding him there.

To make matters even worse, she had displayed more sympathy for the miserable fool they had observed being abused than for his plight. If he made an issue of her attitude, it would only serve to strengthen her low opinion of his ability to defend them. He shook his fist at a passing gull, and too hungry to rant any longer, he fetched his newly fashioned spear and went out to attack the fish.

Lost in thought, Delphine paused to rest at Michael's stone encampment. She sank down in the center and, laying her journal aside, rested her head in her hands. She had never been subjected to such a distasteful interlude, but now having had time to reflect, she felt very foolish for having expected Michael to charge down the bluff to save a man who had survived well enough on his own.

"What an absurd fantasy," she moaned, and in the next breath realized that by questioning Michael's judgment, she had broken one of her mother's cardinal rules. Surely he had taken her childish desire to mount an impossible rescue as an insult to his authority and was sorely provoked with her as a result.

Thank goodness she knew how her mother would lessen the consequences of such a thoughtless error. Françoise would approach him, coil her arm around his, and rest her head lightly against his shoulder while she offered a flattering apology for behaving in such a silly manner. Delphine feared she would only appear ridiculous should she make such a transparent attempt to win his forgiveness, but she could find no less painful alternative.

Shoving to her feet, she bent to pick up her journal and continued on around the island.

When she reached the cottage, she found Michael standing out on the rocks. He looked up and waved to her. Startled by the welcoming gesture, Delphine made her way over the rocks. He had speared several bonito, and when he smiled proudly she was relieved that he did not seem inclined to scold her.

"I did not mean to criticize you for being cautious," she blurted out. "I fear I've lived too long in my own imagination to have a practical approach to life."

Considering that she thought nothing of parading about in varying states of undress, Michael was astonished by the embarrassment coloring her cheeks. Too amused to remark upon his earlier concern for her misplaced sympathy, he responded politely.

"Nonsense, your sense of adventure is most appealing. Perhaps you'd care to join me for a swim later this afternoon."

Certain he must be mocking her, Delphine cocked her head slightly. "If you wish."

"When there is so little to do here," he replied, "I hate to ignore one of the most diverting pastimes."

Delphine nodded and turned back toward the shore. He had been so affectionate that morning that for a brief instant, she had hoped he would again seek her favors, but he had pointedly chosen otherwise. Then, recalling the hunger in his gaze before he had sighted the boat, she loosened the neckline of her nightgown to free her breasts, then knotted the sleeves at her waist.

To avoid discovery, Michael had hastily kicked sand into their fire pit, but she found several glowing coals partially buried at the bottom and by adding bits of driftwood, soon coaxed the embers into dancing flames. After adding more wood, she sat down, leaned back on her elbows, licked her lips, and dug a toe into the sand.

As Michael placed the fish on the grill, he pointedly ignored her provocative pose. "We're both losing weight on a diet of fish and mangoes. I hope there is enough of us left to rescue at the end of the week."

"By the time Guy appears, you might not regard it as a rescue," Delphine replied in a sultry whisper.

"You are a great beauty, Delphine, but I have important work awaiting me at home."

"Really? From what Guy swore, you did little other than sip brandy."

Her observation was so damnably accurate, Michael had to grit his teeth. That he had spent so many months in a spirits-laced haze now appalled him. "I oversee my estates, manage my investments, and respond to near endless appeals for contributions to worthy causes."

"An earl has a great many demands upon his time."

"None of which can be attended to here." Michael flipped the fish. They were nicely browned, and his stomach growled in anticipation.

Deftly pursuing her cause, Delphine's smile grew even more enticing. "I'll be more than happy to attend to you, my lord."

She had left him drunk on passion last night, and he was deeply grateful their unwanted visitors had not found him still sprawled on the beach. "I'll not question your generosity, but we ought not to allow the crew of the next boat to take us by surprise."

Chilled that he shared her fears, she sat up abruptly, sending her hair spilling over her breasts in a silken veil. "Do you wish to take turns standing watch?"

"That won't be necessary, but let's keep our wits about us."

"No one would ever describe you as witless, my lord."

Michael scraped the fish from the grill onto their pewter plates and handed her one. He made the mistake of looking directly into her lovely green eyes, and the whole island seemed to lurch beneath him. He fumbled with his plate, dropped his fork in the sand, and cleaned it off on his shirt tail.

The woman could seduce a stone! What chance did a mere mortal have to resist her? He refused to look her way again while he ate, but that only made the husky edge to her voice all the more magical. Once finished with his fish, he took a bite of a plump mango and was instantly reminded of her gently rounded breasts.

He caressed the succulent fruit in his hands and tried not to recall how eagerly he had succumbed to her charms last night. To his continuing shame, he had sought her out that morning for the very same purpose. Now he was torn between being disgusted with himself for wanting her and furious with the men who had gotten in his way.

He ate the mango down to the large seed while considering his dilemma and reluctantly decided he would be a great fool to allow his displeasure at being marooned there to prevent him from taking all that Delphine so generously offered.

He leaned back on his elbows and gazed past her to the sea. "You swim very well for a woman."

Delphine laughed. "That's scarcely a compliment when most women don't swim at all."

He shrugged. "True, but that doesn't diminish your skill."

"Thank you. You mentioned going for a swim later. Am I to assume that you swim equally well?"

He raked her with a skeptical glance. "Are you challenging me to a race?"

"Why not? If we've few pastimes here, we ought to make the most of each."

Her lower lip was no longer swollen from his angry kisses, and he thought her mouth the prettiest he had ever seen. Then he recalled just how skilled her lips and tongue truly were. She had undoubtedly been tutored by her mother, and he could now more fully appreciate how Françoise prompted the depth of Guy's devotion.

Still, he stubbornly fought to delay the inevitable. "I've no need of a mistress," he announced abruptly.

"I don't recall remarking that you did," Delphine replied sweetly. She adjusted her pose to flaunt her breasts and smiled when his attention was immediately drawn to the small golden ring piercing her left nipple.

"Of course," she reminded him, "a man always has need of an obliging woman."

A day earlier he would have argued her pronouncement applied only to other men, but now he would not waste his breath. However, he was still unwilling to share just how eager he was to experience all her tricks. "We ought to rest a while before we swim," he suggested instead.

"Rest if you like, I'm not sleepy." Delphine shook out her hair and sat up. "I think I'll just stroll the beach and keep watch."

"Yes, do. The next visitors might merely be seeking good fishing and provide the means to return home."

Delphine rose with a graceful stretch then dipped her head to smile at him before walking away. "Dream whatever you wish. I'll look forward to our swim."

She had left her journal behind, and Michael promptly reached for it. Accented with artistic swirls, her handwriting was as beautiful as she was, but even her most recent notations were in French. It was enough to inspire him to learn the language, but lacking the opportunity, he closed the small book and carefully replaced it where she had left it.

He scrubbed his hands through his hair and scratched idly at his beard before stretching out to rest. Michael deepened his breathing, but when he closed his eyes, he again saw Delphine turning away with a coquettish wave and knew he would never sleep. He rose, brushed the sand from his clothes and followed her down to the beach.

Delphine felt his silent approach but waited for him to come even with her to speak. "Surely the Caribbean is the most beautiful sea on earth. I love the clarity of the water, and its warmth is most inviting."

Michael pulled his shirt off over his head and then unbuttoned his trousers. "Shall we race to Kingston?" he asked.

"You're forgetting that I've no reason to leave here, so I'd scarcely give you a race."

"Around the island then?"

She doubted that he would stray more than a few feet from her. "If you like," she responded graciously, and setting her hat aside on the sand, she untied the sleeves at her waist and let the gown pool around her feet.

She was already diving beneath the waves before Michael could shed the last of his clothing, but he quickly overtook her. Rather than attempt to outdistance him, however, she turned over on her back and began to float.

"Have you ever made love in the sea?" she called to him.

He had meant to swim first, but intrigued, began to tread water beside her. They were out past the breakers where gentle swells rose up and rolled on toward the shore.

"Isn't there a risk of drowning?" he responded.

Delphine slid under the water in a smooth backward somersault and came up behind him. She tapped him on the shoulder and exclaimed, "I believe that's part of the fun."

He reached out to catch her, but she disappeared beneath the water and resurfaced several feet away. Her hair floated around her shoulders in a silvery cape as she waved to him and watched him dive toward her.

The water had a crystalline purity, but with her golden skin and pale hair, she was nearly invisible against the sparkling sand. Her fingertips grazed his hip and he surfaced and spun to find her, but she again proved elusive. Certain she would eventually have to seek air, he waited, turning slowly so as not to miss her.

Delphine came up behind him and slid her arms around his neck. "Would you really rather race?" she breathed out against his ear.

Michael caught her hand and pulled her around to face him. "Another time, perhaps."

Delphine leaned back to dip her hair in the sea and then shook her head to pelt his face and shoulders with a fine spray. When he laughed, she reached for his ribs to tickle him.

He caught both her wrists. Tiny droplets of water spiked her long lashes, and her eyes reflected the turquoise Caribbean so clearly that for a frightening instant, he feared he could see right through her. Then she wrapped her legs around his waist and became all too real.

Michael edged closer to the shore until he could stand comfortably. He cupped her buttocks and bent his head to kiss her, but she ducked to nip his shoulder with a playful bite. He responded by pulling her exposed earlobe through his teeth.

She raised her hand to caress his cheek and laughed with him. Their bodies were sleek and slippery, and she freed a hand to align his cock to her cleft and slid down the hardened length. Delphine studied his reaction as she rode him with an undulating curl that matched the ageless rhythm of the sea.

She looked so pleased with herself that he would have taken offense had he not been enjoying himself so. He released her hand, but caught hold of her hair to force her mouth to his. Pressing her close, he kissed her until her abandon made it impossible to stand.

He sank below the surface then kicked off the sandy bottom and rose to half drag, half carry her ashore. He collapsed on the wet sand and pulled her down atop him. Michael wanted to watch as she sucked his cock deep, but she began by licking his testicles, and his eyes closed in grateful surrender.

Breathless from his hungry kisses, Delphine molded herself to his thigh and continued to tease him. Now that she knew him, it was even more fun than it had been on the first night they had spent together. She ran the tip of his cock over the cool flesh of her breasts before flicking him with her tongue.

"Tell me what you like," she whispered while her hands closed around him and began to pump.

"Everything," he moaned.

She swirled her tongue around his corona, then blew on the damp trail. "You taste so good."

Michael thought he probably tasted salty like the sea, but when she handled him so artfully, he had no desire to correct her. He just wanted more and more of her warm, sweet mouth and graceful hands. Each time she eased away, he thrust his hips toward her in a silent plea for more. Her hair grazed his chest, and he hung on until all hope of restraint was lost and another shuddering climax left him too sated to grasp more than air.

Delphine raked her fingernails up his inner thigh as she pushed back on her heels. He was easy to please, but as she brushed her fingertips across her still tingling lips, she was sorry she had let him kiss her. Regretting the mistake, she left him and made her way up the beach to retrieve her nightgown. She went on to the cottage to rinse out her hair before he found her looking like a rain-soaked cat.

She had always loved to swim, but he had made moving through the water so much more fun. If he was as agreeable when he awoke, he might not notice how adeptly she avoided his kiss. She dared not sit and dream of him while her hair dried. Instead she chose to make much better use of her time and took up their knife to fashion a second spear.

Chapter 5

*Life's web unwound
Loving promises forgotten
Tenderness remains*

Michael approached Delphine. "Just what is it you're doing?" he asked.

When she looked up, he blocked the afternoon sun and cast only his golden-rimmed silhouette. "I thought we might have need of another spear or two."

"So you've sharpened the ends of all the fishing poles?"

She ignored his incredulous chuckle and bit her tongue rather than reveal how badly she wished them to be better armed. "Why not? You did well spear fishing."

He knelt beside her and smoothed her hair behind her ear. "You needn't fish. I can provide plenty for us."

She smiled as though food had been her only concern. "Yes, I know, but I have always enjoyed fishing."

He had failed in his best efforts to resist her charms, but beneath her enchanting abandon, he sensed an intriguing complexity. His own mother had never hidden her intelligence, but Delphine appeared

67

to be more comfortable flaunting her perfect body than her private thoughts.

"You are an unusual woman in all respects. Let's go catch our supper." He took the knife from her hand, rose, and drew her to her feet.

He had donned only his trousers, and when she skimmed her fingertips over his broad chest to comb the springy curls, he caught her wrist. "Did Guy ask you to keep a tally of how often you torture me with your hands and lips? Is that what your journal really contains?"

His expression was teasing, his voice honey-smooth, but she answered truthfully. "No, Guy overlooked that detail, along with our provisions. Shall I begin counting now?"

He laced his fingers in hers, bent down to take another pole, and swung her toward the beach. "No, do not confide in him."

"As you wish," she promised. The thought of making Guy privy to anything that transpired between them was as distasteful to her as it was to him. "It would only make him jealous of your prowess."

"Prowess isn't the word I'd use."

"Virility then. Is that the better term? It's a compliment, isn't it?"

"Most assuredly, but I value my privacy more."

She wondered if perhaps he weren't merely appalled to have discovered a weakness for her. It had not occurred to her that he might be ashamed to crave her affection. He was so attractive that there was no cause for shame on her part, merely a twinge of regret that he had been kidnapped.

They found the shoreline bathed in amber light.

They usually fished off the rocks on their left, but this time she pointed in the opposite direction. "Perhaps we should try another tide pool."

"The fish will surely be the same," he argued.

She pulled her hand from his and, abandoning their usual spot, crossed the beach and made her way over the jumbled rocks. After a brief search, she found an inviting pool, but rather than trapped fish, it held a small wooden keg which probably contained rum. Alarmed, she turned to retrace her steps, but Michael was already at her elbow.

"If it's been discarded, it's empty," he said. "It might even have belonged to the men who were here earlier."

The keg was floating rather high in the water, but she thought it would still contain a few drops of rum, if not enough to make him forget he wasn't there alone. She tensed as he waded down into the pool, but after scooping up the keg he hurled it out into the sea.

"I've never been fond of rum," he claimed, and with an agile leap climbed back atop the rocks. "Now let's spear some fish."

Even if he had not been eager to sample what the keg held, she was grateful he had not kept the small barrel to carry fresh water to the other side of the island. Apparently he had forgotten all about his half-built sanctuary, and she would certainly not remind him.

"I fell before I had the chance to spear anything this morning," she mused thoughtfully, "but I believe I understand how it's done."

While fish weren't carried into the pool with every wave, whenever one was swept along, it would swim in a slow circle seeking an escape. She angled her spear and was ready to strike the moment a fat fish appeared, but for a long while, only water streamed into the pool.

"Except for your provocative invitations," Michael murmured, "you're a remarkably taciturn young woman."

She sent him a slyly appraising glance. "Is that a compliment or complaint, my lord?"

"A compliment, of course. Most women could not be quiet long enough to fish."

She refocused her attention on the pool. "I could say the same of most men."

Michael responded with hushed laughter. "You are either a treasure or a curse, Delphine. I've yet to decide just which."

He had such a deep, rich laugh that she became even more convinced that humor was the way to his heart. In the next instant, a good-sized bonito washed into the pool, and she speared it with a vicious jab.

"Ah ha!" she cried. "This is almost too easy."

Her eyes flashed with mischief, and captivated anew, Michael caught hold of her shoulder to draw her near for a congratulatory kiss. Her taste was delicious, and as he deepened the embrace, she dropped her spear and coiled her arms around his waist.

Desperate for still more, Michael stumbled backward, then caught her hand and led her up on the sand. He tossed his spear aside, stripped off her nightgown with a single tug and eased her down on her hands and knees. Then after unbuttoning his trousers to free his sex, he knelt behind her and rubbed against her bottom.

"Hold still," he urged, as he wrapped his arms around her midriff to cup her breasts and leaned forward to spread tender kisses across her shoulders. His shaft surged along her back in a far more insistent caress.

She dropped her head between her arms, and her hair brushed the sand in a silken tent. Enclosed in that pale world, his ragged breathing washed over her as a husky echo of the surf's roar. She pushed back against his thighs to heighten his thrill, and with a final lunge his whole body tensed and his climax spattered across her spine.

He pulled her down beside him on the sand, and with her back still pressed against his chest, he cradled her snugly in his arms. But unlike the times she had brought him to a shuddering release, he had been the one controling every move. She was left feeling oddly detached rather than proud of her artistry.

It was also insulting to think he could have used any willing woman in a similar fashion with the same stunning result. She hoped that possibility would not occur to him as well, and began to pull away, but he tightened his embrace to prevent her escape.

"No, stay with me this time," he whispered against her ear.

While catering to his desires served her purpose, it was an effort to relax and rest her cheek along his outstretched arm. The sand's warmth rivaled his heat, but she found little comfort in either. Just as she thought he had fallen asleep, he slid his free hand over her hip and down between her thighs to lazily invade her feminine folds.

Raising up slightly, he shifted position to lick the gold ring in her nipple and suck on the tip of her breast. He dipped a finger into her wetness and spread it along her cleft to ease his way. His touch was incredibly light.

Welcoming his intimate caress, she angled her hips toward him and slid her foot across his leg. His beard tickled the tender swell of her breast, but his mouth was soft and sweet. She could have floated on that bliss for hours, but adept at lovemaking, he quickened his strokes to push her over the edge, and then smothered her grateful sighs with a flurry of gentle kisses.

"I wasn't certain you were real," he confessed softly. He wrapped her even more tightly in his arms, then added an affectionate squeeze. "It's almost enough to make me forgive Guy for stranding me here."

While Delphine still lay pooled in exquisite heat, Françoise's voice whispered an urgent warning against becoming lost in the passion meant to enslave Michael. She swallowed hard to clear her mind, but her mother's timely reminder rang true. When men loved the chase, a wise woman remained tantalizingly aloof rather than desperately eager for her lover's affection.

Her mother had sworn that men were concerned only with their own pleasure, and until that afternoon, Michael's behavior had served to confirm that opinion. But now he had turned adoring, and she had not dreamed how gratefully she would respond to his touch.

She closed her eyes for what seemed only a moment, but when she opened them, night had fallen and the starry heavens were ablaze with light. Disoriented, she sat up but was relieved to find Michael, while awake, still lay at her side. His trousers were again neatly buttoned, and he flashed a ready grin. She used both hands to cover a wide yawn.

"I'm sorry. I didn't mean to fall asleep."

"You needn't apologize," he assured her. "We've nothing to do here that can't be postponed."

She plucked her nightgown from the sand and slipped it over her head. "You'll swiftly reconsider when we're forced to share a single fish for supper."

He stretched and propped his hands behind his head. "I'd rather just lie here and gaze at the stars. I can't recall a more spectacular night."

"It is pretty, isn't it?" She hugged her knees and searched for a falling star to make a wish that she had not lost all hope of becoming his mistress. No man prized a woman who became so drunk on passion that she neglected his needs. She understood that principle completely, but it was difficult to apply any sensible rule where Michael was concerned. He was to be her first lover, but she could not bear to think he might swiftly tire of her and pass her along to a friend.

Panicked by that wretched fate, she shoved herself to her feet. "It's already dark. We have only one fish, and I'm afraid I might not find it."

"Delphine," Michael cajoled. "We'll fetch the fish later. Come back here."

She was not even tempted to wait and clenched her fists at her sides to strengthen her resolve. She had to preserve her distance because the pattern she set now would be the one he followed. She took a step toward the shore.

"I'm hungry even if you're not," she exclaimed and headed toward the tide pools with a long, purposeful stride.

Michael was at her side in an instant. "You've fallen once today. You'll not risk another accident in the dark. Wait here."

She halted so abruptly that he nearly slid into her. "I did not mean to disturb you."

"Oh no, you mean to disturb me clear to my soul." But he brushed her cheek with a kiss before attending to his errand.

The water reflected enough light for her to observe his progress over the rocks. "Be careful," she called after him, and then bit her lip for he possessed a natural grace and a sure step even in the dark.

The fish, still pinned to the end of her spear, had lain in the pool and been drenched with each new wave. Certain it was still fresh, Michael knelt to clean it, and then carried it up to the cottage.

"I fear the fire's gone out again," he complained.

"No, I see a faint spark of red among the ashes." Grateful for the distraction, she blew on the coals and carefully added more wood. "There, it's catching."

"Thank you. Can you find a mango or two?" he asked.

She knew exactly where to look and returned promptly with one in each hand. "I'll count the mangoes in the morning," she offered. "There should be enough left to last us through the week."

"If there aren't, you may have my share," he replied.

Determined to be an irresistible minx, she nearly purred her response. "That's very generous of you, my lord."

"Not when I care so little for the fruit."

Relying upon her practiced wiles, she struck a saucy pose. "My mistake then. I thought you simply cared for me."

Michael laid the fish on the grill before glancing up. In the fire's bright glow, his eyes also shone with a teasing sparkle. "No gentleman worthy of the name would allow a lovely lady to go hungry."

"How wonderfully reassuring, but tomorrow we must make it a point to catch plenty of fish first thing."

"You've only yourself to blame for distracting me so thoroughly this afternoon."

In her view, he had been the one providing all the distraction. "Then to save us both, tomorrow I'll fish on the opposite side of the isle."

"Oh no, you won't," he swore. "There's too great a danger that you'll come to some harm. I simply can't allow you to roam freely."

She licked her lips. "Can't allow it, my lord?" Her mother claimed a man cared little what his mistress did when he wasn't in her bed, and she expected that freedom. It would be silly to argue the issue now though. Instead, she dropped a mango into his lap and took her place on the opposite side of the fire.

Distracted by the gift of fruit, Michael rolled it between his palms. "I can't hold a mango now without feeling the weight of your breast in my hand."

"I'm flattered, but I'd no idea that you possessed such a poetic nature."

He shrugged. "Neither did I. Perhaps I've simply lacked the proper inspiration."

Pleased she had again seized control of the situation, she vowed to retain it. After all, she had been taught to artfully lead a man, not blindly trail after him. He handed her the first plate with what appeared to be the larger filet, and she thanked him.

She took a bite and murmured appreciatively, "The fish is especially good tonight, isn't it?"

"Perfection," he replied, but his gaze remained fixed on her as he licked his lips.

She took a bite of mango and slurped the juice before it dripped down her chin. "Maybe it's only the beauty of the night, but this mango is particularly delicious as well."

Her mother would be proud of her for eliciting such an admiring gaze and affectionate banter. When she considered how furious Michael had been with her at first, she was all the more pleased. Then she began to wonder if he would be as wonderfully attentive had she not enticed him so boldly. Surely no man would be charmed by a shy girl who quoted her own poetry.

A warm gust brushed her cheek, and she looked up toward the wispy clouds floating across the stars. "The breeze has shifted. Can you smell a hint of rain?"

"It's only the fragrance of the sea," he replied between flavorful nibbles of mango.

"No, it's an approaching squall, and we'll soon be drenched." A moment later, she laughed as huge raindrops fell into the fire pit with a sputtering hiss.

She stood, but rather than dash indoors, she stepped out of her nightgown and turned to catch the rain on her bare shoulders. She shook out her hair and smiled invitingly. "Have you never danced in the rain?"

What remained of their fire molded her breasts with bewitching shadows, and he marveled at her innocent delight. She moved with an exotic grace while the raindrops left sparkling trails on her pale skin.

It was an enchanting sight, and like everything else about her, totally unexpected. He had never imagined such an uninhibited creature might exist, but having found her, he knew precisely what to do. He stood and flung out his arms as though he meant to join her provocative whirl, but instead, he caught her around the waist and carried her into the cottage. He tossed her down upon the bed.

She laughed at his haste until he pulled her legs over the side of the mattress, shoved her thighs apart, and knelt on the floor between them. She grabbed for his hair, but he slapped her hand away.

"I mean to taste you," he swore, "and you'll not stop me."

His tongue swept her cleft, the stroke warm and wet before he tarried at the peak to tease her most sensitive flesh. He braced his arms against her thighs to hold her open while he probed her folds with his fingertips.

"I'm going to do this again in the morning so I can see all of you," he promised before piercing her with the tip of his tongue.

She bucked beneath him, but he slid an arm around her knee to hold her down and continued to caress her with his tongue. He flicked her delicate folds, her swollen nub, and drank up her wetness before easing a finger inside her to stroke slowly in time with his gentle lapping.

Delphine had known it was possible for a man to work the same exquisite magic with his mouth that she worked on him, but it had been no more than a scrap of knowledge gleaned from her mother's naughty pen and ink sketches. Now she was swimming in the thrill, but nothing she had seen or heard had prepared her for a pleasure so intense it bordered pain.

Nearly limp with rapture, she pressed against Michael's mouth, silently begging for more and still more until, in a shattering release, her whole body screamed, *enough!* She reached out for him, but her fingertips barely grazed his hair.

Michael lapped up the last drop of her cream. Then he slid his damp fingers through the fair curls veiling her mound. "Is that enough, or do you want more?"

She heard the seductively whispered question, but it took a long while for her to find the strength to sigh, "More would surely kill me."

"I'll stop then, for how could I possibly defend myself if I committed such a heinous crime?" He crawled up beside her on the bed and pulled her into his arms.

His chest made the perfect pillow and, melting into him, she slid her arm around his waist. Her elbow brushed his trousers, and she was surprised to find him still dressed.

"How indeed?" she asked. "I suppose you would have to find a willing lass and provide the court with a reenactment."

"Delphine!" he cried, highly amused. He laughed at her shocking suggestion.

She tongued his nipple. "I imagine women would line up for blocks to volunteer to aid in your defense."

"You are wicked," he scolded, but his hand had moved to her breast where he toyed with the gold ring.

"Is it wicked to speak the truth? Haven't other women praised you to the skies for the lavish affection you've just shown me?"

He sucked in a deep breath and released it slowly. "I've never even been tempted to kiss another woman in that way, but now you've whet my appetite."

Delphine raised up slightly, but they had not lit the lamp and the cottage was too dark to make out more than the gleam of his eyes. She was surprised to learn that he had never given his wife such intimate kisses, but knew better than to ask why and remind him of the unfortunate girl. Perhaps like most wellborn young ladies, she had been kept so ignorant of the pleasures of the flesh that she would have been too scandalized to enjoy it.

She leaned up to kiss him and tasted her own essence on his lips. "I do taste very good, don't I?"

"Are you simply shameless?" he asked through a deep chuckle.

"Only where you are concerned, my lord." She sat up then and unbuttoned his pants. "I have a bottle of oil in my trunk that is especially made for lovers. It will smooth my hand on your cock. Would you like me to fetch it?"

"Please do." He rolled off the bed to toss his trousers aside, then lay down and propped his hands behind his head. "It's a shame the rain has forced us inside."

"Yes, it only compounds the tragedy of being stranded here." She placed a few drops of the fragrant oil in her palm and then rubbed her hands together to warm them. She returned to the bed and knelt between his outstretched legs, then waited to let the tension build before touching him.

After counting to ten, she slid her fingers around the base of his cock and slowly turned her hands in opposite directions. "There, doesn't that feel good?"

He gasped, "Far better than good."

"I'm sorry there's no judge here to observe, for such a demonstration would undoubtedly aid in your defense."

"Undoubtedly," he struggled to reply.

"Of course, judges do wear long robes. Do you suppose he would slide his hand into his own trousers to get a better feel for your case?"

"Oh yes," he hissed. Delphine was rolling him like

pastry dough between her palms, but he was already hard and growing harder. "Use more oil," he begged.

"The bottle is on the table beside you. Hand it to me."

He moved slowly so as not to risk a spill, grasped it firmly, and passed it to her. He held his breath as she poured more into her hands and then passed the bottle back to him. It took great concentration to return it to the table, but rather than lie back to enjoy her slippery touch, he waited for only a few heavenly strokes before he reached out to catch her arm and forced her down on the bed beneath him.

"I'll leave you a virgin," he promised, "but just let me slip inside." With a sure aim, he probed gently, then withdrew. "God, you feel so good."

He had gotten ahead of her again, she realized and cursed her own stupidity. She rocked her hips against him, but it only sent him deeper before he withdrew. Then he slid his hand between them to rub her in teasing circles. Already tender, she grabbed hold of his wrist, but he kept rocking slowly against her, entering her with short, slippery thrusts.

His next lunge brought a sharp twinge of pain, and she tensed beneath him. "Stop, you're hurting me," she cried.

He withdrew, but then slid the blunt tip of his cock along her crease to again coax her toward bliss. When she began to tremble, he leaned down to whisper, "You were made for this." Then with a sudden stab, he dipped into her again and came in a warm torrent that filled her and dripped down between her thighs.

Both shocked and sated, she lay beneath him again awash in pleasure, and slowly sifted his thick, black hair through her fingers. It was now plain that he had intentionally requested more oil to ease his way inside her. She wondered if she could still be considered a virgin because he had not penetrated her completely.

Probably not truly, she decided, but he was her first lover, and he knew the truth. She shifted her position slightly, but she liked having him sprawled across her. It was a marvelous sensation to have a man of his size and strength cradled so peacefully in her arms.

They fit together beautifully, but even without echoes of her mother's tiresome warnings, she knew she was becoming far too fond of him. It wasn't the attachment in itself that was dangerous; it was the foolish expression of it—the incessant demands and tearful pleas. What man wouldn't flee such a pathetic assault?

She would regard a man who begged for her love as beneath contempt. Affection was a gift, or in the case of a mistress, a commodity exchanged for the lavish benefits a wealthy man could provide. If the mistress was clever, she willingly accepted his love, and created an elaborate fantasy to inspire hope within him that one day she might love him in return.

Michael was a far more wily devil than she and her mother had anticipated, but after she had overcome his initial hostile dismay, he had shown her an appealing charm. He admired her figure and her abandon, and she would rely upon those attributes. Her growing fondness for him would have to remain hidden.

She awakened the next morning caught in a tangled nest of sheets, while Michael, dressed in his trousers, stood at the washstand shaving. She held her breath while he drew the razor up his throat. She had wanted him clean-shaven, but when he toweled away the soap clinging to his cheeks and turned to face her, she feared he now held an unfair advantage.

"Good morning," he greeted her.

Day four, she counted silently. Sunlight streamed in the door and windows. "*Bonjour.*"

"Stay in bed if you like. I'll catch our breakfast."

"Our bed is a sticky mess. After I bathe, I'll change the sheets and launder these for tomorrow."

"So it's now *our* bed rather than yours?" He rested his hands on his hips, and his smile grew wide. His hair was damp and curved over his forehead. "How generous you've become, my lady. I am truly honored."

With sparkling white teeth and deeply tanned skin, he had such a handsome smile. It took a real effort on her part to glance away. "If you continue to gloat, you'll swiftly learn the limits of my generosity."

"I'll attend to the fish rather than risk that dire consequence," he swore on his way out, but his laughter lingered on the moist air.

Delphine waited a moment, then pulled free of the twisted sheets and got up. She took soap and a towel around to the back of the cottage where a convenient bamboo screen and bench made it possible to bathe comfortably beneath the cistern. She used the privy, then washed her hair and scrubbed her body clean. She had returned to the cottage and had just opened her trunk to select a fresh nightgown when Michael reappeared.

"I forgot something," he announced, and he scooped her up and laid her on the side of the bed. He knelt and pulled her hips forward to slide her legs over his shoulders. "Hold still, I just want to look at you."

As outraged as an overturned turtle, she tried to

scoot away, but he caught her waist to keep her in place. "I'm not an anatomy text," she scolded.

"Well, I say that you are, but perhaps you would prefer this approach."

He dipped his head and slid his tongue up the length of her, pausing to trace slow circles around her clitoris with the tip of his tongue. "You are so pink and pretty," he whispered and then resumed his soft, swirling strokes.

Her complaint swallowed, she arched her back to press against his mouth. This was trouble her mother had never described, and she gasped as he slid first one finger and then two up into her. Her whole body began to tingle with a craving that flowed over her skin and down between her legs where it throbbed in time with the beat of her heart.

She heard him unbutton his trousers and then he stood and rubbed the head of his cock along the trail he had bathed with his tongue. She looked up at him through half-closed eyes and found him watching her with a rapt expression. He dipped into her, skating on her own wetness, then stroked her again.

She crossed her ankles behind his hips to pull him closer still, and he slid inside her with another careful nudge. Her heat pooled around him as he massaged her tender flesh with both his fingertips and cock. He made her ache with wanting him, and her only fear was that he might stop.

But her spell over him was equally strong, and the instant she came in fluttering spasms, he shot his come all over her breasts. When the last drop fell, he leaned down to kiss her hard on the mouth, then pushed away from the bed and buttoned his trousers on his way out.

She lay with her legs angled off the bed until the last glimmer of bliss faded away. Still, when she tried to rise, she slid off the bed and landed on the sandy floor with a painful thump. Michael wreaked havoc on her senses, but she feared it was only play to him.

He had been insistent rather than rough, but he had rudely ignored her objections. Well, perhaps more smoothly than rudely, but he had definitely taken advantage of her. She could not abide that.

While the pleasure he gave was undeniable, she refused to be no more than a pretty doll he tossed this way and that. Cursing him soundly, she bathed again, donned a clean nightgown, and with her damp hair flying, made her way down to the rocky tide pools to confront him.

"You are never to treat me so disrespectfully ever again!" she shouted. "I'd not tolerate it from another man, and I most certainly will not tolerate it from you. Do you understand me?"

" 'Disrespectfully,' " he repeated incredulously. "Would you go as far as to say that I handled you as though you were drugged and unable to object?"

Even without the dangerous glint in his eye, Delphine would have understood his meaning. While appalled, she could see no way to dispute his complaint.

"You're an attractive man, and I was curious; I'll admit to taking liberties, but I wanted to learn how best to please you. I thought we'd reached an accord since then, but obviously I was mistaken. No gentleman harbors grudges, sir, and I no longer trust you."

Too angry to continue, she turned and flew over the rocks with the speed of a furious angel.

Chapter 6

Sunlight scattered dreams
Sea-tossed glass, scarred vitrine
Footprints swept away

Intending to shun Michael for the remainder of the day, Delphine plucked a mango from the tree and took a furious bite. He was very nice to look at, but that scarcely made up for the way he behaved. Her mother was as easily insulted, and even years later would remark upon some small slight others had completely forgotten. Michael had just shown himself to be of the same ilk, and that flaw doomed him in her view.

She would never be able to justify her rejection to her mother, however, when Françoise would regard it as doubly insulting. But she and Michael were a disastrous match, and regardless of whatever mistakes she might have made, they probably always had been.

Françoise had insisted that she be able to converse intelligently on a variety of subjects to better hold a man's interest. Delphine had studied with a succession of exceptional tutors, who had encouraged her to use her fine mind. Fortunately for her, if not her mother, she had been taught to see beneath the surface, to thoughtfully analyze another's actions rather than merely accept or condemn them.

For the time being, she was as much a prisoner as Michael, but that did not mean she would have to remain as such once Guy returned. She would capitalize on her mother's desire for her to become independent. There were many wealthy men with property on Jamaica, and from what she had overheard, several had shown an interest in her. Surely one would not be as ill-tempered as Michael.

"And then, it will be good riddance to him," she exclaimed. Her future settled, she began to scan the damp shoreline in search of unusual shells.

Ravenously hungry, Michael waited until he had caught four bonito to return to the cottage. He was dismayed not to find a fire crackling in the pit and even more annoyed that Delphine was nowhere to be found. He had not wanted her roaming about on her own, but because she could not possibly become lost, he set to building a fire and roasting the fish.

He ate three and left the last on her plate, then carried it inside to the table. Their bed was still in wild disarray, and the taunting scent of sex lingered in the air. Instantly aroused, he cursed Delphine as he ripped off the sheets; but when he came upon the bandage he had tied on her arm, it was a sharp reminder of how fragile she truly was. He tossed the stained linen strips into the fire, then carried the bedclothes outside. He rinsed them out under the cistern and hung them on the drooping line strung between the cottage roof and the mango tree.

Inspired to complete the task, he gathered fresh sheets, but remaking the bed proved surprisingly difficult. He had either too great a length at the head or the foot, and wasted what he considered far too much of his valuable time before striking an appropriate balance. He smoothed the top sheet carefully, stepped back to admire his handiwork, and thought he had done a fine job. Not that he would ever be called upon to make his own bed once he returned home, but he was accustomed to living in a neat house, and he would not tolerate chaos here.

Outside, the translucent sea beckoned invitingly, but swimming alone would not be much fun. His imagination supplied diverting possibilities, but without Delphine, it was impossible to act upon any. Infuriated to actually miss her tormenting company, he trudged up the trail to the bluff.

He shaded his eyes with his hand and turned slowly to search the surrounding beach for the elusive blonde. It took a while to locate her, and then he stared in wonder. She was dancing on the damp sand, toes pointed, gracefully tracing figures as though she had the most attentive of partners for the minuet.

It was a breathtaking sight, but he was saddened to think that while she might dip and curtsy with a ballerina's grace, she would never be accepted by polite society or entertained in glittering ballrooms. It was a loss that made his chest ache for her.

His anger forgotten, he made his way down the bluff and circled the island to approach her with a stealth that allowed him to take her hand before she had noted his presence.

"I beg your forgiveness, my lady, but you're a fine figure of a woman, and I was curious; I'll admit to taking liberties, but I wanted to learn how best to please you."

Startled by his sudden appearance, as well as his choice of words, Delphine inclined her head slightly to study his expression and was astonished to find it touchingly sincere. Françoise had insisted a man would rather slit his own throat than apologize to a woman, but clearly, Michael had just disproved another of her mother's strongly held opinions.

His grasp was light, and yet so warm and comfortable that she left her hand resting in his. "It was your lack of forgiveness that caused the problem, my lord. If you are going to recall each of my misdeeds and thoughtless words whenever it suits your purpose to hurt me, we shall never get along."

He opened his mouth to remind her that it had been her fierce anger at him that had sparked the memory of her provocative attentions, but he swiftly thought better of it. "We've only been here three days, so it's unfair of you to accuse me of holding grudges."

"This is day four," she offered.

He frowned. "Four? Are you certain?"

"Yes. Count the nights if you prefer. The first, you reluctantly joined me in the bed. The second night, you came to me on the beach. I'm sure you can recall last night well enough on your own."

"That does indeed make this day four. Just now you were dancing so beautifully, I suggest we continue." He brought her hand to his lips and bowed invitingly.

He had an almost irresistible smile, but with a great force of will, she refused to leave things unsettled. "No more grudges?"

He would always remember their arguments, as well as their passion, but he nodded agreeably. "I fear you are the one who will regret we've promised to forgive and forget, but yes, you have my word on it."

"Thank you. I've danced only with my tutors," she apologized. "So I'll not be nearly as accomplished as your usual partners."

"My usual partners are empty-headed twits who contemplate naught save fashion and gossip incessantly. You could hop around the beach like a rabbit and still outshine them."

She could not help but laugh at that absurd image, but she also wondered if he would describe his late wife in such unflattering terms. She certainly hoped not. He deserved a woman who possessed not merely beauty and grace, but also the wit to keep him amused. Greatly saddened to think he might not have had such an admirable mate, she adjusted her hat to conceal a threat of tears.

"Delphine, we are dancing barefoot in the sand. You needn't fear you'll disappoint me."

She forced a smile. "I'll still try my best." He was at least wearing his shirt now, and she held her nightgown out as though it were a ball gown's cascading satin skirt. "We should probably hum the same tune."

"The sea provides ample music." He raised her hand to continue the minuet he had interrupted, and even without a highly polished parquet floor, she seemed almost to float at his side. Delphine dipped her head to regard him with a coquettish glance, and he was enormously grateful they were on a deserted isle rather than surrounded by a hundred others.

On the last bow, he reached for her, but she laid her hands on his chest. "Could you please show me how to waltz? My last tutor condemned it as scandalous, but I've heard it's extremely popular."

"It is, but I'll warn you now that when I take you in my arms like this and pull you close, it's going to be very difficult to recall we're supposed to be dancing."

"Really? Perhaps you should demonstrate the step first," she suggested.

"No, I'd look too ridiculous. Just follow my lead." He held her in a gentle clasp and then turned to trace wide circles across the damp sand. She moved so easily in time with his steps that he began to hum a favorite Strauss waltz in her ear. Before long, they were dizzy, convulsing with laughter as they clung to each other.

He caught her around the waist and apologized. "We're not supposed to become dizzy. Perhaps we were dancing too fast."

In her opinion, everything had happened too fast between them, but that was her fault rather than his. She held onto his arms to catch her balance. "I don't know if it's the waltz, or simply you, but that was wonderful fun."

This time when he ducked his head, she did not stop him, but instead stood on her tiptoes to meet his kiss. With the next breath, he wrapped himself around her and ground his hips against hers. She closed her eyes to savor his muscular heat. He made his own magic, and she doubted he had been carefully tutored in the art of love.

"I nearly forgot your arm," he recalled suddenly, and pushed up her sleeve to find the cut healing nicely. He leaned down to kiss it, then gathered her into a hug and lifted her clear off her feet.

She could feel where his thoughts lay, but rather than stroke him through his trousers, she kissed him only lightly. She wanted to make the day last, rather than become lost in him and miss so many sunlit hours.

"Let's go swimming again," she encouraged. "I love being able to swim here without having to worry our nudity will shock passersby."

Michael regarded her with a knowing smile as he began to remove his shirt. He had a gentleman's grace in all his actions, but now he moved at a slow, teasing pace.

"What happened to our race?" she asked as she watched him peel away his clothes.

"Race?" He dimly recalled the mention of a race. "I believe it was a tie."

"Then I demand a rematch." She shrugged off her nightgown and ran into the surf.

Michael tore off his trousers and ran after her. She was a streak of peach against the aqua sea, and he let her swim just out of reach.

Wise to his game, she ducked under the cresting wave and came up behind him. Delphine slid her hands over his shoulders and rested her head against his. "Couldn't we just float here all day?"

"We'd become as wrinkled as raisins," he complained, "and I like you much better exactly as you are."

"Well, I think you'd make a very handsome raisin."

"Perhaps, but I'd rather be a man." He turned to face her, caught her legs and pulled them around his hips. "A race was your idea, but you're not giving me much in the way of competition."

Allowing him to support her lower body, she lay back upon the water and spread her arms wide. She gazed up at the cloudless sky and sighed softly. "This is paradise."

He cupped her bottom to align his cock with her cleft and rubbed slowly. They were floating in a trough between swells. The sky above was a huge azure bowl, and her inner heat magnified the sea's seductive warmth. He had grown up in Jamaica, and swum in the rivers and sea thousands of times, but never with an abandoned nymph who made everything new.

"You are paradise."

"And you are an earl with too many tedious responsibilities."

"Not today," he argued, and he caught her hands to draw her back into his arms. She coiled herself around him like a silken vine, and while he loved the feel of her tightly puckered nipples against his chest, he could not deny that she had changed. Or perhaps he had, for she no longer issued the scandalous invitations that had shocked him so badly on their first day together.

Now her suggestions made such perfect sense, they seemed like his own. "I fear you have corrupted me."

She kissed the sparkling drops of water from his eyelashes and then ran the tip of her tongue across his lower lip. "You were in desperate need of corrupting, my lord. All I did was my duty."

He was treading water easily, with the tip of his cock pressed against her navel. He adjusted her hips for a better fit and caught her mouth in a demanding kiss. "You make me come out here, and we'll both drown."

"Whales manage," she teased.

"So they do, but they can hold their breath a lot longer." He kept one arm around her waist to angle her face toward the sky and began to swim on his side toward the shore. "We'll have a race another day."

They had only a few days left, but rather than remind him, she kicked her feet to help propel them to the beach. Once they were through the surf, she broke away from him to run and fetch her nightgown. She spread it out on the dry sand and lay down.

"Straddle me and come between my breasts," she invited, and she pushed them up proudly.

She had not changed at all, he realized, which meant he was the one with new eyes. For a virgin, she had an endless store of entrancing desires, and he did not wish to disappoint her. Michael stepped over her, then knelt at her waist and thrust up between the soft swell of her breasts. It was a heavenly sensation, but best of all, she dipped her tongue to lick the tip of his cock when he shoved forward. Then she reached down to cup his testicles, and the bolt of pleasure made him moan.

She liked watching him. He had been handsomely built when he had arrived on the isle, but now that he was a bit leaner, the muscles rippled down his torso in time with each lunge. She licked her lips, inched forward to angle his cock into her mouth and sucked him deep. She slid her fingers along the shaft, meaning to find the spot behind his scrotum, but he caught her wrists and flattened her hands into the sand.

He was breathing rapidly now, his climax seconds away, when he swung back to escape her mouth and ejaculated over her breasts in a lacy trail. But rather than collapse in her arms as he usually did, he drew in a deep breath to steady himself and slid slowly down her still slippery body.

Michael paused to spread kisses on the smooth skin of her inner thigh, then licked a path to her knee. He sat back on his heels and began to massage her foot. She had beautiful feet with dainty, kissable toes. He began to suck on one perfect toe at a time.

She propped herself on her elbows and rubbed his cream into her breasts with slow, easy circles that mirrored the motion of his hands. "I'd no idea you were so fond of feet," she observed softly.

"Only yours, but there's not a speck of you that isn't perfect."

He was twisting his finger between her toes, and she curled them around his hand. He cupped her heel, sucked another toe into his mouth, and his eyes lit with a mischievous gleam.

Holding his gaze, she tugged her nipple ring. "Thank you, but don't you consider me too tall for a woman?"

"Not for my woman," he swore convincingly.

Her heart skipped a beat, but she licked her lips as though she were merely savoring the moment. Perhaps he now wanted a charming mistress and would strike a bargain advantageous to them both when Guy and her mother returned. On the other hand, his remark could have been no more than an idle compliment.

"I've never had a man rub my feet, and I'm surprised by how wonderful it feels." She pointed her toe to encourage him to continue.

"I know something that feels even better," he replied. He stretched out, pulled her legs over his shoulders, angled her hips toward his mouth, and began to kiss her with slow, deep licks.

She arched her back to press closer, and flung out her arms in abject surrender. This was even better than floating in the sea, and while her eyes remained closed, she saw him clearly. He had none of the foppish mannerisms other young men displayed on the street. He was simply all male, and a splendid specimen at that.

He used his fingers in time with his tongue, and she inhaled sharply. Then he reached up to pinch her nipples playfully, and her climax poured into his mouth in a convulsive stream. Savoring her taste, he moved forward and entered her with short, gentle thrusts.

He nudged at the barrier of her innocence, but ventured no further. She tensed beneath him and marveled at his control. He was again rock-hard, and it would have been so easy to impale herself with a forceful shove. Tantalized by desire she inhaled and would have done it, but in that same instant, he withdrew.

"You have such beautiful skin," he whispered against her temple. "I'd lie out here all day, but I don't want you to get burned. Let's go back to the cottage."

Her legs had turned to liquid, and too content to move, she was delighted when he rose and scooped her up along with her nightgown and his trousers. She wrapped her arms around his neck and snuggled against him. Her mother had patiently taught Guy how to return her affection in kind, but Michael already knew more than his friend would ever master.

She nibbled his ear. "You are a wonderful lover."

He shrugged. "Thank you, but you provide the inspiration."

"Yes, an inspiration is most helpful for me as well, and all of you is handsome, not simply your cock."

The cottage lay beyond the next bend, but while her slight weight was no burden, her outrageous commentary drove him to distraction. "When you talk like that, it's difficult to recall where we're bound."

She slid her fingers through the curls on his chest. "Must we have a destination other than bliss?"

"Not here, certainly."

When she fit so comfortably in his arms, she refused to think beyond the moment, but he soon carried her past the smoking coals in the fire pit and into the cottage. "You made the bed!" she exclaimed, and he dropped her upon it.

He tossed their clothing across a chair. "I am not totally lacking in useful skills. I saved you a fish. Are you hungry?"

She eyed him with an appreciative glance that slowly drifted over his muscular body to focus on his proudly jutting manhood. "Only for you. Come here." The bottle of oil sat upon the small table, and she reached for it.

He circled the bed to lie down beside her and propped his hands behind his head. "When did your mother begin teaching you how to become such an attentive mistress?"

She moved to his feet and removed the stopper from the bottle before answering, but it pleased her to think he really was entertaining the notion of keeping her for himself. "When did your father begin teaching you how to fulfill your obligations as the Earl of Clairbourne?"

"Those were the only conversations we ever had. I'm curious as to when Françoise began grooming you."

She glanced away as if to summon her memories, but she was in fact weighing her choices. Then with a slight nod, she began to spin a truthful tale, carefully omitting any mention of her mother's strict rules.

"You must first realize that my mother has studied men with the concentration of a scientist fascinated by his subject. When I was small, I thought everyone lived as we did, in a beautiful apartment, with lovely furnishings and pretty clothes provided by a generous gentleman, who brought armloads of flowers and presents."

Michael reached up to plump his pillow. "Just how many of these 'generous gentlemen' do you recall?"

"While there may have been others before him, the first I remember was Jean Claude. He was the only one who spoke French to me. He brought me such beautiful dolls. Then there was Thomas, no wait, I believe Randolph might have come before him, but neither was particularly fond of me.

"Then my mother met Guy. He has always been very kind to us, and treated me as though I were one of his children."

"How fortunate," he responded. "But you've not answered my question."

She poured a drop of oil in her palm and held it. "You may have noticed that my mother's every gesture is calculated for effect. She has always wanted me to have as comfortable a life as she and I have enjoyed. Isn't that what any mother would wish for her daughter?"

He hesitated a moment too long. "Well . . . yes."

She was annoyed by that hint of reproach. "We are not common prostitutes who, for a pittance, rent out our vaginas."

"Good lord!"

He appeared horrified, but she simply shrugged. "Did you think I wouldn't know the proper word? What about penis or testicles? They are merely nouns, are they not, which name valuable parts of the body? Why should they be any different than an arm or a leg?"

She was impossible to control, but he shut his eyes and fought to tamp down his arousal. Now sorry he had ever begun the conversation, he sat up slightly. "I just wondered how old you were when your mother taught you how to please a man."

She set the bottle aside and rubbed the oil between her palms to warm it. "My whole life has been focused on pleasing men, but first only by being an adorable child. It wasn't until I was a woman myself that her instruction became more specific, but you don't really expect me to reveal all my mother's secrets, do you?"

Her hair fell in tangles over her bare breasts, her fair skin was flushed, and her expression so inviting his voice grew hoarse. "Just show me."

She smiled warmly. "I've already shown you quite a few."

She began to stroke him with a soft, slippery touch that made the disgraceful way she had been raised of no further consequence, and he fell back onto his pillow. She was more delightfully feminine than any highborn woman he had ever met, and he was no longer ashamed to need her so badly. At the first caress of her lips, he twisted his fingers in her hair and vowed never to let go.

She loved his throaty gasps and the way his long, dark eyelashes fluttered against his cheeks. Best of all, she loved the way his whole body shuddered as an ageless ecstasy washed through him, leaving him to float down in grateful surrender. She had discovered an unexpected joy of her own in pleasuring him. Delphine lay her cheek against the smooth hollow of his hip and rested her arm over his thigh. The surf's soothing roar lulled her to sleep, and she welcomed dreams of him.

When she awoke, he was stroking her hair as though she were a devoted pet. She smothered a yawn as she sat up. "I'm sorry. I didn't mean to fall asleep yet again."

An easy smile played across his lips. "You needn't apologize. But I'd forgotten you hadn't eaten, and I need to get up and catch more fish."

"I'm really not hungry." She moved toward him, and he welcomed her into his arms. "When we came here with Guy, we always had picnic baskets filled with delicious treats: tasty little rolls, cold meats and cheeses, berry tarts and heavenly soft cakes. There would always be lemonade and wine. I don't recall ever being hungry."

Resting in Michael's arms was better than those days, though. This was such a quiet, peaceful moment, and it saddened her to think that even if he kept her in a lavishly appointed apartment, they might never again share such unhurried days and near endless bliss.

Michael waited until Delphine's breathing again became even and deep to carefully reposition her head upon his pillow. He grabbed his trousers on the way out the door and picked up what had become his favorite pole.

Outside, the waves crested with an emerald splash, and the fish slid into the tide pools in slippery silver streams. He looked back toward the shimmering sand, where the sun-bleached cottage seemed to glow with an angelic halo.

Surrounded by the beauty he had been too distracted to appreciate earlier, he knelt to spear the first fish, and then stood to pierce the next three. He was embarrassed to have such fun fishing when the pastime had always struck him as the province of men too lazy for the more strenuous pursuits he enjoyed.

Now he was almost afraid to push his mind in other directions for fear none of his long-held ideas had been valid. He still felt like killing Guy, but if his friend had not kidnapped him, he might never have known Delphine. That he had already spent so much of his life without her struck him as a great tragedy, but he would proceed very carefully now that he had found her.

Her mother would demand a meticulously detailed contract, and he would lose Delphine's respect if he did not present an argument to at least a few of the requests. Of course he would provide well for her; he wanted her to enjoy every comfort, but he would retain control. After all, she was to be his mistress, not he her slave.

That such a distressing possibility even existed gave him a moments pause, but he had lived without love too long to ever become any woman's adoring pet, not even a goddess named Delphine.

Chapter 7

Spiral shell, pale blush
Crystalline, radiant dawn
A haunting perfume

Michael's spear missed his target and the fortunate fish was swept out of the tide pool before he had a second shot. He was hungry and knew Delphine must be starving, but as he looked up to judge the length of the day, a white speck appeared on the horizon.

Dreading what might come, he left his catch floating in a shallow pool and ran ashore with the knife and pole. The bed was now empty and with few places to search, he quickly found Delphine standing beneath the cistern washing her hair. He had often seen her nude, but it was always a thrill, and he hated to interrupt her.

"I've sighted another ship. It may only be passing by, but we ought to go up on the bluff rather than be caught unawares."

Delphine rinsed away the last of the soap, ran her fingers through her hair, and donned the clean night-gown she had brought outside. "At least this time we have more spears."

"Is that why you made so many? You don't trust me to protect you?"

His furious glance made it plain he was ready to rip off heads and kick them into the sea, but she was in no danger from him. "You're an honorable man. I know how hard you would fight to defend us, but I'll not watch you die trying. Now please consider the advantages of having what appears to be an innocuous bamboo pole, when in fact, it is a deadly spear."

The woman was actually plotting to ambush some as yet unseen foe, and Michael did not know whether to laugh or cry. "Do you actually see yourself as some warrior goddess?"

"Of course not. They're popular in myth, not history, and this ship may pose a real threat."

"That's at least an accurate assessment. Go on up the bluff and wait for me."

"Bring all the spears."

"Go!" He turned away before she drove him beyond the limit of his endurance, but when he joined her he was carrying all the spears. "Have you sighted the ship?" he asked.

"Yes, but there are two. The second is right behind the first, but if you look closely, you can make out the shape of two distinct vessels. I wish we had a spyglass."

He stifled a derisive snort as he stretched out beside her. "Are you that eager for a fight?"

Her glance remained focused on the horizon. "No, but let's watch awhile longer. Guy once owned a racing sloop. My mother wouldn't set foot on it, but I went out with him several times when he raced his friends. It was quite exhilarating."

Michael dimly recalled a mention of the boat, but

he had never sailed on it. Now all he could envision was how beautiful Delphine must have been with the wind whipping through her hair. She would have laughed at the wet spray and clung to Guy. It made him sick to think another man had ever touched her, no matter how innocently.

"The first ship is drawing ahead," she noted. "You can see the second more easily now."

Nearly choking on his jealousy, Michael stared out at the sea. The setting sun had turned the sky to flame, but the ships were near enough to sight clearly. They swept the horizon, graceful as swans, now obviously bound for Jamaica.

Delphine grasped Michael's wrist. "I'm relieved they'll not put in here, but we still ought to have a plan."

Despite her denial, he feared that she really did see herself as a warrior goddess. That he could so easily imagine her driving a golden chariot drawn by a team of snowy white stallions only made matters worse.

"What do you suggest?" he nearly snarled. "Shall we dig a pit, fill it with sharpened stakes, cover it with dried kelp, and if scoundrels appear, lure them over it?"

She responded with a delighted gasp. "Why yes, that's a splendid plan. It works in the jungles, doesn't it?"

He groaned. "It might, but it would be ludicrous here where one of us would probably stumble into our own trap."

Annoyed that he had not been serious after all, she pushed herself to her feet. She understood that women were meant to be affectionate ornaments, but she refused to pretend that was all she was. "I really wish you wouldn't trivialize my thoughts."

He let go of the spears to stand and grabbed her arm before she could again flee the bluff with her nose in the air. "That wasn't my intention, but I'll be the one to plan whatever defense we might need."

"Go right ahead, I would not dream of stopping you with my ludicrous ideas."

"Oh blast!" He released her to rake his fingers through his hair. "I don't want to fight with you. Maybe I'm still drugged, you really are a magnificent warrior goddess, and all I have to do is hang on until I wake."

He did not appear to be pleased by that possibility either. "Now who's being ludicrous?" she countered. "I'm a real woman, not some fanciful illusion you can wish away."

That he might hope she would vanish as quickly as a dream struck her as unspeakably cruel. Her heart fell as she considered how long she would like to remain with him. Obviously she was a great fool for caring about a man who was so eager to escape her.

Michael watched a hint of tears brighten the sparkle in her pretty green eyes and cursed his own folly. "I didn't mean to hurt you, but—"

She bent down to pick up a spear. "Be careful, my lord. It's never wise to insult a warrior goddess within reach of a spear. Now, I neglected to count the remaining mangoes this morning, and it must be done before sunset."

She left him to attend to the chore, but Michael sat down where he stood and put his head in his hands. Guy would surely return the morning of the seventh day. That meant they had only two days left before they could flee their island prison. He could survive two more days easily, but it was the nights that would be an excruciating torment.

More than a dozen mangoes remained on the tree. A few could be eaten now, and the rest would ripen in a day or two. They still had plenty of fruit, but Delphine did not feel like eating.

She had foolishly believed she was doing well with Michael, but apparently he merely found her amusing. Once he returned home, he might recall the pleasure she had given him, but he would swiftly forget her name.

Françoise had always insisted a mistress must enchant her lover so that whenever they were apart, he thought only of being with her again. She had failed to enchant Michael, but an older gentleman might more readily become attached to her. The thought gave her a flicker of hope, as did the fact that many silver-haired men were quite dashing.

The tide was coming in, and when she walked down to the surf's edge, the water's lingering warmth was too inviting to ignore. Much preferring a swim to a disagreeable companion, she tossed away her nightgown and ran into the welcoming waves.

Michael sat on the bluff until the gathering dusk made the way down treacherous. That he had found no creative solutions to any of his present problems made the trek all the more depressing. Then he reached the empty cottage and spotted Delphine's rumpled gown on the sand.

He had swum at night and been no worse for it, but when he scanned the sea and didn't find her immediately, he was terrified. He raced over the sand, calling her name, but the surf's roar swallowed both his shout and any reply she might have made.

Frantic, he screamed, "Delphine!" To his immense relief, she rose from the sea and came toward him. Lit by the water's silvery sheen, she was as majestic as any dream goddess, and he no longer wished to wake. He waded out to meet her and scooped her up in his arms.

"What's happened now?" she asked. "More bad dreams?"

Michael choked back a joyful sob and silenced her with a long, hungry kiss. He realized too late how much the desperate gesture revealed. He carried her over the sand into the cottage where it no longer mattered that the bed had not been remade.

He pulled her down onto the rumpled sheets, spread light kisses down her throat, and licked her sweetly puckered nipples. He drew the gold ring through his teeth, flipped it with his tongue, and thought how delicious she tasted all slippery wet.

His stubble grazed her breasts, but she ran her fingers through his hair to press him close. They had been apart only briefly, but clearly he had missed her terribly. Either that, or he simply could not bring himself to apologize to her another time today.

Then she considered that the twilight could have triggered an unexpected memory of his late wife, and he might have simply longed for a woman's comfort. Whatever his reason, she loved having him sprawled across her. Enormously pleased by his change in mood, she arched against him as her stomach growled a noisy protest.

She giggled and slid her hands down his back. "You must be hungry too," she whispered.

"Only for you." He pressed a sloppy kiss in her navel, then sat up. "But part of providing a strong defense is to keep you well fed. Perhaps not all that well, but at least fed. I caught a couple of fish before sighting the ships. I'll fetch them now."

Delphine glanced over the side of the bed. "What happened to my gown?"

"I'm afraid I left it on the sand. I'll bring it back with me."

"Please do." She opened the small trunk to select another, then decided it might be more fun to remain nude until he returned.

Guy had at least left a tin of matches to light the oil lamp and start the fire, but a hasty count revealed they would have to be careful not to run out. If they could just leave the fire burning low they would be fine, but she hadn't seen much driftwood wash up, and the stack beside the cottage was growing low.

They would survive two more days well enough, but they ought to search for wood on the morrow. It would be something new, and as easily as Michael was distracted, it could take the whole day.

Michael was surprised to find Delphine tending the fire unclothed, but then everything she did was unconventional. He handed her the nightgown he had retrieved from the beach, and laid the fish on the grill.

"I'd only caught these two before the ships appeared, but they're of a good size."

"Just like you, my lord."

Her glance was focused on his crotch, and he just

shook his head. She brushed off the nightgown to re-move the loose sand, but she didn't appear to be in any hurry to dress.

"You were right, that ring in your nipple is impossi-ble to ignore or forget."

"I'm so pleased that you've learned to like it." She slid her fingertips through her triangle of pale curls. "Some women have rings here. Would you like me to get one?"

"Good lord, Delphine!" He knelt to check the fish, but his face felt as hot as the flames.

"I didn't mean to shock you again, but think how pleasurable it would be to tongue a ring here."

He dared not glance up to follow the path of her fingers. "I'll be able to think of little else!" Then he had a truly horrible thought. "Does your mother have such a ring?"

"No, but I'm not her twin, and if I didn't enjoy having a pierced clitoris, I could always remove the ring and let the hole close."

He stood, but could barely draw in enough breath to speak. "Just where would you go for such an inti-mate piercing?"

Delphine had yet to don her gown and left it folded over her arm. "Physicians have needles."

"But surely no reputable one would pierce you there."

"Michael, really, have you no idea how many dis-reputable doctors there are? But I suppose I'd proba-bly visit the woman who pierced my nipple. She's meticulous with her tools."

"You mean she's an abortionist?" Michael clenched his fists at his sides. "Not another word on this sub-ject, Delphine, not one."

Delphine had failed to anticipate where her comment would lead him, but she nodded and pulled her nightgown over her head. "Tomorrow, we must gather driftwood for the fire. The heap is growing low."

"Driftwood," he repeated numbly, but his mind took him in another direction entirely.

There were men who sired children with their mistress, but the great beauties never seemed to conceive. He had not given their perpetually youthful figures any thought, but now realized why Delphine and her mother would know a woman who pierced nipples and performed whatever other service an elegant mistress might require.

It was something he would forbid in their contract. Startled that he was even considering the terms of such a document when he had so recently sworn he had no need of a mistress, he had to turn away from the fire. Surely it was being stranded with a nubile beauty who thought of sex even more often than he did that was the root of his trouble. Unfortunately, that comparison only served to make him hard again.

"I believe the fish are done," she called to him softly. "I'll fetch the plates."

He was relieved when she remained on the opposite side of the fire to eat. "Once we're off this cursed isle, I'll not consume another bite of fish," he swore.

"I think it's a lovely island," she argued. "I'd like to plant more fruit trees, but I'm not averse to eating fish or coming here again."

"I'd not come without my own boat."

"You've not mentioned that you own one." She licked her fingers and sent him a questioning glance.

"I don't, unless you count the rowboats we use on the rivers. We spent so much time in Jamaica, my father thought it imperative that I learn to sail. I learned, but I lack Guy's passion for it."

Delphine excused herself to select a couple of mangoes, but quickly returned and handed him one. "I've felt one of your passions," she remarked sweetly, "tell me about the others."

"No, little matters to me now." He set his plate aside and rolled the plump mango between his palms before biting into it.

"You are a very young man to give up whatever brought you joy. Surely your horses are still an important source of pride."

He nodded grudgingly. "Yes, here I own a remarkable stallion and several fine brood mares. I have another stable that is equally fine at my estate in Devon."

"What do you grow on your estate here in Jamaica?"

"Sugar cane and allspice, but though my father was a fine amateur botanist, I can barely distinguish one plant from another."

"You have a competent manager then?" While he did not seem particularly interested in their conversation, she longed to know every detail of his life.

"Yes, I do, but you needn't worry that I can't provide for you."

There, he had said it, and while she was pleased, there was still a wild darkness to the man. Brandy had failed to dissolve it, and though she could make it fade for hours at a time, his deep melancholy always returned. She sat up a bit straighter.

"Why should my welfare concern you, my lord? As I recall, you claimed to have no need of a mistress."

While he had been stubbornly opposed to the idea a few days ago, the alternative was now unthinkable. He caught her gaze and held it. "No, I don't need just any obliging woman, but I do need you. Now come here."

"In a moment. First, I want to finish my supper." She took a bite of mango and chewed slowly.

What she truly needed was a moment to consider a future with him. Losing his wife and child must have hurt him so badly that his heart might never heal. He was still a virile young man who definitely appreciated her beauty, but what he offered was simply a business arrangement advantageous to them both.

Her mother discounted marriage as a tiresome social obligation. Françoise much preferred being the wife of Guy's heart. It didn't bother her mother at all to share Guy, but Delphine would have to compete with a dead woman. It would be even more perplexing if she were to succeed in restoring Michael's soul to the point he took a second wife. That would be a catastrophe of her own making.

Fearing her thoughts were swiftly becoming as bleak as his, she finished the mango and chucked the pit into the fire. She stretched languidly and smiled. "It is another lovely night."

"All the nights are beautiful in the Caribbean," he replied. As the words left his lips, the time when he could not have appreciated the night's fragrant warmth without brandy seemed long past. That it had been less than a week was a tribute to Delphine.

She correctly gauged his frown, stood, untied the ribbon at her neckline, and let her nightgown slide to her feet before stepping out of it. She rounded the fire to sit down in his lap, and circled her right breast with her fingertip.

"Why don't you begin here?"

Unwilling to do her bidding, Michael grasped her

hair to tilt her head and kissed her with the same passionate frenzy that had seized him on the beach. She tasted of mango and warm, willing woman, but he longed to go slowly and savor every delectable inch. He kissed her until they were both gasping for breath before he lowered his head to lave her nipples. Delphine arched her back to thrust more of her breasts into his mouth, and he slid his fingertips down her ribs in a grateful caress. When he finally raised his head, he wore a wicked grin.

"Rather than risk rolling into the fire, let's go inside."

She braced her hand on his shoulder to rise. "I should rinse out my hair first, or in the morning, I'll resemble Medusa too closely to please either of us."

"That's impossible, but I want you to be comfortable."

She swept him with an appreciative glance. "I'll hurry." She picked up her nightgown, then went around the side of the cottage. The air was still warm, and the cistern's contents had been heated by the sun. She opened the spigot and stepped beneath the stream of deliciously soft rainwater, but before she could turn, Michael pressed his nude body against her back. He cupped her breasts, and pinched her nipples gently.

She leaned into him. A mistress was a refuge, after all, and she would be a sweet haven for him. She rubbed against him as he slid his hands over her. He seemed eager to memorize her curves, and she was as enchanted as he. She reached up to shut off the spigot and turned in his arms.

"I saw you once on the street in Kingston. You were arguing with Guy, and I thought you were the handsomest man I'd ever seen."

He cupped her bottom to pull her against his shaft. "You'd not seen many men though, had you?"

"No, but I'd seen enough to recognize how remarkable you are. Even surrounded by a thousand others, you'd be noticed."

"Thank you, but you needn't flatter me."

"It's the truth!" She raised up on her tiptoes to kiss him with an enthusiasm that sparked a lengthy exchange before she drew away. "I'm sorry for that first night. I promise never to take advantage of you again."

"It's forgotten," he stressed, "but now that I'm awake, let's create some new memories. I want you to do everything you did that night all over again."

Delphine laughed low in her throat. "Are you sure you can stand it?"

He responded by wrapping his arms around her waist and lifting her off her feet. "Do you doubt my strength?"

"Not at all," she insisted, "merely your tolerance for limitless pleasure." She left her nightgown outside to wear in the morning and led the way into the cottage, where she plucked a towel from the linen chest and dried him off with affectionate pats.

"I don't believe you'll be able to affect the same lack of interest you showed that night, but I know you'll do your best," she teased.

Michael stretched out on the bed and rested his hands at his sides. "I wasn't disinterested. That was the best dream I've ever had."

She ran the towel over her hair. "Your memory may be more vivid than mine. Do remind me if I forget something important."

"You may rest assured that I will. Now stop stalling and begin."

She lay the towel aside, climbed up on the side of the bed, and straddled his leg. "Close your eyes. That night, I'd no idea they were such a clear blue."

"Are you partial to blue eyes?"

"Only yours, but you're supposed to be asleep, so please be quiet."

She remembered nuzzling his crotch to savor his musky aroma. He had a warm, seductive scent, but wanting to tease him a bit, she raked her nails up his inner thighs before combing the dark curls cradling his sex.

"Just what is it you're doing?" he whispered.

"I was preparing to suck your balls into my mouth, one at a time, and then trace my name on them with my tongue."

He choked back a strangled gasp. "And I slept through that?"

"Yes, but the drug was to blame." She leaned over to lick the length of his now rock-hard cock but drew only the tip into her mouth. His whole body seemed to be twitching, and she had to sit back.

"I can't do anything with you jumping around like that. Perhaps you should go to sleep before I begin."

He drew in a deep breath and released it slowly. "Just give me a few seconds."

"You may have all night if you wish." She slid the tip of her tongue into his navel. Five nights ago, he could have been any attractive man, but now he was quite dear to her. She sat back to wait, but when his hands tangled in the sheets, it was plain he could not relax.

"We can't go back to that night, Michael. I can satisfy you with my mouth and hands, but you can't possibly pretend to be asleep, so why try?"

He opened his eyes and smiled sheepishly. "You're

right, but before I give up on recreating that night, do what you just described."

She widened her eyes to affect a bewitching innocence. "You want me to trace my initials with my tongue?"

He shifted his shoulders to get more comfortable. "Yes, please."

"I'm only here to please you, my lord." She stretched out on his leg, pressed his cock against his belly, and with an exquisite stealth, drew a testicle into her mouth. She had barely begun to trace her name when he caught her hair.

"Stop and turn around," he ordered. "That way I can pleasure you at the same time."

"Oh, I doubt that," she murmured, but she turned as directed to straddle his chest, and pressed her cleft against his mouth. She used her elbows for support and grasped his cock. They had forgotten to light the lamp, but the remnants of the fire filled the cottage with a romantic glow. She rested her head against his thigh to lick his balls, and while this position made it more difficult, she was willing to try.

Then he began to spread oil over and up into her, and she was swiftly as distracted as he. Michael sucked her bud and turned his finger to enter her heat with a slow twist. She responded by rubbing the head of his cock against the roof her mouth. She could feel as well as hear his breath quicken, but the sensation he coaxed from her was so incredibly sweet, she feared she could not satisfy him in time.

Delphine squirmed as he moved his hands over her bottom and thighs in a roving caress, his touch feather-light. Warmth slid clear down to her quivering toes. She felt adored, and overwhelmed by his easy affection, she gave up all hope of pleasing him to lie atop him in a languid sprawl.

He knew precisely where to press and lick, and when the joy he created finally crested in a stunning peak, she felt so weak she would have tumbled right off the bed had he not caught her. She laughed, but it came out as a muffled purr.

He drew her into his arms and pressed her cheek against his shoulder. "You're welcome," he whispered.

She grazed his chest in an ineffectual caress. "Just give me a moment please, and then—"

"No, it feels too good just to hold you. Go to sleep."

Delphine discounted the generosity of his gesture, and meant only to rest until the last of the glorious peace washing through her faded. But his heartbeat beneath her ear was so soothing that she yawned, and fell asleep.

Afloat on her bliss, Michael ran her hair through his fingers. She was such an extraordinary woman. She challenged and shocked him, yet continually filled him with a rapture that left him wondering how he had ever lived without her.

While Françoise may have taught her more than any gently-bred young woman should ever know, Delphine was his now, and he meant to keep her, on his own unapologetically demanding terms.

Chapter 8

*A light golden mist
Sun-warmed skin, a lover's kiss
Shooting stars collide*

Delphine strolled along the beach gathering seashells, but her mind wandered so terribly that she had collected only three small scallop shells by the time she reached Michael's abandoned camp. She paused there to rest, set the shells in a line, and traced lazy patterns around them with her fingertips. Their ridges were perfect, their edges unchipped, but all trace of the small creatures that had inhabited them had been washed away.

As a child, she had had such fun there searching for pretty seashells. It had been a game to her then. She had classified them by type, compared their beauty, and kept a tally of how many she had collected on each visit. She had taken only the prettiest ones home and added them to a large glass jar that still sat on a shelf in her bedroom.

Now she was a grown woman and expected to collect lovers rather than seashells, but it was impossible to regard Michael as merely the first of many. It simply hurt too much to think of him as someone to be used up and cast aside like a broken seashell. He was already hurt so badly that she would never be able to bring herself to leave him. That meant she would have to remain with him until he tired of her, and how would she bear such a sad fate? Unwilling to leave, unable to stay, the only way to avoid breaking both their hearts was not to create a liaison between them in the first place.

She glanced out over the sea. How she loved its primal scent! Its roar was the voice of the father she had never known, and now its strength and beauty would always remind her of Michael. It was already too late to guard her own tender heart, but not too late to protect his shattered emotions.

When Michael awoke, he was annoyed to find Delphine gone, but annoyance failed to dim his eagerness to find her. As he hurried to shave and don his shirt, his glance fell upon her journal lying on the table.

On the first page, she had written her name in her beautifully distinctive script, and seized with a sudden desire to have a keepsake, he used the razor to slit the page from the book. He folded the single sheet neatly and hid it in his boot. He doubted that she would ever discover it was missing, but he would not deny taking it if she did.

He had never sought a token from a woman, and it amused him to want one now. If he again succeeded in waking before her, he would cut a lock of fair hair.

This was already day five, and while she had made what was in actuality an imprisonment enjoyable, he could not wait to take her home. Once back on Jamaica, there were so many pretty things he could buy her. She deserved to be pampered, and he rather liked the idea of spoiling her shamefully.

He whistled a jaunty tune as he set out to find her, but he had begun to run and was out of breath by the time he did. He bent over to rest his hands on his knees. "Why didn't you wake me?" he asked.

Delphine looked up. A hasty glance revealed his hair was damp, and he was freshly shaven, so he had taken the time to look his best before seeking her company. Perhaps he had been bored, lonely even, but not desperately eager to see her. Hopefully, that would work to her advantage.

"I'm used to rising early, but when there is so little to do here, I hated to disturb you."

He sat down beside her and drew her into his arms. "I'd say we have a great deal to occupy us here, but maybe you've already tired of me."

She caressed his cheek. "We can sit here trading compliments, but I fear we're wasting time that would be better spent gathering driftwood. I've neg- lected the chore, and we need a fire to cook our meals, such as they are."

Michael would have preferred to exchange compli- ments, but he could not argue with her more practical suggestion. "If it's driftwood you want, then let's col- lect some at once." He got to his feet and lifted her gracefully to hers. He dropped an arm around her shoulders and gave her a quick hug.

"Then we'll fish and roast another fine breakfast. Or would you rather go for a swim before we fish. What's your pleasure?"

She rested her hand on his flat belly, then let it drift

lower. "We definitely need the driftwood and fish, but we could take our time before going for a swim."

He caught her wrist, but she had already felt him harden at her touch. "Wait," he insisted, "you needn't do that here. There's an enormous difference between servicing a man and making love. Let's just see to the chores, and then devote the remainder of the day to making love."

His confident smile was so utterly charming she had to nod. Her task had been so simple when all she had to do was touch him, but now that she had felt his affectionate caress, nothing was easy. A flood of unshed tears filled her throat with a painful knot, and she adjusted the angle of her hat, as though the breeze had caught it. The shells forgotten, she walked down to the edge of the water.

"Delphine, look at me."

His voice had deepened to a commanding tone, and she had to remind herself that there was no past, no future, but only the glorious present. As her mother had taught her, she would create a fascinating illusion and weep for him later alone. She smiled brightly as she turned. "Yes?"

Disarmed by her relaxed expression, he shrugged. "I'm sorry, I feared something might be amiss. I know you're probably hungry and sick of this tiny isle."

"No, not at all. I love this place. Now let's make the effort to gather driftwood on our way home."

He caught himself before he laughed at her absurd description of the simple cottage. He wanted so much more for her. "I'd challenge you to a contest to see who finds the most, but I already know I'll be the one to carry it."

GET UP TO
4 FREE BOOKS!

You can have the best romance delivered to your door for less than what you'd pay in a bookstore or online. Sign up for one of our book clubs today, and we'll send you **FREE* BOOKS** just for trying it out...**with no obligation to buy, ever!**

HISTORICAL ROMANCE BOOK CLUB

Travel from the Scottish Highlands to the American West, the decadent ballrooms of Regency England to Viking ships. Your shipments will include authors such as CONNIE MASON, CASSIE EDWARDS, LYNSAY SANDS, LEIGH GREENWOOD, and many, many more.

LOVE SPELL BOOK CLUB

Bring a little magic into your life with the romances of Love Spell—fun contemporaries, paranormals, time-travels, futuristics, and more. Your shipments will include authors such as KATIE MACALISTER, SUSAN GRANT, NINA BANGS, SANDRA HILL, and more.

As a book club member you also receive the following special benefits:

- **30% OFF all orders through our website & telecenter!**
  (Plus, you still get 1 book FREE for every 5 books you buy!)
- **Exclusive access to special discounts!**
- **Convenient home delivery and 10 days to return any books you don't want to keep.**

There is no minimum number of books to buy, and you may cancel membership at any time. See back to sign up!

*Please include $2.00 for shipping and handling.

YES! ☐

Sign me up for the **Historical Romance Book Club** and send my TWO FREE BOOKS! If I choose to stay in the club, I will pay only $8.50* each month, a savings of $5.48!

YES! ☐

Sign me up for the **Love Spell Book Club** and send my TWO FREE BOOKS! If I choose to stay in the club, I will pay only $8.50* each month, a savings of $5.48!

NAME: _____

ADDRESS: _____

_____

TELEPHONE: _____

E-MAIL: _____

☐ **I WANT TO PAY BY CREDIT CARD.**

☐ VISA   ☐ MasterCard   ☐ DISCOVER

ACCOUNT #: _____

EXPIRATION DATE: _____

SIGNATURE: _____

Send this card along with $2.00 shipping & handling for each club you wish to join, to:

**Romance Book Clubs
1 Mechanic Street
Norwalk, CT 06850-3431**

Or fax (must include credit card information!) to: 610.995.9274.
You can also sign up online at www.dorchesterpub.com.

*Plus $2.00 for shipping. Offer open to residents of the U.S. and Canada only.
Canadian residents please call 1.800.481.9191 for pricing information.

If under 18, a parent or guardian must sign. Terms, prices and conditions subject to change. Subscription subject
to acceptance. Dorchester Publishing reserves the right to reject any order or cancel any subscription.

JOIN NOW!

"Then you've already won," she teased, and skipping along the damp sand, she swished the skirt of her nightgown as though she were dancing.

He just shook his head and followed, but the real joy was in watching her.

They were too distracted by each other to taste their breakfast, and Delphine easily coaxed Michael into the cottage. She brushed the tips of her hair as he removed his clothes, and as soon as he was stretched out on the bed, she cast aside her nightgown and joined him.

She knelt between his legs and bent her head to caress his torso and groin with her shimmering tresses. "If I had some silk scarves, I'd tie you to the bed," she murmured, letting her hair drift over his cock.

"Although I suppose we could rip up one of my nightgowns," she added.

Michael was already gripping the rails of the headboard. "I've no wish to be bound, so there's no need to sacrifice one of your pretty gowns."

"They can all be replaced, so should you change your mind, please let me know." She backed away to drag her hair over his thighs. "I have a needle and thread. Would you like me to pierce your nipple?"

"Delphine! Good lord, no. Are there actually men who wear rings like yours?"

"Intriguing thought, isn't it?" She moved up again to slide her hair over his shoulders.

"No, it isn't. Do you think of nothing but ways to torture me?"

She laughed as though he were the one doing the teasing. "I think only of how to delight you, and you might have enjoyed being bound or pierced."

"You have to know me better than that," he choked out gruffly.

"I know every inch of your handsome body," she nearly purred, "but little else, my lord."

"What if I'd been short and stout?"

She bent down to slide her tongue into his navel. "Then you'd be here alone. My mother would never have sent me to an ugly earl."

"Not even if he were Guy's closest and richest friend?"

"No. She admires beauty in a man as greatly as I do." Delphine twisted the ends of her hair and whisked them across his nipples. He rocked beneath her, and she slid her free hand up his ribs. Then she skipped her fingertips from his elbow to his wrist.

"Arms are a neglected part of a man's anatomy, but yours are quite sensitive, aren't they?"

He sucked in a breath and rubbed his arm to dispel the tingle. "Obviously, but wait a minute, let's consider appearance in more depth. If you were to begin with a homely man, you'd not have to worry that his money might outlast his looks."

She sat back on his ankles. "Hmm, yes, definitely a point to consider, but you're forgetting that the choice was made for me."

Michael frowned slightly. "Am I not your choice now also?"

She dragged a nail in a light trail down his belly and watched him flinch. "You have provided an abundance of fish."

"Is that all you'll consider?"

She leaned back to shake out her hair and flaunt her breasts. Straightening up, she wrapped both hands around his cock. "There is this fine asset as well."

"Why not let me show you what I can really do with it?"

"Oh no, that wasn't part of the bargain," she cautioned.

It was all he could do to lie still as she stroked him, and he spoke through clenched teeth, "I'm not the one who made it though, so let's strike a new one."

"I wish I could, but my mother would never forgive me." She leaned down to lick him with an enticing swirl.

He had to close his eyes to shut out the sight before he could draw a breath to argue. "Of course she will, because I'll give you every advantage."

She again laved his corona, and sat back to pump him slowly. "I'd say I already hold it."

"There's far more to me than a hard cock."

She did not doubt that he was serious, but she would not allow herself to be. "A great deal more, I'll agree. You're not only handsome, but also quite charming, although you could do better things with that smooth tongue of yours than simply argue."

Tempted to wrap his hands around her lovely throat, he gripped the rails with a new intensity. "I want you now, Delphine. Write your own terms in your journal, and I'll sign it."

She released him, but rested her hands on his thighs. "No. I have absolutely no head for business. My talents lie elsewhere."

He could not argue with her boast. She knew precisely where to press, lick, or stroke, and she did it with such imaginative flair he would have promised her anything. That she was such a rare beauty only served to intensify the heartstopping pleasure.

Sick of Guy's and Françoise's game, he raised up to

gain Delphine's full attention. "I'm not playing. I want you now. Let's forge our own contract. Your mother needn't be involved."

She dipped her head and looked up at him through the gentle sweep of her eyelashes. "I understand your frustration, my lord, but I'm serious, too. I've no wish to sully the delight I've found in your arms with some dryly worded document."

She also refused to sign an agreement she had no intention of honoring. He had placed her in a most uncomfortable position. She already knew he did not enjoy being crossed, but when his gaze darkened to a menacing glare, she scrambled off the bed and snatched up her nightgown on the way out the door.

Michael stared at the space where she had been perched on his legs and cursed his own aching need. Delphine was maddeningly independent, and he had made such a clumsy grab for her it was no wonder she had been infuriated, or God forbid, frightened away.

She had made him so damn hard he swore as he dragged on his pants. He could solve the problem with a few brisk strokes of his own, but he would not allow her to wonder or fret for the few minutes it would take to achieve momentary relief on his own.

He went flying out of the cottage, but the surrounding beach was empty, all sparkling sand and no winsome woman. He hated chasing her, but the hair on his neck rose in a warning wave, and he turned to find her observing him from the bluff.

"Damn," he muttered under his breath; he had not spent half the time courting his wife that he had in pursuing Delphine. That bitter realization stopped him in mid-stride, but unwilling to relive that horror, he started up the path. He was uncertain what to say, but he would not apologize for what he felt when his whole body ached to make her his own.

Unfortunately, she was ready for him. "You will always have the superior strength," she challenged, "but I'll not be forced into anything I don't wish to do. Is that clear?"

He raised his hand in an abrupt plea for silence. As the Earl of Clairbourne, he was unfamiliar with ultimatums, and yet her willful defiance was a large measure of her charm.

"All right," he agreed with feigned reluctance. "I won't be forced either. Now may we have a truce?"

"A truce?" she drew out the word as though it were a ridiculous request, and then stepped into his arms and kissed the pulse in his throat.

Michael savored the lush fullness of her breasts against his chest, but he took a firm hold on her shoulders and pushed her back a step. He still wanted to hammer out an agreement, but not if it meant sacrificing a moment with her now.

"I'll agree to postpone the inevitable discussion of terms, but I mean to have you, Delphine. I'll be more generous than either you or Françoise could have dreamed."

She relied upon a wistful smile to convince him he would have his way. Once off the isle, however, she would vanish so completely, he would wonder if she had ever been more than a glorious erotic dream.

"I trust you to protect my interests as well as your own," she assured him softly.

"It's settled for the moment then." He drew her back into his arms and hugged her so tightly neither of them could breathe.

His forceful embrace left her both puzzled and panicked. She had not expected him to care this deeply, and it made her situation all the more heartwrenching. She stretched up to suck his earlobe, and he released her with a good-natured chuckle.

"Shall we continue as though we hadn't been interrupted?" he asked.

She spoke honestly now. "I certainly hope so, my love. I've no wish to waste another moment of this beautiful day."

He gestured for her to precede him down the path. The past year had been a painful blur, but he now found an acute pleasure in such simple things. The sky was a vibrant blue, the sea shinning with a near blinding sparkle, and his lithe companion was easily the most beguiling creature since Eve. Overwhelmed with his good fortune, it was all he could do not to race her back to the cottage.

As they entered, he tugged off his shirt. "I swear we waste far too much time removing our clothes. Let's simply go without them from now on."

Delphine let her nightgown pool at her feet, then laid it over the trunk. "It would certainly save time, but if I became too sunburned to share the bed, you'd blame yourself rather than the sun."

"True." He waited for her to climb up on the bed, then swiftly moved over her and pressed her into the mattress. She smiled as he slanted his mouth over hers, and he was swiftly lost in her mango-flavored kiss.

He gasped for breath when he broke away to reach for the oil. "Does this have a taste?" he asked.

"Yes, but it's neither salty nor sweet."

He rubbed a drop on her right breast, circling the pale areola before rolling the nipple between his thumb and fingers. He bent down to lick her gently, then sucked away the oil. "Hmm, yes, it's rather like the way you taste when you come. I like it."

She ruffled his hair as he moved to her left breast. She loved his heated kisses and arched her back to encourage more. Even the lightest sucking sent a thrill through her, and she pressed him closer still.

He pushed back on his elbows. "Maybe I should tie you to the bed. We did rip up one sheet to bandage your arm, and—"

"No, not when I enjoy touching you so much. Your whole body sizzles with life. I'd make a most disagreeable captive." She framed his face to bring his lips up to hers. She could taste the oil now, but thought he had flavored it with his imagination.

He slid his tongue over hers, longing to enter her. Michael doubted his ability to keep his behavior in check much longer. He rubbed his erection against her thigh and deepened his kiss. He had never known desire this intense, like fire under his skin, and he pushed away to spread fevered kisses over her breasts.

She made a grab for his hair, but he was too quick to be caught, and pulled her legs over his shoulders. He cupped her bottom in a forceful grasp and watched her eyes close as he slid a thumb into her. She bucked beneath him as he twisted his hand but rather than slow down, he stretched out to swirl his tongue around her clitoris. He circled the tender nub, teasing, tasting, brushing it with his lips and tongue until she writhed with a passion that matched his own.

He did not pause to taste the oil this time, but after dribbling it over her, he shifted position to tease her with his cock rather than his hands. He felt the tension coil within her, winding to tighten around him as he edged deeper. The oil made it so easy to slide forward into her heat, but he fought the compulsion to end her body's last bit of resistance.

Certain he was either the finest of gentlemen or a stupid fool, he withdrew and used his fingers and mouth instead to bring her to climax. Then gripping her hips, he held her tight while he drank in her cream and licked her to a second shuddering release.

"Stop," she mumbled weakly.

"I'm not tired," he insisted with another long swipe against her now swollen folds.

"You will be when I finish with you," she swore, but she was too sated to rise from where she lay sprawled. "Come between my breasts again. You liked that, didn't you?"

Rather than straddle her, he rolled her onto her side, moved behind her, and slid his cock between her legs. He stroked her clitoris with each thrust, while he pinched her nipples with an enticing rhythm.

"I like all of you," he whispered against her ear. "Your scent, your taste, it's all delicious."

He rocked against her thighs, then slowed to a stop to prolong his pleasure. Her skin was so smooth and sweet. He held her close as he moved again, fitting her cleft like a locomotive to the rails while she pressed her thighs together obligingly. He sank deeper with each thrust, then bathed in her heat, came against her clitoris.

Exhausted by that rippling joy, he fell asleep still wrapped around her. When he awakened bound to the bed's iron rails, he was more amused than angry. "Determined to have your way with me again, are you?"

Delphine kissed him full on the mouth, then turned and left the cottage.

He yanked on the sheeting ropes and rattled the

whole bed. "Delphine!" he yelled. She had fallen into a rapture-drugged sleep in his arms and this was how she repaid him?

"Delphine!" What had she done to him? If she planned to leave him tied to the bed until Guy and Françoise returned, she would have more than a taste of his anger. He yanked his wrists, but rather than break free, he merely tightened the knots.

She had lashed his ankles together and secured them to the rails at the foot of the bed. And he had slept through that? He was furiously angry both with himself and her until she came through the door, nude, dripping wet, and trailing a length of kelp.

"What is it you think you are doing?" he shouted.

She coiled the kelp around her arm as she approached the bed. "I thought you might appreciate a challenge."

"Not this one, I don't!"

She climbed over the end of the bed, unfurled the slippery kelp with an agile toss and flung it over his chest. She then withdrew it with a tantalizing hand over hand motion. "Why don't you pretend that you're a pirate and I'm a willful mermaid?" she coaxed.

"I'm no pirate, but you are too damn willful!" he countered, but to his shame, his cock rose in eager anticipation of such lively sport.

She trailed the damp kelp across his groin, then with a flip of the wrist, dragged it under his balls.

"Delphine!" he shrieked.

Alarmed, she leaned over him. "Have I hurt you? It's supposed to feel incredibly good with a silk scarf."

He grit his teeth. "Untie me this instant."

"As you wish." She let the kelp slip to the floor and freed first his feet and then his hands.

He sat up and rubbed his wrists. His first impulse was to haul her over his lap and spank her soundly, but she was watching him with such a befuddled gaze his anger dissolved in a renewed burst of desire. He pulled her into his arms.

"I'm not hurt. You just shocked me is all. You ought to warn me before you try something that wild."

When she failed to respond, he tilted her chin to force her to meet his gaze. "I never know what to expect from you. Now I don't care what your mother or Guy may have told you, you needn't keep me constantly entertained. Being here like this is enough."

She licked her lips. She had wanted him too distracted to recall his demands for a contract, but obviously she had failed. She would have happily settled for a righteous anger that would have sent him back into an icy retreat. Any response would have been preferable to his affectionate understanding.

"It isn't like you to be so quiet," he whispered against her temple. He nibbled her earlobe and hugged her. "I ought to be furiously angry with you, in fact I was until you strolled through the door clad in no more than a handful of seaweed.

"My God, I want off this island so badly it hurts. There's so much we could do back home. I know a chef who prepares the most delicious meals anyone's ever tasted and musicians who play such beautiful music we could dance all night."

Delphine hushed him with her fingertips. "That sounds wonderful, but could you please teach me how to ride?"

A slow smile spread across his lips. "Do you really wish to learn?"

"You're a horseman as I recall. Why wouldn't I want to learn?"

All he could envision was Delphine in her filmy nightgown astride a pretty pale mare. It took his breath away, and he rested his forehead against hers. "Yes, it will be a pleasure to teach you everything I know about horses and riding. You'll need a proper riding habit, perhaps a whole new wardrobe if you own nothing but silk nightgowns."

She nestled against him. "I have a great many beautiful clothes, and I'd be happy to wear them for you," she lied.

"You must teach me French," Michael urged.

She kissed him before repeating his question. "Do you really wish to learn?"

"Yes, I want to read your poetry."

"It's meaningful only to me," she apologized, "or I'd translate it into English to save you the trouble of mastering French."

He nuzzled her throat. "You'll not discourage me so easily when I'm fascinated by your thoughts."

She refused to believe him and add to the pain of their parting. Instead, she regarded him with a playful smile. "I'd assumed you were fascinated by my more obvious assets."

He pushed her down on the bed. "From your silvery hair to your dainty pink toes, there's not an inch of you that doesn't fascinate me. Learning French to gain access to your thoughts is a small price to pay."

"Have you forgotten your many obligations as an earl?" she queried softly. "Once home, you may lack the time to acquire a new language."

He propped his head on his elbow, but kept her close. "Is your real question if I will still have time for you?"

"Sprawled across a bed on a tiny isle, it's difficult to imagine another life; but yes, there are your prize horses, and—"

"Delphine," he chided in a husky whisper. "I was barely alive before I met you, and now, I even enjoy fishing."

She drank in his deep chuckle before responding. "Is that such an amazing transformation, my lord?"

"Monumental, but please call me Michael, or my darling, or simply beloved, if you prefer."

She savored the thrill of that request for the length of a heartbeat, then tickled his ribs. "Must every woman you meet fall at your feet and swear undying love?"

He caught her hands and muffled her laughter with a hungry kiss. "I care not at all for other women when you're the one in my bed."

"Must I remind you again that this is in fact my bed? Even if it were yours, would you care for me only as long as we share it and forget me once we were apart?"

He slid his fingers through her hair and kissed her with a languid perfection that left them both breathless. "Why would we ever be apart for more than a few hours at a time?" he asked.

She pulled back slightly. "Won't you return to London every year?"

"Only if I must, and even then, I'd take you with me."

"What would you do, dress me as one of your servants and pass me off as a new upstairs maid?"

He touched his fingertip to her lips. "Never. I'd

dress you in silks and satins and introduce you as Mademoiselle Antoine."

Playing the flirt, she continued to regard him with a curious glance. "I have no reputation to lose, but what would you gain by flaunting your mistress?"

He sat up to adjust their positions and rubbed her shoulders gently. "Envy certainly, but I'd never expose you to scorn. Don't you know that?"

Even with his hot breath against her cheek, she knew she would never see his estate in Devon, but it was senseless to argue over something that could never be. "So I'd be subjected to a tedious voyage only to be hidden away?"

"When have you ever spent a tedious moment with me?"

She laughed way back in her throat. "I can recall several in our first day together."

He slid his arms across her bosom and hugged her tight. "That was another man entirely. I've been reborn with you."

Delphine rested her cheek against his arm and wished with all her heart she could say the same; but rather than being reborn in his arms, the wanton woman who had been raised to seduce wealthy men and profit from their generosity had simply ceased to exist. She was no one now, and would soon disappear rather than confess his love had been her undoing.

Chapter 9

Passion sears the heart
Starry nights fall open
Moonbeams float on dreams

Delphine eased herself from Michael's arms to leave their bed before dawn. She bathed and brushed her hair until it shone, then dressed in a fresh nightgown adorned with tiny tucks and pale pink ribbons. As the sky lightened, she leaned against the cottage doorway and watched her lover sleep.

Day six, and her heart ached for all she had found with Michael and would soon lose. When she returned to the bed, she sat cross-legged at the foot and slowed her breathing to the rhythm of his. She memorized the width of his shoulders, the slant of his cheekbones, and the slight curl that made his glossy black hair dip low on his forehead.

She was well acquainted with his stubborn pride and knew how furiously angry he would be when she refused to become his mistress. Yet she had only two equally horrid choices: to appear heartless now, or unspeakably cruel tomorrow. Filled with dread, she failed to notice when Michael awoke until he reached out to grab her shoulders and pulled her down into his arms.

"Finally, you've stayed with me." He rolled her beneath him and nuzzled her throat. "Let's celebrate."

His stubble tickled, and she laughed in spite of the darkness of her mood. She rubbed against him, but his fiery heat melted only the frayed hem of her fears. Now intent upon giving him pleasure, she rocked her hips against his erection, and he muffled an appreciative groan in her hair.

"Don't make me beg," he whispered.

She traced light circles on his back. "What is a delay of a day or two?"

"A lifetime."

"We have already shared a lifetime," she assured him sweetly.

"No, we've not even begun."

He had her nightgown bunched around her shoulders and with a hasty tug, she tossed it to the floor. It was impossible to summon rational thought while he lapped at her nipples with lazy swirls, and she arched into his mouth. Men loved the chase, and only a single challenge remained to keep him enchanted. It was much too soon, even on their last day, to give up her last and most highly cherished prize.

He raised up, moved over her, and kissed her with a deep, thorough passion. When he finally broke away, he caressed her cheek fondly. "I'm sorry our first kiss wasn't as enjoyable."

"What do you mean? I certainly enjoyed it, and as you must recall, I asked for another."

"True, but you meant only to torment me." He fingered the ring in her nipple as if the exotic jewelry were ample proof.

"Torment was never my intention." She licked her lips and leaned into his kiss. She was lost in him, but even that bliss was tinged with sorrow.

Michael broke away when he tasted her tears and wiped the moisture from her cheeks with his fingertips. "Please don't cry. I thought you were happy with me. If there's something you want, just name it."

She was embarrassed to have been betrayed by her emotions. "I am very happy to be with you, but I'm sorry we're leaving tomorrow."

"I'm not." He kissed the tender hollow beneath her collar bone, then slid down to her navel. "I can't wait to take you home."

She combed his hair with her fingertips. "You know I can't set foot in your home."

He glanced up to flash a quick grin. "I'll decide who belongs there, no one else."

His defiant confidence was awe-inspiring, but it was irrelevant when their time together was swiftly drawing to a close. "I admire your certainty," she claimed.

"Shall I describe all I admire about you?" he countered.

Delphine undulated beneath him. "I'd rather that you showed me."

He laughed at her provocative pose. "Now there's a challenge we'll both enjoy."

She closed her eyes to savor the moment, but a sharp pang of guilt brought a stark clarity. Love demanded the truth, and such a fine man deserved it. She drew in a deep breath and forced out the most painful confession she would ever have to make.

"I can't become your mistress."

Michael froze. "What did you say?" He propped himself on his outstretched arms to better gauge her reply.

In an instant, she glimpsed the hostile stranger he had been on the first day. Unwilling to back down, she remained calm. "I can no longer play at something that will never be."

"You're not making any sense," he scolded crossly.

"Just let me go." She tried to escape his embrace, but any effort to leave the bed only increased the delicious friction between their bare bodies.

"Never." He slid his cock along her cleft with a light thrust meant to tease rather than satisfy. "We are too finely matched a pair, Delphine. I'll never let you go."

She had expected him to be angry, but rather than rage, it was a chilling determination that darkened his gaze. None of her naive assumptions about him had ever proven correct, and while frightened, she feigned a confidence to rival his.

"Am I to be your prisoner now?" she asked.

He dipped lower to slide on her wetness. "Yes, if there is no other way. Now be still," he ordered.

She grabbed for the rails above her head. "You'll not keep me against my will."

"The hell I won't. I'll hire a dozen men to guard you."

Each stroke of his cock brought an exquisite burst of heat, and she had to taunt him through clenched teeth. "I'll seduce them and escape."

"Not the men I'll hire," he responded darkly.

She regarded him with a knowing smile. "If I could seduce you, they'll pose no challenge at all."

He entered her then, but withdrew when he felt her flinch with the first twinge of pain. "Mistress or prisoner," he vowed, "the choice is yours, but I mean to keep you."

He shifted position to tilt her hips, and dropping between her thighs, licked her hungrily. He slid a finger into her and with slow, deliberate strokes swiftly brought her to the brink of release before withdrawing.

"You'll choose me willingly, or the choice will be made for you."

He left her suspended on the cusp of rapture, but even with her breath coming in sharp gasps, she refused him the satisfaction of a reply. She had already chosen him in her heart, but if he wished to hate her, she would welcome it. If he would not bring her to climax, then she would do it herself, but as she slid her hand down between her legs, he caught her wrist.

"You are shameless," he swore. Drunk on desire, he rolled his tongue into her, and she came with a grateful shudder. He swallowed each shimmering drop of her essence, then moved up to thrust the tip of his cock into her.

He held her gaze, daring her to welcome or refuse him, but when she did neither, he fought to remain still and filled her with his own release. Completely spent, he stretched out to share the pillows, but still held her captive in his arms.

By the time he felt her stir, he had had a long while to consider how to deal with a woman who was as perverse as any ancient goddess. Steeling himself for their next battle, he released her with a gentle pat.

"What you need, my darling, is a perfumed bath,

some pretty new clothes, and a fine meal that doesn't consist of fish and mangoes. Then the prospect of living on my terms will have an irresistible appeal."

Delphine swore under her breath, scrambled off the bed, plucked her nightgown from the floor, and drew it over her head. "I'd no idea you were such an arrogant ass. No, that's not true. I've known it all along."

Michael rolled off the bed. "Clearly you're delirious with hunger or you'd never have voiced such an insulting opinion. I'll catch our breakfast, or perhaps by now, it will be the midday meal. That's sure to put you in a better mood."

"I doubt it." She strode out the door and turned right to circle the isle. That he was not heartbroken was a relief, but it stung that he had swiftly discounted the sincerity of her declaration. It also forced her back into a most uncomfortable role.

Delphine picked up a smooth stone and hurled it out into the surf. She had circled half the island before it occurred to her that if she were convincingly contrite, it would be that much easier to escape him tomorrow. Unfortunately, that still left their last day to survive.

"A day unlike any other," she mumbled to herself. She sat down in the sand and hugged her knees. She smelled like Michael, which was not at all unpleasant, but nevertheless, a painful remainder of how close they had been. So close in fact, she was rapidly becoming as anxious to leave the island as he.

Michael attacked the fish with a spear, but a plentiful catch was a far easier prize to attain than Delphine's heart. He had certainly never met another woman like her, and one probably did not even exist. At the very least, a beauty with the courage to defy him was a rare breed.

As he jabbed the third bonito, he vowed to make her eat more than the few mouthfuls she usually consumed. Then perhaps she would see her way clear to confide in him the real reason for her distress. He would quickly provide whatever was lacking, and then once their cursed contract was signed, he would truly make love to her until she begged him to stop.

He chuckled at that thought and could not even recall the last time he had looked forward to anything with such amused abandon. While his life had not been dull prior to his marriage, it had been utterly predictable. He had fulfilled every challenge befitting the Earl of Clairbourne, but the accomplishment had left him feeling hollow rather than proud.

Now after a week of Delphine's marvelously distracting company, he felt compelled to make his own mark on the world. Better still, he felt confident he would succeed at whatever he chose to pursue. He had not felt such driving ambition in years, and although the task at present required no more than the spearing of a few fish, he relished each triumph.

When he returned to the cottage, he was relieved to find Delphine tending the fire, and thought it might be best to forget their earlier confrontation. It had ended as their hostile exchanges usually did, with her setting out alone, but she had come back. Buoyed by that thought, he placed his catch on the grill.

"I'm going to buy you a gold bracelet with delicate fish charms, and each time you wear it, I want you to recall the days we've spent here together."

"Do you actually expect to command my thoughts?"

she responded incredulously. "I would naturally treasure any of your gifts, but you've no right to tell me what to think, or feel, when I enjoy them."

She was seated beside the fire, poking the coals with a slender stick, and he was disappointed to find her still in an intractable mood. "Nay, I can only suggest you hold a kind thought for me, but I know you'll do exactly what you please."

"Which will annoy you no end."

"Probably, but as long as you share my bed with the enthusiasm you've shown here, I'll forgive you."

"I doubt I shall appear sufficiently grateful to please you."

He knelt beside her and smoothed her silky hair behind her ear. "You needn't worry about pleasing me, Delphine, although I am deeply worried about pleasing you."

His husky tone drew her gaze to his lips, and it was all she could do to swallow a sob. "Turn the fish or they'll burn," she murmured softly, but she could not draw a deep breath until he moved toward the fire.

He frowned pensively. "Are you worried that I'll drink to excess once we return home?"

While startled by the question, she shook her head emphatically. "No. Guy had hoped a week with me would restore your former good humor, and I believe it has."

He turned the fish before resuming their conversation. "Yes, for the time being at least, but rest assured I found no answers in liquor, and shan't seek them there ever again."

Intrigued, she sat forward slightly. "Answers for what?"

He laughed at her sudden show of interest. "Quite

frankly, you're such a beautiful distraction, I really can't recall."

A *beautiful distraction,* she repeated silently. He had meant to flatter her, but the compliment scraped her already tattered feelings raw. She had succeeded in her initial quest to enchant him, but took no joy in the feat.

Now she was fast becoming as melancholy as he had been upon his arrival, and she had to force a smile. "Guy will be so pleased."

"I should be your only concern now," he reminded her with an inviting grin.

"Perhaps, but I do have another. I haven't found the perfect shell for this visit, and I always collect one."

"We'll search all afternoon if you like," he promised. "I haven't gathered sea shells since I was a child."

"You must have been a very handsome boy." Even numb with the pain of impending loss, the compliments came easily to her.

"No, I was far too tall and thin to be appealing."

"You would have appealed to me," she assured him.

He began to remove a fish from the grill, and it landed on her plate in a flaky heap. "You weren't even born, Delphine. Now here, I insist that you eat every bite of this delicious meal."

She had never felt less like eating, but took the plate and fork he offered and broke off a bite. "I'll grant you that I may have been born too late to be a childhood friend, but time is only a single factor. With so many people scattered over the world, separated by mountains and oceans, it's amazing that any of us ever meet."

"Geography is scarcely a problem compared to

how carefully our parents orchestrate our friendships, indeed every last one of our ancestors appears to have had a say. Whom we meet is never an accident."

Delphine dipped her head as though she concurred, but she doubted he had considered her mother, whose ability to advance her own interests rivaled the cunning of any warrior king. Of course, had Michael's bride not died so young, they would not be together now. She would not bring that sad trick of fate to his attention, however.

"You're really referring to social class, aren't you?" she asked. "And yes, class definitely limits our social circles, but fate also plays a vital part," she argued persuasively.

He shrugged. "It might, but I prefer to rely on my own resources rather than wait for the vagaries of fate. Now I must insist that you eat."

She took another bite of fish, then set her plate aside to reach for one of the last mangoes. She appeared to appreciate its subtle aroma, and then replaced it on the plate.

"I'm really not hungry, and if you force me to eat, I'll simply become ill and be of no further use to you for the remainder of the day."

He licked his fingers before replying. "As long as you recover by this evening, I'll not complain."

She tossed her head to send her flowing hair out of her eyes. "It's a long while until nightfall. Are you sure you can wait?"

"You are a terrible flirt."

"You mean that I don't do it well?" she inquired innocently. "I shall have to practice more diligently whenever the opportunity arises."

He straightened up. "You'll do no such thing.

You're not to flirt with any man but me, ever. Is that clear?"

She softened her pose and regarded him seductively. "Actually, I don't flirt with you. A flirt offers a mere hint of her charms, a tantalizing glimpse of what she might share to inflame a gentleman's desire. I leave nothing veiled, nor do I tease and leave you unsatisfied."

"You have denied me one exquisite pleasure," he reminded her.

"I've not denied it, merely postponed it." She loosened the ribbon tie at her neckline and let the tucked bodice slip to flash her gold nipple ring. She then rose with a gentle sway.

"You'll need your strength. Finish my fish for me, please. I'm going down to the water to look for shells."

"We should wait for low tide in the morning," he called after her.

"I may search then too." She turned away before he could forbid her to go. She needed to escape him for a while at least.

Her mother had sworn men heard only what they wished to hear, and Michael had dismissed her refusal to become his mistress with an astonishing haste. Did he hear anything she said, she wondered, or did he look at her and hear only the echoes of his own deepest longing?

She had not been gone for more than two minutes before Michael realized how accurately she had described him. He was an arrogant ass, who had referred to a life of hereditary privilege as though she shared it.

But damn it all, he swore silently, she was the equal of any daughter of the peerage. No, she was a great deal more intelligent than most, and far more beautiful. Any man with a choice would choose Delphine, but he had had ample evidence that she was decidedly reluctant to choose him.

With less than a day to improve her dismissive attitude, he had no time to lose. He ate the last of his fish, and hers as well, then saw to his grooming before he set out to find her. She had not gone far, but he still took the precaution of approaching her slowly.

She was seated in the sand, knees bent, apparently studying something hidden from his view. She was a most introspective woman, and yet he would not apologize for interrupting her solitude.

Sensing his presence, Delphine turned toward him when he was still several feet away. "Come and look," she invited. "I've found a hermit crab. They're such fascinating little creatures."

She had found a tiny hermit crab lugging a cumbersome shell several sizes too large for his home toward the tide pools. Fighting its way through a thick tangle of sandy kelp to reach the water, the industrious crab was indeed curiously appealing to observe.

Michael knelt beside Delphine. "Determined fellow, isn't he?"

She looked up and smiled. "Not unlike you, my lord."

"Michael," he reminded her. He raised his hands to frame her face and caressed her lips with a gentle kiss. "I hope that you are referring to his tenacious spirit rather than his looks."

He had shaved after she had left him, and she slid her hand along the smooth curve of his cheek. "From a passing carriage I thought you extraordinarily handsome. This close, you are beyond compare. Is that what you wanted to hear?"

"Only if it's what you truly believe. I wish that I'd seen you the day I caught your eye."

"You would have glimpsed only a pretty child and done no more than wave," she insisted.

There was a stunning honesty to her cool emerald gaze that touched his heart. "It can't have been all that long ago."

Nothing before the day they had met held any meaning, and she could not agree. "Time can't always be measured in months and years."

Perplexed, he followed the hermit crab's progress for a long moment and then nodded. "That's why it's so important that you stay with me, so we'll not miss a single hour that we might share."

His impossible hopes were too painful to bear. She shoved him off balance and leapt to her feet. As she sprinted down to the water, she dropped her nightgown to the sand. She ran into the sea, dove beneath the waves, and then with a long, desperate stroke, rode the swift current away from the man who would never understand why she had to leave him.

Michael laughed at what he mistook for her high spirits. He left his pants atop her gown and followed her into the sea. When she failed to swim parallel to the shore as she usually did, he called to her, but seemingly oblivious to his cry of alarm, she widened the distance between them.

He refused to believe that she actually meant to escape him by drowning, but they were a long way from shore before he finally overtook her. Treading water, he locked his hand around her wrist and made no effort to disguise his anger.

"Were you bent on drowning? Or did you merely wish to be rescued?"

She lay her free hand on his shoulder to tread water in time with his beat. Looking back over her shoulder, she was startled by just how far they had come, but she had already risked telling him the truth once that day and not been believed. There was no point in re-living that humiliation.

"I'm sorry," she lied. "It's such a beautiful day, and the water is so inviting and warm that—"

He wound his hand in her hair to pull her into a punishing kiss. He intended to spank her long and hard for scaring him so badly, but it would have to wait until they returned to shore. If they even could reach the island.

He pulled her against his chest and swam on his side, but with her slender body all slippery, and the fullness of her breasts pressed against his arm, it was all he could do to stay focused on the swim rather than ravish her right there in the water. Had he not feared they really might drown, he would have done it, but when he finally touched down and felt sand, Delphine provided the longed-for request.

"Make love to me here," she begged against his lips. "We can spread out my gown again to make a fine bed."

"Oh no, first I mean to—" His angry outburst caught in his throat as she cupped his balls and began to stroke him.

Their vigorous swim had left her too worn out to delay the inevitable surrender. "We've no need of contracts," she coaxed, mistaking his intention. "All we need is ourselves."

She bent her head to lick his nipple and felt his heart thundering from exertion rather than passion, but ample evidence of his stamina weighed heavily in her hands.

Too hard to think of anything other than the surprising timing of her invitation, he was not about to risk having her change her mind. He steadied himself with a deep breath, then scanned the beach for their pile of clothes. It wasn't far off, and he carried her easily to where her nightgown lay.

He then kicked his pants out of their way and set her down. He waited for her to smooth out their makeshift bed, then stretched out beside her. The afternoon sun was still bright, but a gentle breeze caressed their skin, and he believed the scene sufficiently romantic to please her poet's soul.

"I had never made love in broad daylight until I met you," he confided. He pulled her gold ring through his teeth, and she slid her hands through his hair.

Intent upon pleasing her, he whispered against the full curve of her breast, "We needn't rush. Let's go slow."

Now that she finally understood his earlier impatience, what she craved was a tender urgency. She wanted all of him and right now. She nipped at his shoulder and raked his inner thigh with her nails.

He caught her hand and laced his fingers in hers. "For once, pretend you know nothing about men and allow me to show you all there is to making love."

His smile was warm and inviting, but the gently worded rebuke still stung. "Forget I'm a whore? Is that what you mean?"

"No," he denied with an anguished sigh. He sat up and raked his hands through his hair. "Good lord, Delphine, I just want, oh blast, what difference does it make? I should have let you drown."

She stared at him, her head titled slightly, seawater dripping from her hair in sparkling trails over her breasts. "We can't change what we are, Michael, and I'm so tired of acting a part."

He nearly choked on disgust. "Then you don't want me after all?"

"No, I do!" she cried. They were on the beach, nude, dripping wet, and arguing as though any decision they reached would not be the absolute worst for each of them. Utterly defeated, she rose shakily to her feet, but Michael reached out to catch her knees and pulled her right back down on the now damp nightgown.

"Where do you think you're going?" he shouted.

"Does it matter?"

He looked up to judge the angle of the sun. "Yes, it matters a great deal. I know precisely what I want, and despite your childish attempts to dissuade me, it's you."

He was sorely tempted to toss her over his shoulder and paddle her bare bottom all the way back to the cottage. He abandoned the idea only because it was a poor prelude to what he truly wanted them to share.

Michael leaned across her to force her to lie down. "Not another word from you," he warned.

Unable to provide a rational explanation for her chaotic moods, she clamped her jaws shut, but remained pliant in his arms. This was what she wanted after all, to take him deep and be completely filled. Rather than offer the slightest complaint, she willed him to hurry.

Grateful she had hushed, he played his fingertips over the smooth flatness of her stomach, then whispered, "Yes, relax, that's exactly what I want."

She closed her eyes and wondered if he were making love to his late wife, a fragile bride who must have been a true innocent. She fought to convince herself his thoughts were irrelevant when she was so full of him, but the uncertainty still pained her.

He kissed her palms, and sucked her fingers one at a time, but with no loving promises, she doubted she was more appealing than a memory. He licked the tender skin at her elbow, his breath barely grazing her breasts, and she responded with a restless sigh. Each of his gentle caresses and tender kisses carried an unspoken devotion, but Delphine feared none of it was for her.

Then he kissed her with a hunger that matched her own, and she ceased to care. He lavished affection on every inch of her satin smooth flesh, the small of her back, and the tender spot behind her knee. He rubbed her feet, and kissed her toes before licking a loving path up her inner thighs. He parted her feminine folds with his fingertips, then his tongue.

That he cared so much for her pleasure made her ache with longing, and it was impossible to hold still. She rolled her hips, thrust against his mouth, and the surrounding world took on a bright golden glow. He slid two fingers into her, stretching her, gliding on her own wetness. She grabbed for his hair, but he kept licking her, tickling her with the tip of his tongue, until her whole body throbbed on the brink of a shattering release.

She felt him shift positions, but rather than enter her with a shallow nudge, this time he lunged and went deep. There was an instant of searing pain and then a heated rush of rapture so intense she cried his name. Her inner muscles clenched to hold him, but he withdrew and plunged again, riding her ecstasy until it became his own.

With his last thrust, he made his possession complete and vowed to take her a thousand times if he must, until he won her promise to be his forever.

Chapter 10

Whispers on the wind
Laughter, sighs, a lover's cry
A taunting memory

Delphine paced the dock with a distracted stride until the sails of Guy's boat appeared like gulls' wings against the rose-hued sky. Confident her mother would arrive with the dawn, she had left a blissfully exhausted Michael asleep in their bed.

When the sleek sailboat reached the dock, she returned Guy's wave and secured the mooring line. But certain things could not possibly go well with her mother; she clenched her fists at her sides and steeled herself for the worst.

Beautifully groomed and attired in a peach silk gown, Françoise took Guy's hand to step down to the dock. She circled her daughter, took in her windblown hair and lightly tanned skin, and shook her head in gentle reproach.

Then she noted Delphine's desolate gaze, and in an instant, her expression filled with a furious rage. She drew back her gloved hand, and struck her daughter such a fierce backhanded blow Delphine might have tumbled off the narrow dock had Guy not rushed to catch her.

"Leave her be," Françoise cried. "Can't you see what's happened? Clearly she's no longer a virgin, and I doubt Michael is solely to blame."

Flabbergasted by how brutally Françoise had treated her only child, Guy gave Delphine an affectionate squeeze before releasing her. He peered at the young woman, intent upon discovering what his mistress had seen. Delphine was certainly no less beautiful, but he also recognized the dramatic change in her demeanor.

"Well, yes, now that you bring it to my attention, Delphine does look a mite, what shall I say, fatigued?" he remarked. "If her affair with Michael has progressed further than we'd anticipated, then his mood must be greatly improved. I, for one, am deeply grateful."

Françoise thumped him soundly on the upper arm. "Well, you shouldn't be. I warned you things might go horribly wrong, but you insisted Michael could be trusted."

Delphine paused to make certain her jaw was not broken before she interrupted. "Please, that we failed to wait for a signed contract wasn't Michael's fault. I can't become his mistress, so there was no reason to delay what we both wanted."

Even more horrified by that bizarre announcement, Françoise turned in a tight circle. "*Mon Dieu*! The girl has lost her mind!"

Guy looked for a bench so his mistress might sit down and compose herself, but one had never been added to the weatherbeaten dock. "This is no place to discuss anything," he insisted. "Now where is Michael? Is he awake?"

"No," Delphine responded, "and you mustn't wake him. Please take me back to Kingston at once; I can avoid him indefinitely there, and you can return for him before noon."

Françoise stared at her coldly. "Why would you wish to avoid a man who'll provide for you generously?" When Delphine failed to respond, she became even more insistent. "Did you actually inform him that you'd not become his mistress?"

Delphine shrugged unhappily. "Yes, but he refused to believe me."

Encouraged, Françoise took a step closer. "Are you certain?"

"Yes, he wants me too badly to believe I'm sincere."

Françoise nodded thoughtfully. "That changes everything. It won't be easy to save you from your own foolishness, and we'll have to hurry for any hope of success. We'll let Michael believe that you've returned to Kingston, but in fact, you'll remain here. A few days of solitude should jar you to your senses. Now go quickly to the other side of the island and remain there until after we've sailed."

Astonished, Guy touched her arm. "I'm sorry, my dearest, but I simply don't understand what it is you mean to do."

Françoise rolled her eyes in dismay. "There's no time to plot romantic intrigues, but you'll thank me later. Now go, child, before Michael comes seeking your company, and give some serious thought to how poorly you'll fare in the world without him."

Delphine had no wish to see Michael that morning, and was happy to hide, but she offered a condition of her own. "First, promise me you'll not be angry with Michael."

Guy shook his head. "I'll not offer a single promise until I understand precisely what's happened here. Did Michael abuse you in some way?"

"You don't regard stealing her virtue as abuse?" Françoise cried.

"Mother, please," Delphine chided. "Hit me again if you wish, but Michael hasn't caused me the slightest harm. Now I'll go. I wish you all a safe return to Kingston."

Guy had always admired the pride in Delphine's graceful walk and waited until she had reached the sand before he made his thoughts plain to Françoise. "You must never strike her again. I forbid it."

"You also forbid Michael to make love to her, and look where that's gotten us." She turned away, fixed her gaze on the brightening heavens, and began to methodically plot how best to avert this catastrophe.

"You must hold your tongue," she insisted, "and rely upon me to salvage my daughter's future."

"I'll not lie to my best friend," Guy swore.

Françoise responded with a forced laugh. "You've already drugged and kidnapped him, why would a small prevarication trouble you?"

Guy rocked back on his heels. "You have a point, but I still don't like it."

"You don't have to approve, just keep still and allow me to lead Michael where we wish him to go."

Guy nodded reluctantly, but he was not pleased.

A short while later, Michael hurried from the cottage still yanking on his boots. He stopped to search the beach for Delphine, and not finding her, rushed on out to the dock to meet Guy and Françoise.

"Where's Delphine?" he asked, looking past them to the boat. "Has she already gone aboard?"

Françoise flashed her most enchanting smile. "She returned to Kingston earlier, and we'll escort you home now."

"She left without me?" He turned to Guy for an explanation, but received only an apologetic shrug.

Badly disappointed, he swallowed a bitter curse. "There was no need to separate us, Françoise. I'm more than willing to strike a fair bargain."

Relieved to find Michael as determined as Delphine had claimed, Françoise coiled herself around his right arm. "After a week here, Delphine's beautiful skin was all sunburned and her hair like straw. She needs time to soak in a milk bath and recuperate. Please understand how eager she is to look her best for you. You must give her a few days to rest and primp before you call on her."

Michael could barely tolerate her cloying touch and brushed her hands aside. "I intend to do far more than merely call on your daughter, and you know it. Now let's stop wasting time and be on our way."

Guy gestured toward his boat. "I'm relieved you're not angry about the way we arranged for you and Delphine to meet."

"What makes you think I'm not thoroughly disgusted with you both?" Michael shot right back at him. "You invited yourselves into my home and then took advantage of my hospitality to bring me here against my will. It's not something I'll soon forgive, but we'll settle that score after I've spoken with Delphine."

Guy nodded agreeably, and boarding the sailboat, Michael missed the frantic glance his friend sent Françoise. The French woman raised a fingertip to her

lips in a silent warning, and she gave Michael no reason to suspect anything was amiss on the voyage home.

Delphine waited until mid-morning to climb the
bluff, but when she found Guy's boat had sailed, she
was overwhelmed with sorrow. She had been able to
avoid facing Michael, but now that he was gone, she
felt terribly alone.

When they had finally returned to the cottage yesterday, he had insisted upon shampooing her hair and
bathing her as gently as he would a babe. She had repaid the favor in kind, but when he had quickly become
aroused, he had refused to cause her additional pain,
and she had satisfied him with her mouth and hands.

She dimly recalled eating a mango rather than interrupt their loving play to fish, but she still had no
appetite. She made her way down to the cottage, but a
quick search revealed Michael had left nothing behind. She wished she had cut a lock of his hair while
she had had the chance, and picking up her journal,
she went out to the shore to write an account of
everything that had transpired between them.

She had assured Michael that she was writing poetry rather than keeping a diary of their time together,
but now she was consumed by the need to record his
every word and gesture before all but her most vivid
memories began to fade.

Once they reached the docks in Kingston, Michael refused the loan of Guy's carriage and hired one to return home. He was surprised to find the tropical
forest had not overgrown the estate and had to remind himself he had been absent only a week, rather
than several years.

"Good afternoon, my lord," his butler greeted him. "How was your fishing trip?"

"What fishing trip, Percy?" Michael asked in dismay.

"Why, the one with Mr. Barnett. I hope there was no trouble, but how did you lose your clothes?"

Michael looked down at his wrinkled shirt and faded pants, then up at the meticulously groomed and dressed butler. "Yes, you might say we had a bit of trouble, but the fishing was excellent. Now, while I dress, please summon my manager. I need to catch up on the plantation business."

"I'll see to it at once, my lord," Percy responded, enormously relieved to find the somewhat disheveled earl showing such practical concern.

Hoskins, Michael's valet, appeared at the top of the stairs as Michael made his way up to his room. Like the butler, Hoskins had also served his father. He was now stoop-shouldered, near-sighted, and slightly hard of hearing, but he saw to his duties with a touching devotion, and Michael would never have suggested he ought to retire.

"Good day, my lord. You found the fishing diverting, I trust?"

Michael could not help but laugh. "You could say that it surpassed all my expectations."

"What splendid news. If I might say so, it's good to hear you laugh again. You used to be such a jolly sort."

Michael could dimly recall those days, but the joy he had found with Delphine was infinitely better. He dressed quickly to meet with his manager, and was pleasantly surprised to learn that despite his neglect, the plantation continued to be extremely profitable.

Once he had dismissed the man, he leaned back in his chair. His first impulse was to fetch Delphine that very afternoon, but he absolutely refused to be the slave to her that Guy was to her mother. If he waited a few days, it would surely unsettle Françoise, which would also work to his advantage. He did not care how exorbitant her demands might be, he would feign reluctance at first, but ultimately agree to insure Delphine's welfare. Their arrangement, however, would be on his terms.

His stomach growled noisily, and his thoughts turned to food for the first time all day. He could not wait to share a fine meal with Delphine for the first time. They would definitely skip the fish course.

He rose, stretched his arms above his head and wished for the freedom of movement he had enjoyed on the island where he had often gone without a shirt. Now dressed as a proper earl, he was clad in several layers of expensive garments and felt rather constrained.

Clothes were not the real problem, however; he simply missed Delphine. Françoise had not been so indelicate as to refer to the real reason her daughter would need time to rest, but he understood that she would require a few days to heal. It pained him to have hurt her, but she had been no less affectionate afterward.

Frustrated not to have her with him now, he left the house to stroll the gardens, but in the beauty of the flowers saw only the lovely Delphine. He did not return to the house until dark, but when he sat down to dine alone, the superbly prepared meal was as tasteless as sawdust. He feared it would be a very long night indeed.

While the self-imposed delay had been torturous, Michael remained on his plantation for three days before going into Kingston to call on Delphine. He could not have said which was worse, the loneliness of the days or the agonizing nights. Now a storm was brewing, and the darkening sky matched his surly mood.

He just beat the rain to Françoise's apartment, where Guy's carriage was parked in front. He looked up at the second floor and wondered which of the tall windows was Delphine's. He stood there a moment, hoping for a glimpse of her, then he rapped insistently upon the door.

He was swiftly admitted by a tiny woman who greeted him in French. He waited for her to announce his arrival and then followed her to the parlor where Françoise was seated on a blue damask love seat only a single shade darker than her gown. Guy came forward to greet him, but Michael was annoyed to find the pair alone.

"I've come to see Delphine," he announced. "Where is she?"

"She's at the dressmaker's," Françoise explained smoothly, "but won't you stay and visit with us awhile?" She gestured toward an ornate golden samovar, topped with a small matching tea kettle. "Perhaps you'd care for a cup of tea."

"No, thank you." Michael had dressed in gray, and while his waistcoat had a maroon stripe, he suddenly felt as though he ought to have chosen less somber attire. Too anxious to sit, he strolled over to the front window and glanced out at the street.

"What time do you expect Delphine to return?"

"She may be gone for hours, but her absence provides us with an excellent opportunity to talk. Won't you take a seat? I know you want to provide for my daughter's comfort, and I'm confident we can come to an amicable agreement as to her apartment and furnishings as well as her clothing and allowance."

Michael barely glanced over his shoulder. "My

agreement will be with Delphine, Madame, not you. As for an apartment, she'll have no need of one. There is a dower house on my estate, built years ago for the dowager countess, and although it's seen little use, I've kept it in good repair. Delphine may redecorate it as she pleases, but she'll reside there."

Guy cocked his head. "You mean to have her live on your estate?" he asked incredulously.

Michael made a failed attempt not to snarl. "I just said so, didn't I?"

Alarmed, Françoise fanned herself with her ivory fan. "I'm afraid that just won't do. Delphine needs her own home."

Michael turned to face her. "As I explained, the dower house will be hers to do with as she sees fit."

"Michael, really," Guy interjected. "You're obviously fond of Delphine, but she ought to reside at a discreet distance here in Kingston."

Michael folded his hands behind his back. "No. I insist that she live on my estate. Wait until she arrives. I seriously doubt that she'll refuse."

Françoise shot Guy an imploring glance, but he appeared to be as flustered as she. "My daughter adores you, but we must think of her security. One day, you'll remarry, and—"

"One wife was more than enough for me," Michael vowed darkly, "but I intend to provide generously for any children Delphine and I might produce. I'll put such a promise in our contract, along with the demand that should Delphine ever conceive, she will give birth to our child.

"Do not misunderstand, Madame. I'll not tolerate evil potions to force a miscarriage nor visits to an abortionist. Is that clear?"

Absolutely horrified by that shocking demand, Françoise extended her hand, and Guy helped her to her feet. "What I understand, my lord, is that we have made a grave error in assuming you would treat my daughter well. I'll not have her imprisoned on your estate, nor allow her to be used as your brood mare."

Fearful that everything had gotten badly out of hand, Guy slipped his arm around her tiny waist. "My dearest, let's not judge Michael's motives so harshly."

"I don't care what Françoise thinks of me," Michael proclaimed. "My agreement will be with Delphine. Now what is her dressmaker's address? I'll go there and provide her with an escort home."

When Guy and Françoise exchanged startled glances, he grew suspicious. "Has she been here all this time?" He promptly left the room, went to the bottom of the stairs, and called her name.

Guy came up behind him and smoothed his hand across Michael's shoulders. "She's not here. Now it would be best for all of us if you returned home. Let's plan to meet another day to discuss what's best for Delphine."

Michael was sick of his own company and desperate for hers. "No, I'm not leaving here without seeing her." He walked back into the parlor and sat down in the only chair which appeared sturdy enough to bear his weight.

"She will return before nightfall, won't she?"

Françoise sank back down on the love seat. "You may sit there for days if you wish, but you'll not see my daughter when you offer such intractable demands rather than a comfortable life."

Ignoring her taunt, Michael folded his arms across

his chest. "Must I repeat that Delphine will be the one to decide, not you, Madame. She told me her father was a Danish ship's captain. While we're waiting, why don't you tell me the truth?"

Guy sat down beside his mistress and nodded his encouragement. "It's an exciting story, my dearest, why not share it?"

Françoise stared at him coldly. "I'll not relate the tale as idle entertainment."

"I've not asked to be entertained," Michael insisted. "I merely want to know the truth about Delphine, and I doubt that she knows it."

"She doesn't," Guy replied.

"Hush!" Françoise swatted his knee with her fan.

Michael sat forward slightly. "I promise you I am the soul of discretion."

Françoise feared she had seriously misjudged him, but on the chance he would listen and then depart, she cleared her throat, and took a soothing sip of tea. "I prefer not to dwell on what was lost in France, but most of my family perished in the revolution. A faithful gardener saved me from the guillotine by hiding me amongst his children. Those are years I wish forgotten, but as soon as I was able, I fled France for England, where I caught the eye of a Russian count."

Michael doubted this tale held any more truth than the story about the Danish captain, but he was undeniably intrigued. "You don't say," he murmured.

"Yes, Alexi was a dashing figure, and I loved him dearly, but the faithless bastard was slain in a duel over another woman. The instant I learned of his fate, I packed everything I could steal from his apartment—that samovar was one of his treasures—and bought passage on a ship sailing the next morning for Jamaica.

"The Danish captain was very kind to me. I might have led him to believe Delphine was his, but he was lost at sea on his return voyage to England. He was a very handsome and charming man, and I preferred to let Delphine believe he was her father rather than a Russian nobleman who had betrayed us both."

"Remarkable," Michael complimented. "You're admitting to being both a thief and a liar. You don't even possess a conscience, do you?"

"I did what had to be done to survive and provide for my daughter," Françoise exclaimed. "I'll not apologize for it."

"Nor should you, my darling. You must keep that story to yourself, Michael," Guy urged.

"You needn't worry that I'll burden Delphine with her mother's lies. She feels a special affinity for the sea because of the Dane, and I'll not spoil it for her. Now I'd like to see her room, if I may."

"That's not at all proper," Françoise argued.

"Neither is what you two did to me," Michael reminded her. He rose and turned toward the stairs. "And no proper mother would have made Delphine so adept in the erotic arts. Don't bother to summon your maid. I'll find her room myself."

"No, I'll show you." Guy kissed Françoise's cheek before he rose and crossed the parlor. As he and Michael reached the stairs, he lowered his voice. "You needn't be so belligerent, when there's absolutely no point in making an enemy of Françoise. Delphine's room is the first to the left."

Michael turned the crystal knob and shoved the door open. The spacious bed chamber was painted a pale sea foam green, and the gilt furniture appropriately delicate. The bed was covered in white lace and heaped with ruffled and embroidered pillows he felt certain Delphine had stitched herself.

The collection of seashells in a jar upon a shelf near the window lured him further into the room. The cool air held a faint hint of perfume, but he was puzzled by the absence of any feminine clutter. He traced the inlaid design on the tortoiseshell hand-mirror atop the vanity and then touched Delphine's hairbrush. He had never seen a room in such perfect order, and he feared he knew why. As he turned to Guy, he caught a glimpse of himself in the vanity mirror. His well-tailored clothing was now loose, but he was still surprised to look so thin and deeply tanned.

It was all he could do not to shout at the man he now doubted had ever been a true friend, but his voice still held a menacing edge. "Women always leave something lying about, a cast-off slipper, a mismatched glove or bit of lace. This room hasn't been occupied in days. What have you done with Delphine?"

Guy had cautiously remained at the doorway. He did not wish to anger Michael, but his friend had proven to be surprisingly headstrong, and Françoise was no less stubborn. He loved them both, and rather than allow them to trade further insults, he stepped into the room and pulled the door closed behind him.

"Delphine needed some time alone to consider her future. We'd planned to return to the island for her today, but the weather was deteriorating, and—"

Michael crossed the distance between them in a single hostile stride, grabbed Guy's lapels, and lifted him clear off his feet. "Dear God, you left her alone there?"

Guy's toes scraped the floor as he tried to break free. "She knows the island well, and she'll come to no harm."

Michael released him so quickly Guy stumbled back against the door. "If she's alone she won't, but a boatload of brigands came ashore while I was with her. What if they return?"

"What brigands? You'd not mentioned them before."

Michael described them briefly. "They appeared to know their way around the island. Are they friends of yours?"

Guy frowned, then nodded slightly. "I know who the tall man could be, and I'm sorry he and his companions troubled you. But with a storm brewing, Delphine will have no unwanted company."

Infuriated anew, Michael reached out to grab him again, but Guy shrank back, and Michael dropped his hands to his sides. "Did you at least leave her some provisions and warm clothing?"

"Well, no, but—"

Michael cursed the pride that had kept him at home for three wretched days while Delphine could have fallen on the rocks, or God forbid, drowned while she swam as though there were no danger in the sea.

"I'll need your boat and the precise heading," he announced as he reached for the door.

"You don't mean it. Not when this storm might be a bad one."

"I'll not leave Delphine to fend for herself when she could so easily be hurt or swept out to sea."

Guy chased him back down the stairs. "Michael, you're not thinking clearly. The cottage is on the leeward side of the island. The bluff protects it from the wind and Delphine will be as safe there as she would be here."

"That's a damn lie and you know it." Michael paused at the entrance to the parlor while Guy hurriedly scrawled the course to the island on a sheet of pale blue stationery.

Michael glanced at it, then slid the paper into his coat pocket. "I'm going after your daughter, Françoise, and if she's suffered even the slightest injury, I'm coming back here to kill you both."

Françoise jumped as he slammed the front door, but she was too frightened to rise. "You told him where Delphine is?"

Guy began to pace in front of her. "I had no choice. He took one look at her room and knew she hadn't been home."

"Well, you needn't worry about Michael Mallory's threat," Françoise swore. "If anything has happened to Delphine, I'll kill you myself."

"I'd rather take my chances with him," Guy responded darkly. He could not understand how such a simple plan had gotten so badly out of hand.

"Delphine is as resourceful a woman as you are, my pet," he mused as he turned. "She'll tame Michael's temper as easily as she must have the first time, and with her wrapped around him, he'll sign whatever contract you put before him."

Françoise was not convinced. "You've forgotten that she's refused him, and now it's obvious why. I fear the lightning they strike together may be far worse than the coming storm."

Chapter 11

Rain-darkened hopes
Rivers swirl into the sea
Ebb tide strands the heart

With such a brisk wind, Michael was confident he could make the island in under an hour. Before he set sail, however, he had to leave his carriage at a livery stable, gather provisions, and purchase warm clothing for a young woman whose size he was forced to illustrate with curving gestures. After one last stop, he boarded Guy's boat, ran up the sails, and set a course for the small island lost over the horizon.

Stung by rain, he kept one eye on the compass and the other on the roiling sea. He had not sailed on his own in years, and then only in fair weather, but Delphine's plight was far too grave for him to waste a moment of concern for his own safety.

As the rainfall grew increasingly heavy, he fought to guide the small pleasure craft through a storm where sky and sea merged in a shimmering blur. He would have never turned back, but if the course Guy had given him was not precise, Delphine would not be only one in dire straits.

* * *

Delphine was seated on the floor, wrapped in a blanket, and leaning back against the bed when Michael came bursting through the door. Silhouetted by a flash of lightning, he dropped sacks and parcels. He shouted her name, but a jarring clap of thunder muffled the sound.

Delphine's heart skipped a beat, but she greeted him calmly, "Won't you please come in? The roof leaks a bit, but not here beside the bed."

Elated to find her unhurt, he sank to his knees in front of her, and framed her dear face with trembling hands. "I would never have left you here all alone. Are you all right? Have you had enough to eat? I've brought food and clothes for you. God, how I've missed you."

Fervent kisses punctuated his frantic questions, and she had to grab his shoulders to remain upright. She had missed him desperately. Now here he was, kissing her and shivering.

"I'm fine, but let me help you out of those wet clothes. There are more blankets in the linen chest. We can wrap up, get in bed, and keep warm while we wait out the storm."

Water had rolled off his overcoat to pool around them, but he had been too anxious to hold her again to notice. He nearly crushed her in his embrace before he realized he should have shed the rain-soaked Garrick at the door.

"I want more than mere warmth from you," he breathed out against her throat.

She combed the wet ringlets off his forehead. Delphine didn't know whether to compliment his bravery or think him a fool for risking his life to reach the island when, while not without leaks, the cottage was as safe a refuge as her home in Jamaica. She chose the most tactful option.

"Thank you for wanting to protect me."

"I always have, but this time, I could."

"Oh, Michael, did you think I doubted your bravery? You were absolutely right, we couldn't attack three armed men. It would have been ridiculous to even try. I thought no less of you for showing the proper restraint."

"At the time, you did."

Delphine shook her head. "No, I was merely being foolish. But you were very brave to venture out in such a violent storm."

A sly smile tugged the corner of his mouth. "The wind wasn't so fierce when I left the harbor."

Even with his teeth chattering, he was teasing her, but nothing had really changed between them. It saddened her to think their argument had merely been postponed, rather than resolved.

"You're still awfully wet," she whispered, and she plucked fretfully at his clothes.

"Wait, it's just my coat," he murmured. "I must have had a hat, but lord knows what's become of it." He rose awkwardly to fling the heavy overcoat over a chair at the table, and then dropped down in front of her again.

This time as he leaned forward to hug her, a corner of the journal resting in her lap jabbed his chest, and stunned, he drew back. "I'd swear your journal was laying on the table that last morning when I went racing down to the dock to meet Guy. I should have realized what it meant and known you'd not have left it behind.

"Your mother speaks nothing but lies, but can you

ever forgive me for believing her when she said you'd returned to Kingston?"

Touched by his anger with himself rather than her, she reached out to set the precious diary on the bedside table. She then gave his cheek a tender caress and kissed his mouth sweetly. "There is nothing to forgive."

"Oh, but there is." He clamped his mouth shut rather than admit he had deliberately waited three days to call on her when that stubborn show of pride could have killed them both.

Another flash of lightning lit the cottage with a near-blinding glare and was swiftly followed by a rafter-rattling roll of thunder. Michael braced himself for the next blast by shifting position to sit beside Delphine. He hugged her shoulders and leaned back against the bed.

"I found warm clothing that I hope is close to your size. I tried to buy everything we'll need: meats, cheeses, bread, apples, oranges, and wine for you, which I'll not share. I'm sorry there was no time to make a jug of lemonade."

Delphine had been lost in such sweet memories of him, and to have him recall her childhood picnics brought tears to her eyes, which she hastily wiped away. "I'll not miss it. The storm provides sufficient light, if in rather unpredictable bursts, but let me up, and I'll prepare us a meal."

The voyage had been so damnably difficult, Michael still felt as if the cottage floor were rolling beneath him. "No, I'll wait awhile, but I want you to eat now. You have to be hungry."

"Hmm, a bit," was all she would admit, but she had had such little appetite since they had parted that she could not recall when she had last eaten. After leaving his embrace, she sorted through the packages littering the floor, carefully separating the clothes from the food she set upon the table.

"This ham smells wonderful. Is it from your plantation?" she asked.

Michael closed his eyes and propped his head against the mattress. "No, but the butcher swore it would be the best I'd ever eaten."

Delphine cut a slice and chewed it slowly. "It's smoked to perfection. Now all I need is a bit of cheese."

Michael held still, which helped to alleviate the rocking sensation somewhat, and enjoyed her appreciative murmurs. "I should have remembered tea," he remarked suddenly.

"We'd need a fire to heat water. Wine will be fine," she assured him, but she left the bottles untouched. "Oh, this bread was baked fresh this morning. It's delicious."

"I'd hoped it would be."

Despite the wonderful abundance he had provided, she ate only a few bites and quickly returned to him. "Now, please, let's get you bundled up and into bed."

He lacked the energy to complain as she yanked off his boots and socks. She tickled his feet and laughed with him. "I've done this before, you know." She crawled up over him to unbutton his jacket and waistcoat. "It wasn't just your coat, you're soaked clear through."

"My clothes will dry."

"I care little for your apparel, my lord, it's you I'm concerned about."

She looked around the cottage, hoping for more

dry spots than he had clothes. He removed his cravat and shirt on his own, unmindful of the bandage encircling his left arm.

"Oh, no, you've been hurt. How?"

"It's nothing. Now, where's the bed?"

"You're leaning against it," she replied in dismay.

Another bright flash of lightning lit his sleek, muscular build as he rose, and when her hands went to his belt, it wasn't only to assure his comfort. She clung to him as the thunder rocked them again and then pushed him down on the bed.

Had the day been sunny, she would have repeated her refusal to become his mistress. But when he could have drowned, to remind him of her decision would have demonstrated a shocking lack of gratitude. There would be time enough tomorrow, or the next day, to set them both free.

Michael's head was still swimming, and he held onto her waist. "I feel as though the cottage were spinning and about to wash out to sea."

"No, the ground is firm beneath us," she assured him as she struggled a bit to get him out of his trousers and drawers. She then fetched the extra blankets. "That's it, wrap up, and we'll cuddle until you're warm."

He draped a soft blue blanket around his shoulders and then pulled her down beside him on the bed. "Let's cuddle later. Just give me a moment until the room stops pitching and rolling."

She had experienced the unsteadiness that comes when moving from the sea to land, but he appeared to be suffering an extreme case. Content to lie beside him, she held him tightly until he finally stopped shivering, but by then, he had fallen asleep. She had not slept well since they had parted, but while the storm howled around them, she slept soundly in his arms until he kissed her awake.

The timbre of the storm had now changed to a piercing howl. The wind buffeted the sturdily built cottage, but protected by the bluff, it had sprung no new leaks. It did, however, offer an occasional menacing creak and groan.

With Michael coiled so tightly around her, she lacked any desire to rise and inspect the cabin. She wanted only to lose herself in him while they were both captives of the storm.

"I'll never let you go," he vowed softly. He spread tender kisses along her jaw and down her throat before pausing to peel away her nightgown. He trailed feathery licks to her gold ring and then laved her breasts. He breathed out her name with a prayerful reverence and repeated his promise, "Never."

Convinced this was no time to argue over their future, Delphine pressed against him to draw in his heat. She had believed their last night together would be the end, and that made this unexpected wild coupling indescribably sweet. Drunk with desire, she welcomed his every kiss and caress, and when he entered her with a single thrust, she was lost.

She undulated beneath him to draw him still deeper into her bliss. The strength of his heated passion matched her own fire, and the tempest they created together was far more intense than the one whipping the island with fiendish strokes. When Delphine next awoke, she was amazed they had not been reduced to a heap of pale ashes.

She flipped her hair from her eyes, and rested her hand on her lover's shoulder. "Michael?"

He didn't stir, and his skin felt much too warm. She quickly touched his forehead. She had thought their passion had erased any lingering chill from his voyage, but clearly he had come down with a fever. Frightened that such a strong man had fallen ill, she threw aside the tangled blankets to cool him as best she could.

The storm had lessened to a steady rain, and she quickly carried his sweat-soaked blanket outside to rinse and wet thoroughly. The rain wasn't as cool as she would have liked, but it was far cooler than Michael's flushed skin. She lay the blanket over him, and then shook him slightly.

"Michael, I need you to wake and help me," she called urgently, but he moaned only an unintelligible reply.

"Oh, damn it all." Rather than survey the clothes he had brought her, she quickly opened her trunk to remove a fresh nightgown. She had not had so much as a slight fever since she had been a small child, and she could not recall what her mother had done to treat it.

They had no healing herbs, and if she couldn't wake him, there was no way for her to carry him down to the sea to soak in a tide pool. Hoping the waters of the Caribbean would be cooler than the rain, she grabbed the pitcher from the washstand and made for the shore.

The beach was strewn with driftwood but she crossed it with nimble zigzagging leaps. The sea was indeed slightly cooler than the rain, and she returned to the cottage to drip the salt water on Michael's chest and arms.

She patted the cool water on his face and when he

smiled in his sleep, Delphine gave his shoulder a hearty shake. "Wake up, Michael. I've no idea what to do, and you can't leave me here to do it all alone!"

If her frantic cry pierced his dreams, he gave no sign of it, and she sat back to watch him. With only a slight shadow of beard, he reminded her all too vividly of the night Guy and her mother had carried him through the door. She had known he would awaken then, but now she could only pray that he would.

She leaned down, rested her ear on his chest, and listened to his heart. The beat was steady and strong, which reassured her, but she knew even grown men in their prime died of fevers. Still, she thought that was a particularly virulent type of fever, not one brought on by exertion and a chill. Uncertain what more to do, she sat down beside him on the bed.

His left arm lay limp at his side, and wondering if whatever injury he had suffered might be a factor, she slowly unwound the bandage. When she found not a deep cut or burn, but instead her own name beautifully tattooed on his flesh, her mouth fell agape. It was on the tender inside of his forearm where it was unlikely to be discovered by others, while he need only turn his palm upward to read it.

Astonished, it took a moment to recognize the graceful script as her own. Doubtful that he could have had time to memorize and duplicate it, she remembered her journal. She had not noticed the first page where she had written her name was missing, but now discovered it was.

"Did you intend to do this all along?" she asked him. "Fine gentlemen don't sport tattoos. What could have prompted this absurd display?"

More stunned than puzzled, she had every intention

of asking that very question just as soon as he awoke; she could not even imagine him wearing her name like a brand through the rest of his life. One day he would take a wife to produce the expected heir to his title and fortune. What would that poor woman think when she found, after their marriage ceremony surely, another woman's name on her new husband's arm? she wondered. At least it wasn't over his heart.

Shaking off such distressing thoughts, she tried to recall, if she had ever been told, how fevers were supposed to be treated. When the only idea that presented itself was her own thirst, she decided he ought to have something to drink as well. With the cistern overflowing from the rain, they had fresh water in abundance. How to pour it down his throat without choking him was the problem.

Terribly frustrated to be so woefully ignorant, she smoothed his tangled hair off his forehead. "I've mastered only the art of sensual pleasure, my lord, and have no practical skills whatsoever. You'd be better off stranded here with a housemaid."

That she had no way to summon competent aid was equally disheartening. She wondered if the boat were still at the dock and hurried outside to see. That Michael could have moored it so skillfully yesterday surprised her as much as finding it was Guy's boat.

Drenched, she looked back toward the cottage to judge the distance, but she could not drag Michael down to the boat alone. Even if she could, she knew little about sailing, and nothing about setting a course to see them safely home.

She spied a dead seagull on her return to the cottage and took it as a very bad sign. Now thoroughly wet herself, she stretched out atop Michael to cool him with her own chill. "Don't you dare die on me," she begged. "I'd never forgive you for that."

Guy drew back the silk curtain and looked up toward the dark clouds billowing overhead. "It might rain for days. I hope Michael and Delphine will survive on their own."

Françoise took another stitch in her embroidery before glancing up. "Neither is the type to fall victim to inclement weather, and my only worry is that Delphine lacked sufficient time to consider how bleak her future would be without him."

"Surely you'd not turn her out." Guy stepped away from the window to approach the fireplace where he faced the flames rather than his lovely companion of so many years.

"In a way, I already have, but with Michael Mallory so determined to rescue her, it has worked to her advantage as well as mine."

Guy shot a glance over his shoulder. "Are men always so predictable?"

Françoise smiled as though the answer to his question was too obvious to merit a response. "Neither of us suspected that Michael would present such intractable terms. He confused me completely, but I trust you'll be able to make him appreciate how desperately Delphine will cling to her independence."

Dumbfounded, Guy began to pace in front of the fire. "Why is that my responsibility? I simply meant for Delphine to fill Michael with hope and desire, not a murderous rage to possess her."

"Well, what you intended and what occurred appear to be two entirely different things, don't they? I wish we could overhear their conversations on the island, but lacking that advantage, let's plan how best to redirect Michael along the rightful path."

"Do you actually believe we'll succeed, considering the complete catastrophe in which we find ourselves?" Guy fumed.

"Are you certain you have no French blood? I really expect an Englishman to be far more coolheaded. Besides, you're the one who put the plan in motion, and I'll not allow you to abandon it now and jeopardize my daughter's future."

"You'll not allow?" Guy repeated incredulously, but when Françoise smoothed her fingertips over the soft swell of her bosom, he could not recall why Michael and Delphine's future even concerned them.

In the afternoon, Delphine repeatedly dunked Michael's blanket in the sea, but if her pitiful effort to break his fever was having any effect, she had yet to see it. She hoped Guy might rent a boat the instant the sky cleared and come to the island to retrieve his own, but she had the awful suspicion that regardless of the weather, he would remain locked in her mother's arms.

Exhausted and forlorn by evening, she ate a few slices of ham and a chunk of cheese. She was about to reach for an apple, when the bag of oranges caught her eye. Orange juice was sweet, and perhaps if she dripped it on Michael's lips, he might lick it off.

Inspired, she sliced an orange into quarters, then struggled to lay him flat on his back. She climbed up on the bed behind him, cradled his head in her lap, and gently squeezed the first wedge. The resulting drops of juice splattered on his lips, but then rolled off toward his ear.

She slapped his cheek lightly. "Michael, please help me here."

He was so relaxed, she found she could pinch his lower lip to create a little cup, which she could then fill and fold closed. While it took a bit of coaxing, using that method her second attempt to fill his mouth with orange juice was a success, and she felt it roll down his throat. Delighted, she wiped his lips and repeated the process with the remainder of the orange.

She needed him to drink water though, and before she could fetch some, he again rolled over on his stomach where his cheek remained firmly pressed to the mattress. "Well, thank you for what help you extended, but you're going to have to do much better the next time. I absolutely refuse to bury you here, so you're going to have to survive."

Scolding a sleeping man brought little satisfaction, but at least she had found a way to make him drink. Her mother was in as robust good health as she was, and this was the first time she had ever attended anyone who was ill. She had swiftly discovered it was exhausting, and should Michael not recover due to her pitiful store of medical knowledge, she would just lie down and die as well.

She stretched out beside him and closed her eyes. If not Guy, then eventually someone would visit the island and find their bodies. With no one to tell their sad story, one would undoubtedly be created for them. The tale might even be sung in seaside taverns from Kingston to Bristol.

To be the subject of some tragic love story did not appeal to her at all, and she got up again to go down to the sea to wet Michael's blanket. There were tears rather than raindrops running down her cheeks when she returned.

The next day Michael was no better, but Delphine was grateful that at least he appeared no worse. She spooned water into his mouth, kept him covered in damp blankets, and never left his side.

"You may be assured that I will purchase the latest medical text at my first opportunity," she told him. "If I had a house with a little plot of land, I could grow medicinal herbs, and support myself in that way. I would have to learn how to brew effective remedies, of course, which unfortunately might require a number of years. God forbid that I should harm anyone with any of my initial cures."

Sobered by that grim possibility, she cast about for another means to survive on her own. "I doubt I would be hired as a governess without references, although I certainly know more than most women. I could become a seamstress, or perhaps a companion to an elderly widow who would enjoy hearing me read. Of course, her son would probably fall in love with me, but I'd not return his affection and have to disappear in the dark of night so he could not pursue me."

She sighed and continued to sift Michael's hair through her fingers. "Maybe I should go to America to seek work as a governess. I could always claim the part of my luggage which had contained my references had been lost during the voyage, and wouldn't anyone there be delighted that I speak French as well as English?"

Michael slept too soundly to respond, but Delphine continued as though he were the most attentive of confidants. "I could be a servant I suppose, but the first time I refused to warm the master's bed, I'd again find myself without any means of livelihood. At least a man can go to sea and seek adventure."

She raised her hands to cover a wide yawn and then gazed out at the rain. It was gradually tapering off, but not nearly quickly enough to suit her. "Do you like rainy days, Michael? I don't. Raindrops always remind me of tears, as though the heavens were weeping for a lost love. I need sunshine to be content."

Michael stirred then, and she shook him a time or two. "Wake up, please," she implored, but he had merely shifted position slightly, not opened his eyes.

"You are beginning to try my patience," she murmured. She left the bed for a bite of cheese and bread, then went out into the rain rather than remain shut in the cottage with her fears.

Chapter 12

Foam-crested waves
Mermaid spinning, arms flung wide
The whole world's atilt

Michael recognized Delphine's voice, but her words were indistinct, as though she were seated in an adjoining room. He still enjoyed listening. Her tempo sped then slowed while her tone rose and fell to a seductive whisper. She appeared to be relating a long, involved tale. It sounded fascinating, but he drifted off before the end came, and she was rewarded with her listener's laughter or tender sympathy.

He was so awfully tired and stretched out to flex the muscles in his legs. He just needed to sleep a while longer while the rain sluiced off the roof in such a soothing lullaby. Then he would ask her to repeat the whole story for him.

"Michael?" Delphine had felt him move and laid her cheek on his shoulder blade. She thought his skin felt a mite cooler, at least she hoped so. When he again failed to respond, she dozed off, then woke with a start.

His blanket was merely damp rather than cool. She pulled it off the bed and trudged across the beach to dunk it in the sea. Her arms ached from the strain of wringing it out yet again, but she carried it back inside and spread it over Michael with the same tenderness she had shown the first time.

If his fever did not break soon, she doubted she would have the energy to tend him another day. Had she left for Kingston with him, he would have had no reason to venture out in the storm. If he died, the fault would be entirely hers. She had hoped to save them both this agonizing pain, but he had failed to play his part.

Fearing all was lost, she curled up beside him, and for the first time, wished her mother had taught her more than a child's sweet bedtime prayers.

Michael swam up from the depths, coughing and sputtering as he jerked himself upright. The wet blanket chained him to the bed, and he fought his way free. The cottage was dark, and he felt by his side for Delphine. When she wasn't there, he shouted her name, but all that came out was a hoarse croak.

She had been fetching water, but when she heard him call, the pitcher slipped from her hands. In her haste to reach him, she nearly fell on the bamboo flooring beneath the cistern, but caught herself and ran inside. While the rain had faded to a lingering drizzle, she was wet from head to toe.

"Yes?" she gasped as she came flying through the doorway.

"We've got to move the bed. It's all wet," Michael replied in a voice he scarcely recognized as his own.

"The whole island is wet!" she responded and ecstatic he was alive to complain, she scrambled up beside him. "Oh, Michael, you gave me such an awful fright."

He covered a yawn and was surprised to find more than his usual morning stubble covering his cheeks. "How long was I asleep?"

"Well, you were dizzy when you arrived, so I believe you were already ill. You went right to sleep, and I couldn't wake you yesterday, nor today. How long does that make? I'm afraid I'm unable to think clearly enough to make a proper tally."

Michael pulled her into his arms for a brief hug, then leaned back. "That's only two days. I heard you talking. Was someone else here?"

Startled, she wondered if he recalled anything she had said, but she relaxed when apparently he did not. "No, only you, but you're a very fine companion. Now we can move the bed if you'd like, but then I intend to sleep a couple of days myself."

"No, the bed is fine where it is. Go on to sleep. I want to clean up." He rolled off the opposite side of the bed, but found his legs all wobbly. He needed a moment to regain the strength to stand. Then, determined to take care of himself rather than continue to rely on her, he shoved off the bed.

He made it out the door before having to sag against the side of the cottage and grab hold. His only consolation was that he felt better than he had on his first morning on the island, and he fully intended to pull himself together by dawn.

Rather than make his way to the cistern to bathe, he stood beside the cottage and let the rain rinse him clean. The rain was cold in Devon, but here it was as warm as tears. Had he not missed Delphine so badly, he might have stayed outside far longer.

When he returned to her, she had lit the oil lamp and was making up the bed with fresh linens. "You should have waited for me to help you," he scolded softly.

"It's no trouble. Now sit down and eat, I really am going to sleep."

Michael looked around for his pants. "I don't believe it's proper for a man to dine without a stitch of clothing."

"Haven't we discussed this before?" Delphine replied through a sleepy yawn. She left the wrinkled linens in a tangled heap on the floor and lay down on the bed.

Michael vaguely recalled a discussion on the need, or lack thereof, for apparel on the island, but he could not recall what decision they had reached. Knowing Delphine, he supposed they had agreed not to bother.

"Won't you join me?" he called invitingly.

When Delphine failed to respond, he crossed to the bed but she had already fallen asleep. He stroked her hair lightly and bent down to kiss her cheek. Even in the dim light, he could see the shadows beneath her eyes and feared she had not slept the whole time that he had.

"I'm so sorry, my love," he murmured softly. "Things will be better for us from now on." He believed it, too, and couldn't wait to explain how they were going to live on his plantation together.

Delphine heard him roll up the soiled linens, but she kept her eyes closed and continued to feign sleep. She was so completely drained she doubted she could have carried on a coherent conversation even if she had remained awake. She was so grateful he was well, but his ordeal had taught her a vital lesson: she would bide her time and wait until they were off the island to leave him a second time.

Her course decided, she sighed softly and sank down into the feather mattress. She stretched her toes and began to count in her mind. Before she reached six, she had fallen into a deep, dreamless sleep.

It had been shortly before dawn when Michael had awakened, and he let Delphine sleep until late that same afternoon. Then he sat down beside her on the bed, peeled away the blanket, and trailed his finger-tips from her toes to her hip. In response, she twitched, and rubbed her foot along her leg to erase his path. When he switched to her arm, she gave up on sleep, and opened her eyes.

The rain had tapered off, and a pale light filled the cottage with a hazy glow. He was again clean-shaven, and as always, his teasing grin touched her heart. He looked relaxed, as though the last few days had been a carefree idyll.

She covered a wide yawn, then pulled the blanket back up to her shoulders and snuggled down. "Are you completely unable to amuse yourself?" she chided.

Michael had spread the linens outside to rinse in the rain and then walked up and down the debris strewn beach. He had sat in the doorway and watched the sea churn for what had seemed like hours. He had eaten a bit of ham and cheese and an apple, then watched her sleep before he had taken another nap himself. None of it had been enjoyable without her.

"I doubt I could catch any fish in this weather, and even if I did, there would be no way to roast them. The only book here is your journal, and because it is written in French, I can't read it."

"Nor should you," she insisted. "My private thoughts are my own."

"I'd rather you shared them with me. Even if no one else was here, you spoke for a long while when I was unable to respond. Tell me what you said."

Delphine licked her lips, but she had no intention of ever revealing her plans to strike out on her own. "I told you how much I disliked rain, and how badly I wanted you to be well. I wondered about your horses too," she added to what she hoped was a believable summary.

He suspected there was far more to relate, but unwilling to pester her with questions, he stood. "I'm sorry I missed it. Now why don't you get up, bathe, and join me for supper. I thought I'd brought a whole bag of oranges. Did you eat them all?"

Delphine angled her legs off the bed. "No, my lord, you did, drip by drip."

"That explains it then. I wish I'd brought along some walnuts. Apples are delicious with them."

"Or with cheese," she offered. "Now you're making me very hungry, so I'll hurry."

"You may have all the time you require." Michael gave her a quick kiss as she walked by. Even all sleep-rumpled, she was still a goddess to him.

Delphine was amazed by Michael's hearty appetite as well as by the fact that he had left the wine unopened. "I hope the weather soon clears, or we may run out of provisions."

"What do you mean? We've half a ham, plenty of cheese, some bread, and a dozen apples. If tomorrow isn't clear, we'll surely have sun again by the next day."

Delphine sliced an apple wafer-thin and took a piece. "If you found the island in a storm, the return to Kingston should be no challenge at all for you. I simply hadn't thought you were fond of sailing."

"I'm not, but you were a compelling inspiration." He smiled slyly as he transferred several slices of apple onto his plate, and ate them.

"I had no idea how great an inspiration I was until I saw your tattoo. Quite frankly, I don't know whether or not to be flattered that you put my name on your arm, and in my own writing too. Was that your intention when you cut the page from my journal?"

He was surprised that she had not mentioned the tattoo earlier. He turned his arm to admire the beauty of the tattoo artist's work and was glad that he had thought of it. "No, I simply wanted a memento. The tattoo was a separate idea altogether. I'll never be in any danger of forgetting you, but still . . ."

She waited, then fearing he was about to make some wonderfully romantic declaration that would reduce her to tears, she stood and began to clear the table. "I shall strive to be flattered then, but you mustn't expect me to ink your name into my skin."

"No, Michael's too common," he agreed. "Of course, Clairbourne would be distinctive."

"And so long it would encircle my arm." She set their plates and utensils outside to be cleansed in the rain, but when she returned to the table, he grabbed her waist and pulled her down on his lap.

He nuzzled her throat and slid his hand underneath her nightgown to caress her leg. "Perhaps it would look best lengthwise on your thigh."

"I think not," she argued, but she looped her arms around his neck. She found it difficult to believe he felt well enough to make love, but she intended for them both to enjoy it if he did.

He raised his hand to caress the smooth swell of her breasts. "Clairbourne would fit quite nicely across here."

"Do you actually believe that I'd disrobe in front of some dockside artisan?"

"A valid point," he murmured as he dipped his head to place a kiss in the valley between her lovely breasts. "What about the woman who pierced your nipple? Do you think she might be inclined to—"

"No, I do not." She raised her hand to his forehead. "With such bizarre thoughts, I fear you're still feverish. I absolutely refuse to wear your name on my person—even tattooed on the bottom of my foot."

"A very pretty foot it is too," he replied. He shifted slightly to kiss her deeply and sent a hand between her legs to open her cleft. "You're right," he whispered against her lips, "this is madness, but it's of the most delicious sort."

She rose up to take his fingers deep, then reached for his belt. "You must conserve your strength. Remain where you are, and I'll slide down your cock."

He was seated in a straight-backed chair, and once she had removed his trousers, she tossed away her nightgown. She swung a leg over him, balanced on her knees, and took him in slowly, inch by inch. His hands tightened on her waist, but she rose to hover above him.

"There's no need to rush; you know where you're bound."

He threw his head back. "Ah, that I do, but . . . Delphine . . ."

She raised up again to keep only the smooth tip of him before sliding down a little farther. "You like this?"

Michael moved his hands to knead her breasts. His breathing had quickened, and he sighed deep in his throat. He rocked slightly, and she moved with him, up and down, then with a slow circular motion that took him to her depths. He thrust up into her, and with her hands on his shoulders, she rode him until he slid his hand between their bodies to massage her into a throbbing climax in time with his own.

He feared he might slide right out of the chair and tumble to the floor, but her back was braced against the table, and she held him steady until the last tremble of pleasure coursed through him.

Spent, Delphine lay her head on his shoulder and fought not to cry. Even without a tattooed reminder, she would never forget him, but she could not resist whispering a naughty suggestion. "I think I'll sit upon you this way each time we dine, my lord. It would make for the most fascinating meals."

Michael's imagination instantly painted the scene at his estate in Devon. The long mahogany table was brightly illuminated by half a dozen gleaming silver candelabras filed with scented candles. Silver serving dishes were piled high with delectable treats, and crystal goblets held the finest wines. The assembled guests were all talking politely to each other until one chanced to note how he and Delphine were occupied.

"I can see it so clearly," he responded. "There's a dinner party at my estate, and you're wearing pale blue satin. Your hair is styled in a crown of curls. Each time you come down on me, you utter a soft, 'Oh, my lord,' and soon everyone at the table is leaning forward to get a better view. The guest of honor would be on my right, and his eyes would nearly pop from his head."

Delphine rolled her hips and felt him growing hard again within her. "You're the one who should be telling the stories. I meant only to suggest the most intimate of dinners, not a party for dozens."

"You needn't worry. I'd never share you with my guests."

"I certainly hope not," Delphine replied in a playful tone, but she was determined not to remain with him long enough to find out.

Without withdrawing, Michael stood and lay Delphine back on the table. He took care to move the lamp aside so that she was at no risk of singeing her hair. Then, standing between her spread thighs, he pinned her wrists to the table and rocked forward.

"Tell me why you remained here on the island." His surprising change in tone conveyed a demand rather than a polite request.

Filled with the whole, hot length of him, Delphine squirmed, but she made no effort to break free. Instead, she smiled invitingly to disarm him. "Now that you've made me think of a dinner party, I wonder what your guests would say to this rapturous display."

He rocked forward again. "They'd probably gasp and then clap their hands in time with my thrusts." He made several slow, sweet lunges to demonstrate. "Let's pursue that theme another time. I insist that you tell me why you didn't leave here when I did."

She closed her eyes a moment to simply feel him slide on the slippery wetness he had helped to create. Then she sighed. "You overwhelm me."

"I could say the same of you," he responded. "But I

did not abandon you, nor would I had I known the truth."

"Truth," she repeated softly. She mixed the truth so freely with lies it was a wonder he accepted anything she said. She shifted position slightly to lock her ankles behind his hips. "Which of us will be the first to move?" she challenged.

"You wish to make a bet? What do you have to wager?"

"Alas, nothing," she admitted. "But then, I intend to win."

Michael relaxed his grip on her wrists as he considered the possibilities. "Perhaps we could agree on the performance of a service."

Feeling him thrust so deeply was such a new and splendid sensation, without the slightest twinge of pain, and she could have lain there all night to enjoy it. She regarded him with a fond gaze. "When have I ever refused to service you?" she purred.

Michael waited a long moment, but her glance held such a delicious promise, he lost interest in gambling for anything more. He slid his hands around her, and drew her up into his arms.

"Let's both move and call it a draw," he offered.

Delphine ground her hips against his. "Yes," she breathed out against his ear. "Let's insist each of our encounters end in a draw."

He grabbed a handful of her hair to force her mouth to his, but even as she lost herself in his possessive kiss, she felt him sway. She broke away and grabbed his shoulders.

"Michael, are you ill?"

He blinked, as though startled by her question, then slid into her. "A little dizzy maybe, but not ill."

She didn't believe him. "Stop." Without waiting for him to withdraw, she scooted back to free herself, and then slid off the table. She reached for his hand. "Come back to bed with me."

She led him to the bed, yanked back the blanket, and gave him a slight shove. Frightened, she swallowed hard, then lay down beside him. "Just go to sleep."

He pulled her back into his arms. "I'm fine," he insisted wearily. "I just need a nap."

Delphine smoothed his hair off his forehead and kissed his brow. "It's too late in the day for a nap. Go to sleep." She was relieved when he relaxed against her, but if they did not leave the island soon, she was in grave danger of losing her sanity, as well as her heart.

The day dawned with sparkling clarity, and when Delphine awoke, Michael was already up and dressed. She looked past him toward the sunlight streaming in the doorway and window, and silently rejoiced. She propped herself on her elbow.

"You look as dashing as always. Do you feel well enough to sail home?" she asked.

"Yes, I do, but you can't step out on the docks in a nightgown. Did you try on the clothes I bought for you?"

She yawned and stretched. "Not yet. Give me a moment to wake first."

"You may have all the time you require." He sliced the ham for their breakfast and laid it on their plates. "I left my carriage in Kingston, and we'll take it home to my estate."

"I beg your pardon?" Positive she could not have understood him, she sat up and hugged her knees.

He laid the knife on his plate, wiped his hands, and approached the bed. "I'm taking you home with me. There's a dower house you may decorate as you choose. The garden could use a woman's touch as well. You'll be very comfortable there, Delphine, and we'll sleep together every night."

She had not believed him the first time he had mentioned taking her home, and she was taken aback by the outlandish pronouncement. "You intend for me to reside on your estate?"

"Yes, I do. I realize it's an unconventional arrangement, but I want you there. Besides, when we have children, which we surely will, they ought to be raised on their father's estate."

Delphine's heart began to pound in her ears and though she fought not to shriek an objection, her expression was unmistakably hostile. "Is that the arrangement you made with my mother?" she asked incredulously.

"I discussed it with her, yes." That Françoise had been no more pleased than Delphine, was not something he cared to reveal. "I'll not insult you with an allowance. Spend as much as you choose on whatever pleases you. You'll find me generous to a fault."

Delphine was still attempting to cope with his mention of children. "What you describe is impossible," she exclaimed. "One day you'll remarry, and you cannot expect your bride to feel welcome in a home that also includes your mistress and bastard offspring."

He scoffed at her objection. "One wife was more than enough for me. I'll never remarry. I'll name our first-born son as my heir, and provide generously for our other children as well." He reached out to caress her cheek. "I intend to take very good care of you and whatever dear little babies you give me."

Delphine scarcely knew how to respond. Once they had returned to Kingston, she had intended to allow him to believe she would become his mistress. Then she would have promptly disappeared. It was a fine plan in her view, one that spared them both, but once shunted off to his estate, she would be his captive, his prisoner.

All she had to do was keep quiet a while longer, and convince him to allow her to stop by her mother's apartment for a day or two to gather her belongings. It was too reasonable a request to refuse. When Delphine glanced up at his confident grin, it was impossible to swallow the furious anger welling up from her toes.

"No, what you wish me to do is act the part of your wife and provide you with an heir; but you cannot breed sons without any thought of the consequences, as though they were prize horses."

Michael had seen her angry, but she was beyond livid now. "I thought you had come to care for me," he murmured softly.

The wistful comment brought tears to her eyes. "I do, but I'll not live on your estate. To do so would subject us both to an unbearable burden of shame and ridicule."

"We're a very long way from London's gossiping shrews," he countered, "and no one who matters has any idea how we behave here."

She wiped her eyes and stared at him coldly. "I matter, and so does my mother."

He responded with a mirthless laugh and then stretched the truth gossamer thin. "I explained my intentions to Françoise, but when I discovered that you were still here, there was no time to waste in forging an agreement."

"You're lying!"

He straightened up, and his stance became not merely proud, but menacing. "I've never lied to you, nor will I ever."

She had not donned her nightgown before joining him last night, and she left the bed, plucked her journal from the bedside table, and still brazenly nude, shook it at him.

"Upon several occasions, you've offered to allow me to draw up a contract which you swore you'd sign. Let's do it now. Your terms are absurd, pure folly for us both, so we'll replace them with mine."

He watched her walk to the table, clad only in her long, silvery hair, and thought she had a most unfair advantage. "Please try on your new clothes first, because my thoughts go in only one direction when you're nude; and at present, I doubt that you wish to seduce me."

At the moment, clothing meant little to her, but knowing she reeked of him, she flounced outside to bathe and shampoo her hair. She returned wrapped in a towel and sorted through the garments he had purchased for her. The ivory silk lingerie was pretty enough, as were the layers of petticoats. She dressed quickly in a chemise and lace-trimmed pantalettes, then having no need of body bands to flatten her stomach or lift her breasts, she tied the petticoats at her waist and shook out the gown.

It was a pale green muslin, high-waisted with ribbon ties and a matching overdress with embroidered trim adorning the sleeves, squared neckline and hem.

She was surprised by how well it fit. "I don't believe I've ever owned such a charmingly respectable gown."

She sat down at the table to pull on the stockings and then tried on the kid slippers. They were a bit large, but not unwearable. She stood, smoothed her skirts, and glanced toward him. "Thank you," she said without a trace of sincerity.

He had undressed women, and enjoyed it too, but she had just yanked on her new clothing with an unladylike haste that had been so unexpectedly arousing he had to cough to find his voice. Even then, with her hair flowing free, she looked so incredibly young and sweet, he feared she might be mistaken for his daughter.

"I could have done better with more time," he apologized.

She turned to take the bottle of ink from the shelf beside the table. "You needn't fret. I am more than capable of selecting my own wardrobe."

"Well, yes, I'm sure you are, but even today, you look lovely."

"Thank you again." She opened her journal to a fresh page. "What is today's date?"

"I've no idea. Leave it blank, and we'll fill it in later." Anxious to convince her his ideas had merit, he began to pace beside the table. "Let's begin with our names. This is an agreement between Delphine Antoine and—"

"You intend to dictate the document?" she asked incredulously.

He paused to turn toward her. "Surely I have had more experience than you at creating binding contacts."

"You undoubtedly have more experience than I do with everything, but I intend for the terms to be mine."

She had shoved their plates aside, but he sat down and took a slice of ham. "Perhaps we should eat first. I know I'm hungry, aren't you?"

"No, not at all." She dipped her pen in the ink, and then realized she was uncertain how to begin. She would ask him only the obvious, however. "Would you like for me to refer to you as the Earl of Clairbourne?"

"Naturally. This is the last bite of bread, are you certain you don't wish to share it?"

"Positive." She glanced out the window, and wished she had given some thought to a contract while he had been ill. Unfortunately, she had been focused solely on leaving him, not creating promises which would fool him into believing she intended to remain as his cherished companion.

Then it occurred to her that she just might present terms so advantageous to her, and onerous to him, that he would refuse to agree, thus solving her problems with him for once and for all. It was then a struggle not to smile too wide.

"While you are undoubtedly as generous as you claim, my lord, you could be lost due to some unforeseen catastrophe, and I would be left having to beg for a pittance from your relatives. To avoid such a disastrous happenstance, I should like an allowance for life that would also be included in your will."

Michael leaned forward so abruptly, his pewter plate nearly shot off the table. "You expect me to support you, even after I am dead?"

"How could you rest in peace knowing that I was

begging on street corners?" she countered with a poignant catch in her voice.

"Good Lord, Delphine. Does your mother have such an ambitious arrangement with Guy?"

She had no intention of revealing her mother's wealth assured a comfortable old age regardless of how long her liaison continued with Guy. "No, but had she thought of it, I'm certain she would have requested one."

Michael sat back and glared at her for a long moment, and then he nodded grudgingly. "As the mother of my children, of course I'll provide for you in my will."

Delphine shook her head. "No, you must insure my comfort regardless of whether or not we produce a single child together. Not every couple does, you know."

His gaze grew even darker. "Oh yes, I'm well aware of that. Perhaps we should agree upon a base figure and then add increments for children."

"What do you mean, if I bore one child I would receive the minimum, but if I bore two, or ten, I'd be rewarded appropriately?"

"Why do you sound so insulted? You're the one demanding to be supported forever!"

This time, Delphine feigned regret. She replaced the lid on the ink and closed her journal. "Oh, now I see. I had not realized that I might be too expensive for you. What a shame."

Michael leapt from his chair with growling roar. "That is the stupidest thing you have ever said. Now I'm going down to the dock to make certain there was no damage to the boat, and when I return, we'll reach an understanding. I can promise you that."

As he stormed out, Delphine reached for a slice of

ham and took a bite. To claim to wish to be his mistress, while at the same time presenting a lengthy list of wholly unacceptable terms was such a brilliant ploy she was elated to have thought of it. She smiled to herself and wondered just how outrageous she dared be.

Chapter 13

Blistering heat
Sun-scorched sand, sea aflame
Molten surrender

Michael swore a string of bitter oaths as he approached the dock. Then scowling, he looked back over his shoulder and added a few more. He had never struck a woman, nor would he, but he had never been so sorely provoked.

He had long known what a manipulative bitch Françoise was, and he was chagrined to have been so easily duped by Delphine. He continued to curse the whole time he inspected the boat, which had weathered the storm quite well, but he no longer felt any great sense of urgency to leave the island.

He refused to leave, in fact, until they had settled upon a contract which would be beneficial to them both. As with any man of means, he had occasionally invested in an enterprise which had ultimately proven unprofitable; but he had never deliberately cheated anyone. Nor would he trick Delphine now with an agreement which appeared to favor her, but would be far more advantageous to him in the long run.

Badly disappointed that she had not shared his enthusiasm for his initial plan, he circled the island as he searched for a creative solution which would appeal to her. Unfortunately, by the time he had reached his rock-strewn encampment, not a single viable idea had presented itself.

What disturbed him most was that after he had been drugged and kidnapped, Delphine had welcomed him to the island with a tender concern and wanton affection. Even when he had been in the worst of moods, even when he knew exactly what she was, she had seduced him with a sparkling grace that he could not bear to lose, *would not lose*.

He stretched his arms, and then, suddenly aware of the driftwood scattered along the shore, he began to gather an armload to carry home. "Home," he laughed to himself, but with Delphine, the tiny house had truly been a home.

As Michael neared the cottage, Delphine was standing in the doorway. She had draped the pale cashmere shawl he had bought her over her shoulders, and as she turned, sunlight danced along the interwoven golden threads.

She looked so delicate and sweet, but as Françoise's daughter she would have been tutored from childhood to seek every advantage for her beauty. It was no accident of fate that he had been stranded there with her. He was there because he possessed all the qualities her mother admired: wealth, youth, and a handsome appearance.

For all of Delphine's carefully nurtured sophistication, she truly knew very little of the world. Most assuredly, she had never been courted by a gentleman. After the way he had left her, it would be unexpected, an approach for which she would be totally unprepared. For that reason, if no other, he was determined to bring her to his bed by affection alone. She might have played her part beautifully with him, but now it was his turn to guide their fate.

He could have cursed Françoise all day, but he would not lose his temper again with Delphine. He would exercise the same care as her mother, but he would teach her the bliss they shared was worth far more than gold. If that tactic failed, then he would bind her to him with babies she would never abandon.

He added the driftwood to the pile at the side of the cottage and brushed off his hands as he greeted her. "I should not have called your remark stupid, when in fact, you're a brilliant young woman. Now we needn't trade insults, when we'll get along so much better by being civil."

She stepped out onto the sand. "I agree, but I must still insist upon a signed contract to protect both our interests."

He brushed her cheek with a kiss and then gazed out toward the sea. The water was again a vivid aqua. Drawing upon what little patience he possessed, he lowered his voice to a hushed whisper.

"Has it not occurred to you that you may already be carrying my child?"

She had failed to consider the possibility and stared at him wide-eyed. "I have been, shall we say, preoccupied."

"Then this is a good time to consider it. There has been ample opportunity for it to have occurred, very pleasurable opportunities I might add."

Her smile was faint compared to his charming grin. She had been compiling a list of demands, which while reasonable in the broadest sense, were intended to discourage him. Children were not among them, however. That she could so easily imagine him running his hands over her swollen belly frightened her badly.

"The wise man sires children with his wife," she cautioned, "not his mistress."

He laughed. "I may be known for many things, but no one has ever complimented my wisdom."

The breeze ruffled his hair, and he raised a hand to rake it off his forehead. It was a careless gesture, yet it was incredibly endearing. She would never tire of studying him.

"Guy's boat is at least afloat. Does it need any repair?" she asked.

"No, it's still seaworthy, but would you mind if we waited a day or two before returning to Kingston?"

She moved toward him, stepped right out of her left shoe and then kicked off the right. "If you're not feeling well enough to sail, then of course we ought not to go. I'll not risk your health for any reason."

The tear in her gaze was touchingly real. Either she was a consummate actress, or she really did care for him. He chose to believe the latter and build on it. "I didn't mean to worry you. I'd just like to clean up the island so that it's as pretty as when we found it. The repairs to the cottage roof will require another visit with the appropriate supplies."

Delphine ran her hands over her skirt. Her new dress was attractive as well as demure, but certainly not meant for cleaning debris from the beach. "I really do like the clothes you bought me, but if we're not leaving, would you mind awfully if I wore one of my nightgowns?"

"Not at all. I'm very fond of them." He leaned

down and brushed her lips with a light kiss. He left his boots and socks at the cottage and then walked down to the shore to begin working.

Delphine pulled her lower lip through her teeth. He had been so angry when he had left, but returned in such an agreeable mood. It usually took him several hours to calm down, and she feared that he had simply lost interest in offering her a contract. It was precisely what she wanted, and at the same time, not what she wanted at all.

Perplexed, she quickly shed her new clothes, but left the drawstring of her favorite nightgown's neckline loose to offer a tantalizing glimpse of her breasts. Tears stung her eyes as she followed Michael down to the water, and she could not understand why the rejection she longed for had hurt so badly.

When they had a near mountain of driftwood piled beside the cottage, Michael grabbed a fishing pole and went out on the rocks. He had not thought he would ever look forward to dining on fish, but the day was warm and bright, and while it was a struggle not to glance in Delphine's direction while she was nearby, he enjoyed himself immensely.

He carried his catch up to the cottage and built the fire. He called for Delphine, and she answered from the top of the bluff. "What are you doing up there?" he asked.

"Just making sure we'll remain alone," she answered, but in truth, she was so badly confused, she had barely scanned the sea for sails. She still did not feel like eating, but made her way down to the cottage.

"The sky is so clear, I'm surprised we can't see all

the way to Jamaica today," she remarked as she took her place opposite him on the sand.

"Don't forget the Earth is round," he explained. "We see in a straight line, or we'd surely be able to see the sailors milling about the docks. Frankly, I don't care what they're doing on Jamaica when things are so perfect here."

"Perfect?" she scoffed. "Surely you jest."

"No, the three days I spent without you were more than enough. Did you miss me?"

She dipped her head, and her hair fell away from her brow to reveal a faint greenish tinge along her left cheek. Inside the cottage the light had been too dim to see the mark, and earlier in the day, the breeze had whipped her hair into a lacy veil.

He moved close to trace the fading bruise with his fingertip. "I'm sorry I failed to notice this before now, but either you slipped and fell while I was away, or Françoise slapped you so hard that you were badly bruised. Tell me what happened, and this time I would appreciate the truth as to why you remained here."

This was the quick-tempered Michael she knew. She had forgotten the bruise, but the blow that caused it had been quite painful. "My mother was disappointed in me," she admitted softly.

"In what way?"

She knew his implacable expression all too well and shrugged as though her hesitancy was understandable. "I grew up and became an unfortunate reminder of her own mortality. At the same time, she has difficulty seeing me as a woman rather than a disobedient child."

"Yes, it's a common enough problem between parents and children, but what was the subject of your argument that morning?"

She licked her lips. "You, of course. What did you expect?"

He grit his teeth and silently swore that even if it took until midnight to extract the truth, he would hold his temper in check. Nevertheless, remaining calm was a struggle. "Could you be more specific?"

Again, she merely skirted the truth. "She was furious with us for becoming lovers, and unwilling to insult you, she punished me. Now please don't burn the fish."

He could readily grasp Françoise's fury, but she had then sweetly lied to him about her daughter's whereabouts. Some important element had to be missing from Delphine's account of that fateful morning, but that he could not fathom precisely what left him thoroughly annoyed.

"Before we leave here, you'll tell me the truth," he swore darkly and then turned their meal with an impatient flip.

"I could make the same demand," she replied, and when his gaze remained fixed on the grill, she wondered if he weren't harboring a few secrets of his own. It was an intriguing possibility.

Unwilling to admit to what lengths he was willing to go to keep her, he ignored her comment and scooped up the fish. "It's a shame the mangoes are gone."

"Yes, it is." She took the plate he handed her. After several bites of fish, she complimented him and returned to the main issue. "How long do you intend to delay writing our contract?"

"That all depends on how long it takes to put you in a receptive mood."

She licked her fingers and took note of his rapt glance. All of her tricks still had the desired effect on him, but she was no longer the same single-minded vixen. He had opened a whole new world of emotion, and it was no wonder she found it so difficult to cope.

"It may take forever," she cautioned, "and Guy is sure to come for his boat, if not for us, before then."

"Eventually," he admitted, "but you'll find me very agreeable company until he arrives. How do you spend your time at home? Do you enjoy listening to music?"

She sat up to survey the deserted beach. "Yes, but I fail to see any musicians here, unless you have some hidden nearby?"

"Not today, but I'll hire some as soon as we return home. I know you love to dance."

She laughed at the memory of their minuet. "You were very kind not to make fun of my inexperience."

"Laughter isn't what you inspire."

He had such a charming smile, but his compliment left her feeling empty. "I want to go home," she blurted out suddenly.

The plaintive request jarred him, but failed to diminish his resolve. "We'll go just as soon as we agree on terms, tomorrow perhaps, or the next day."

That she was now the one trapped on the island was not lost on her. Her heart fluttered in her chest like a caged bird's, and she bit her lip rather than cry. A single tear escaped her lashes to slide down her cheek.

"Delphine?" Her anguished expression prompted him to set his plate aside, and then to remove hers from her trembling hands. Wanting to console her in the best way possible, he lifted her into his arms and carried her inside to the bed. He gently lay her face down, then quickly stripped off his own clothing and moved to cover her body with his own.

Propped on his elbows to spare her his weight, he kissed her shoulder and then smoothed her hair aside to kiss her ear. "You're as wild and beautiful as the sea, Delphine, and I've no desire to break your spirit."

He eased her nightgown up out of his way, then rolled his hips to sink into her, but only teased her with the tip of his cock before withdrawing. "You needn't be afraid of me when I'm so good to you," he whispered against her cheek. He pushed forward to plunge deeper. "This is how it will always be between us."

She felt his heat and strength not only across her shoulders, but also along her spine and down her legs. He was pressed so snugly against her whole length that she could barely move, but she rocked her hips against his in a subtle surrender. She knew precisely what he was doing—seizing yet another opportunity to create a child—but she lacked the will to resist when she wanted him so badly.

His thrusts were slow and sweet, gently stretching her until he was buried deep. He held still then, laced his fingers in hers and spread kisses along her cheek. Michael longed to offer poetic promises, but he was too full of her to speak. He could only move, and he slid a hand beneath her to press against her cleft.

Delphine bucked her hips, and he slid out and back in. She was so tight and hot. He buried himself again and again until he could no longer fight the tide racing toward release. He shuddered as it splattered her depths, and he kept her locked tightly in his embrace until their shared rapture blurred into a dreamy calm.

With Michael, Delphine had discovered that her mother's explicit instructions were no more valuable than the paper wrapping a treasured gift. Consumed by their passion, she was still grateful to have mastered so many erotic techniques, but she could not even imagine sharing them with another man.

At the same time, while it was a tempting prospect, she would soon cease to exist if she were no more than a pretty pet he sought on a warm afternoon or chilly evening. Nor would she be his surrogate wife and fill his home with handsome bastards who would probably go off to sea and never return.

When he began to lick her ear, she brushed him away. "You make a most interesting blanket, my lord."

"No more than interesting?" He rolled away, left the bed, and dressed quickly. This was not the courting he had planned. He blamed himself rather than her haunting allure for betraying them both.

"I hope you'll forgive me for not waiting for a contract," he offered apologetically. "I'll spend the night on the other side of the island so it won't happen again. We'll work out an agreement first thing in the morning."

He went out the door before Delphine could stop him, but she remained in the bed savoring his scent on the bedding until the sun had disappeared below the waves.

Michael peeled off his clothes and swam parallel to the shore until he was too tired to manage another stroke. Some gentleman he had turned out to be, he fumed silently. He strode up the beach and shook out the water dripping from his hair. He yanked on his trousers and leaned back against the rock wall he had not bothered to complete.

He thought of Delphine as the wild one, but her tearful gaze was as powerful an aphrodisiac as her nipple ring; and he had taken her without showing the slightest restraint. Indeed, the possibility of merely offering sympathetic words and gestures had not even occurred to him. He had not expected their physical tie to provide such a powerful emotional link.

What had he really missed when he had gone home alone? He could not separate her beauty from her enticing ways, or her defiance from her seductive surrender. He needed the whole array of her charms with an aching hunger she alone could assuage.

And all she longed for was a written document assuring her survival should he swiftly tire of her and toss her aside. Since that improbable happenstance would never occur, it was scarcely a fair trade; and he balked at placing a monetary value on the devotion of a young woman who was so dear to him.

Clearly he needed a better plan. Delphine was a creature of perplexing moods, but she had been wonderfully attentive when his only desire had been to escape the island. Feigning disinterest might be wise, but where was he going to find the resolve for such an outrageous pretense when he had failed so miserably that day?

Exhausted, he spread his shirt over the sandy soil, lay back, and propped his head on his hands to stare up at the sky. The light had begun to fade, and the first stars were faint in the dusk. Perhaps all he needed was a good night's sleep to awaken refreshed. As he drifted off to sleep, he hoped to dream of Delphine.

* * *

Michael awoke when she touched him. "Is something wrong?"

"Yes, you should at least have a blanket upon which to sleep. I brought you one."

He sat up, yawned, and struggled to his feet. "How very thoughtful of you." He tossed his shirt upon the rocks, then reached for the blanket and spread it out on the ground. "I'm surprised you found me in the dark."

"The stars lit the way. The island isn't large, so it wasn't much of a challenge."

"Unlike you," he teased.

"I've provided no challenge at all. Indeed, I have been shameless in my desire for you."

Whether it was her snowy gown or pale hair, she glowed as brightly as the stars. "Perhaps it is a mere trick of the night, but you have the shimmering beauty of a goddess," he whispered. He reached out to draw her into his arms and rested his cheek against her hair. "Stay with me."

She snuggled closer still. "Obviously, I'm unable to stay away."

"We don't need a contract for this." Michael found the ribbon at her neckline already untied and with a gentle tug, her nightgown pooled at her feet. He drew her down onto the blanket and kissed her until they were both so breathless he had to stop for air.

She licked his lips to draw him down into another deep kiss, and he felt as though he were falling into the night. When at last he could bear to break away, he kissed and licked a trail over her cool breasts and down the inviting plane of her stomach. He moved to her feet and rubbed them gently until she almost purred.

He kissed her ankles and calves, slowly nibbled his way up her slender thighs, and then slid his hands beneath her bottom to raise her cleft to his lips. He pierced her with his tongue and lapped and sucked until she writhed beneath him, but he used only his fingers rather than his cock to heighten her pleasure. He coaxed her to the brink time and again before finally sending her catapulting over the edge.

Then, elated with his newfound restraint, he slept with her nestled in his arms until Guy woke him the next morning with a rude shove.

"I must say you two make a handsome pair sprawled there like native lovers, but I feared that you'd been lost at sea. I could not have lived with myself a moment longer without coming to rescue Delphine. Clearly, she does not require it. Or do you, my dear?"

Delphine slipped from Michael's arms and rose with an unabashed nonchalance. She picked up her nightgown, slid it over her head, then reached out to ruffle her lover's hair.

"As a matter of fact," she admitted through a sleepy yawn, "I would like to return home with whichever of you would care to take me."

Michael was on his feet in an instant. "You'll stay with me, Delphine."

Guy perched himself on the adjacent low rock wall. "My goodness, I didn't mean to start an argument. I merely wanted the assurance that you were both safe."

"Clearly we are," Michael grumbled. He bent down to grab their blanket and folded it over his arm. Delphine handed him his shirt, but he did not bother putting it on.

"You must have come in someone else's boat," he said. "Leave it for us and sail your own home."

Guy raised a gloved hand and cleared his throat. "I'm afraid that's impossible. I plan to use mine, and the rented boat must be back in the harbor by noon."

Michael watched Delphine shake out her hair. She would not meet his gaze, so it was clear what she wanted. "All right, on one condition."

Guy chuckled. "Only one?"

"Yes, I want Delphine's promise that she will not go straight to her mother's abortionist friend for a potion to prevent her from giving me a child."

Delphine's head came up with a snap. "I'm not your property, my lord, and you have no right to make any demands whatsoever. As you'll surely recall, you passed on the chance to forge a contract yesterday. Today, I intend to return home with Guy, and we can come to an agreement over terms tomorrow, or next week if you'd rather."

Guy stood and slipped his arm around her waist. "As you know, Delphine is like a daughter to me, and—"

Michael raised his fist. "Don't say another word, or I'll make you eat it along with your front teeth."

There was no mistaking his mood, and Delphine feared he might seriously harm Guy before he realized what he had done. "Please, there's no cause for such violent threats. You have the promise you sought, my lord, now let's return to Kingston where I can finally have a hot bath and the comfort of my own bed."

Michael let her go with Guy, but he was seething clear to his soul.

The following afternoon, Michael called on Delphine accompanied by a Mr. Phineas Finch, a diminutive older gentlemen he introduced as his solicitor. "I know it's a contract you want, so I've brought an expert to handle it," he explained.

Michael was dressed as he had been the day she had seen him on the street in a navy coat and fawn trousers. His black boots shown with a bright gleam, and he had trimmed his hair. He looked like the perfect gentleman, but his gaze was as fierce as when she had left him on the island.

Once they were seated in the parlor, she was grateful Guy wasn't there. She glanced toward her mother, who wore a satisfied smile as though her plans had already come to fruition. But when Françoise spoke to begin the negotiations, Delphine refused to give Michael false hopes and quickly interrupted.

"While I appreciate your interest, my lord, I've chosen to enter a convent," she announced with far more confidence than she felt.

"*Mon Dieu!*" Françoise exclaimed. "Where did you ever get such a bizarre idea?"

"On the island," Delphine responded calmly, although the desperate plan had been inspired that very morning by the sound of distant church bells. "When Michael was ill, I had time to consider my purpose in life and discovered the religious path held great appeal."

Françoise waved her perfumed handkerchief as though she were about to faint, but Michael just laughed. "Which church is it you attend, Delphine? If you mentioned the name, I've forgotten."

"Church?" she repeated numbly. In truth, she had never set foot inside a church. Her mother had insisted that if God had abandoned her father when he was in peril on the sea, then she would abandon God in return. Delphine did not care to relate that excuse to Michael, however.

"I've not actually had the opportunity to attend church," she admitted softly, "but that does not mean that I don't belong in a convent."

Michael left his chair and took a step toward her. "You must at least have some idea whether you wish to become an Anglican or Catholic nun."

Delphine was dressed in pale pink and toyed with the trailing velvet ribbon trim. "Is there a great difference between them?"

Hiding his smile, Michael turned to his solicitor. "What would you say, Mr. Finch?"

"Well, good lord, yes," he responded emphatically. "But there is another matter of perhaps even greater significance. My dear, has it escaped your notice that religious orders are open to virgins rather than young woman with, shall we say, your experience?"

Dismayed by the intimacy of their discussion, the solicitor puffed out his cheeks in a fine imitation of a toad, but Delphine promptly recalled a chance remark by one of their maids. "I believe widows are also welcomed, sir."

Michael nodded thoughtfully. "You plan to present yourself at a convent, be it Anglican or Catholic, as a recent widow?"

Determined to stick to her story, no matter how unlikely it might sound to him, she straightened her shoulders proudly. "Why not?"

"Why not?" he repeated incredulously. "Nuns are noted for their exemplary behavior, Delphine. They're deeply devout, not merely charming liars."

His insult gave her a moment's pause, but she refused to give in. "Isn't forgiveness an integral part of religion?"

"Yes, if you had one," Michael argued. "Well, far be it from me to come between you and your newfound pursuit of religion. Just tell me which convent you wish to enter, and I will take you there now. I'll even pose as your late husband if you so desire, but you mustn't languish here if a spiritual quest is your true calling."

Françoise had grown pale and was so uncharacteristically flustered that she was unable to utter any comment one way or the other. She had offered refreshments when the men had arrived, but now rang for her maid to bring sherry.

Delphine thought it wise to depart before her mother had recovered sufficiently to insist upon a contract with Michael and rose clutching her new cashmere shawl. "Thank you. I'll be happy to go now, if you know where the nearest convent might be located."

"Oh yes, my darling, I certainly do."

It wasn't until Delphine was seated opposite Michael in his carriage that she realized he might be taking her precisely where he wished her to go. He caught her wrist as she reached for the door and made it painfully clear that she had outsmarted only herself.

Chapter 14

Flying, falling up
Delirious angels
Hands brush in passing

Perhaps dreading a scene, Phineas Finch had insisted upon returning to his office on foot, but Michael would have behaved no differently had the attorney remained with them. He softened his hold on Delphine and then released her with a gentle pat.

"You might sustain a serious injury leaping from my carriage, and I can't allow that. Please, just sit back and enjoy the ride. You're lovely in that shade of pink, by the way—but then you're remarkably beautiful in nothing at all."

"You also look splendid today," she remarked absently. Fearing she was merely compounding her mistakes, she focused on the passing scene. They were traveling north through the section of Kingston she knew well, but it was a small comfort.

"Thank you, but nuns mustn't flirt," he scolded with a sly chuckle.

"I've not taken any vows as yet, have I? If you like, I could kneel between your legs and—"

"Delphine!" Michael shook his head. "Even with

219

your hair curled atop your head and wearing an exquisite gown, you merely look like a lady. You'll never behave as one, will you?"

"When it is so easy to reach out and touch you, certainly not. There will be no handsome male distractions in a convent."

"I should hope not. There is an order of Anglican nuns here. I've provided them with several generous donations, and Mother Catherine has been most appreciative. I'll be happy to take you there, but I'll have to instruct the sisters that if you're not on your knees praying, you ought to be scrubbing the cold stone floors to cultivate a true sense of piety."

"Bastard."

"You must learn to control your temper, or you'll surely end up working in the laundry boiling bedclothes in a huge kettle, if they even use linens on their narrow cots."

She shot him a darkly threatening glance. "Have you also made generous donations to the Catholic sisters?"

"No, of course not. But from what I've heard, they're even more strict. If you insist on going to them, I'll be forced to describe you as my mistress. They'll have you scrubbing floors as a penance on their own."

He was seated in a relaxed pose, and Delphine fixed a stare on the inviting bulge between his legs. "I'm surprised you're not already hard. Doesn't threatening me with dire punishments arouse you?"

"Hush, or I will have your face in my lap."

"It would be my pleasure, my lord. You see, you're beginning to swell."

Michael crossed his legs, which only made him more uncomfortable, so he uncrossed them again.

Until that very moment, he had been toying with the idea of leaving her with Mother Catherine for a week or two, but now he was convinced that she would scale the high stone wall and be gone before nightfall. That was his worst fear, that she might simply disappear. He had told his driver he would be returning home, and saw no reason to change their destination.

"I want you to visit my plantation, but you'll not be my prisoner. I'll take you back home in a day or two, or perhaps you'll decide you like it so much there that you'll never wish to leave. Either way, I still have hopes of reaching an agreement on an equitable contract."

Françoise had been equally appalled by Michael's demands, and she had harangued her daughter half the night on the dire need to convince him to see things their way. The ordeal had made Delphine's head ache, and she had slept poorly. Now that entering a convent appeared to be such a poor choice, she needed time to devise another means of escape. To gain at least a few precious days, she approached Michael from a new angle.

"When we have two such different ideas of what my role as your mistress should be, it's imperative that we wait until I'm certain whether or not I've conceived a child."

"Why? I'll provide most generously for you and our children."

Before she could reply, the carriage hit a bump and the back wheels lurched into the air. Delphine nearly slid right off the thickly padded leather seat, but Michael caught her in time to prevent a fall. Flustered, she sat back and braced herself more properly.

"Thank you, my lord. Now where were we? Oh

yes, I'll take the blame for enticing you into disregarding Guy's terms for our week together," she continued, "but my willfulness has changed nothing."

"Delphine," he cajoled.

She raised her hand. "No, listen to me. I know nothing about children, other than having been one. I've never held a baby, or had any desire to become a mother. If I should be carrying your child, then I'll give birth to the babe. I'll place him or her in your care, but I'll not remain with you to provide a half dozen more."

His tone darkened to match his scowl. "And if you're not with child?"

"Then I'll follow my mother's methods to avoid becoming so, which is what I should have done from the beginning to spare us both this terrible uncertainty."

He swore under his breath. "You have no heart at all, do you?"

That he would never understand how much she loved him pained Delphine greatly, but she hid her anguish. She glanced out the window and was surprised to find they had already left Kingston far behind. The narrow road north was bordered here by lush foliage in a thousand shades of green, every leaf shimmering in welcome.

Michael studied her expression, seeking even the smallest hint of regret, but the defiant tilt of her chin was unmistakable, and all too familiar. "Willful is the perfect description for you," he commented dryly.

Delphine had not even begun. She turned back toward him. "How did you choose your wife? Was it for her beauty and charm, or her bloodlines?"

Shocked that she would dare to mention Amelia,

Michael erupted. "You will never speak of my wife ever again. Is that understood?"

Delphine did not even flinch. Instead, she slid from her seat, knelt between his knees, and raked her nails lightly across his crotch. "This is what I understand, my lord, and nothing else."

Michael fought to catch his breath, but she had already unbuttoned his trousers to free a now throbbing erection, and it was all he could do just to breathe as she sucked him deep in her throat. He arched his back and grabbed her hair as she swirled her tongue around the corona and twisted her hands around the shaft.

When she cupped his balls, he exploded in her mouth, and Delphine sucked down each pulsing spurt until he was completely dry. She then eased him back into his trousers and fastened them neatly before returning to her seat.

"That ought to keep you satisfied until tonight," she murmured sweetly. "Then I'll do it again, and as often as you like, but you'll not have me until I'm certain just what my role will be."

Awash in a rapture-drugged haze, all Michael heard was her generous offer of fellatio. It wasn't until later that he realized she expected him to again treat her as a wanton virgin.

When Guy arrived at Françoise's apartment, she wept as she painted the sorry picture of what had transpired earlier that afternoon. "If only you'd been here," she sobbed. "I don't know which of them is more stubborn, but to enter a convent, oh Guy! Can you even imagine Delphine in such a dreary place?"

"I don't imagine it is dreary to the faithful. They must enjoy the serenity and calm."

"That isn't the point!" she scolded. "I wanted a fine man for my daughter, and you assured me that Michael was the perfect choice. They should have come off the island as devoted to each other as we are, but she is still refusing him. What can the little fool want?"

Guy sat down, crossed his legs, and waited for her to end her tearful tirade. "Perhaps all isn't lost. I would go to Michael, but since he has threatened me with grievous bodily harm, I prefer to wait a bit and allow them to work out the matter on their own."

"Coward," Françoise exclaimed, tracing a distracted oval on the pale floral rug. "I've threatened to kill you myself, and you're not afraid of me."

"No, but I probably should be."

"You are incorrigible," she fumed. "What if Michael actually took her to a convent?"

"No, I doubt that. He wants her in his bed too badly. It's his desire for children that surprises me. He should simply marry Delphine, and be done with it."

Françoise collapsed beside him on the settee. "What an extraordinary idea. Would you marry me if your wife died?"

"In an instant, my love, but she's as healthy as a horse and will undoubtedly outlive us all. Why is it the most uninteresting people always have such long lives?"

Françoise leaned back and closed her eyes. "Perhaps it only seems that they do. Michael didn't kill his first wife, did he?"

"Of course not! You know how she died. It was a

shame too, because she was such a pretty little thing, if not very bright."

"What?" Françoise drew herself upright. "They were not a good match then?"

"No one would be a good match for Michael when compared with Delphine, but let's not be morbid. Let's simply have a light supper and enjoy the evening."

Françoise had had such high hopes for Delphine, and now she wasn't even certain where her daughter was. "It is a blessing to have a child," she confided, "But I fear she favors her father and will risk dying for love as an adventure."

Guy seldom thought of that foolhardy Russian count, but then it was always with genuine gratitude that the count had recklessly thrown his life away and left the delightful Françoise all to him.

Delphine was exhausted, and the rocking motion of the carriage soon lulled her to sleep. Her dreams were scattered images of Michael. Although it was already dusk when they rolled to a stop, she awoke far from refreshed.

Before that instant, she had not given any thought to Michael's plantation home. The house was enormous. The first story was built of stone, and the second of native wood. There were spacious verandas and windows fitted with wide louvers to admit the breeze. A profusion of hibiscus and orchids surrounded the house with color.

Michael was smiling, but she could not even pretend not to be impressed. "What a beautiful house."

"Thank you. I'll take you on a tour of the whole plantation tomorrow if you like."

The footman opened the door and Michael exited the carriage first to assist her. He hugged her as he set her on her feet and then stepped back. "I hope you'll feel welcome here," he whispered.

Having kept watch for his master's return, Percy came down the steps to greet them. Michael had alerted him to the possibility he might bring home a guest; but the butler had not expected such a pretty young woman or that she would arrive without a chaperon.

"Welcome home, my lord, my lady."

"Miss Antoine will be visiting with us a few days," Michael informed him. "Did you prepare the dower house as I asked?"

"Yes, my lord, you'll find everything in perfect order, but where is Miss Antoine's luggage?"

Delphine rather enjoyed Michael's perplexed frown. "Oh no, how could we have forgotten my things?" she lamented with hands clasped beneath her chin.

"How indeed," Michael replied. "Please don't fret, we'll find you something to wear."

"I do so hate to impose," she responded, "but we can worry about my clothing later. Is there time to see your stable before dark? I do so want to see your horses."

She was regarding him with an adoring gaze, but Michael did not know whether to be relieved that she was providing such a convincing performance or annoyed by how easily she donned a ladylike pose.

He offered his arm. "If we hurry, we might be able to see my favorites, but we'll have to wait for the morning for riding lessons."

She wrapped her arm around his and fell into step beside him. "If suitable clothing can be found, I shall look forward to it. May I borrow one of your night-shirts to sleep in?"

"Alas, I don't wear them," he replied. He waited until they were on the path to the stables to confide more. "I believe you have Percy completely fooled. It should be no challenge at all to convince the rest of my staff that you're a lady."

"I've never thought of myself as otherwise," she countered. "I've no wish to embarrass you, today or ever. Now, I've never seen horses mate. Could you arrange such an exhibition?"

He glanced over his shoulder to make certain no one was close enough to overhear, but even then took the precaution of lowering his voice. "It's not deemed proper for a lady to be present, but do you recall the day on the beach when I had you on your hands and knees and came on your back?"

What she recalled was how her hair had formed a damp curtain and how lonely she felt. "How could I possibly forget?"

"Good, then simply imagine the stallion covering the mare, but he shoves his cock up into her rather than slide along her rump."

"Yes, I can visualize that easily enough, but still—"

"Delphine," he scolded softly. "There are grooms who work in the stable, and I'd rather you didn't shock them with questions about breeding."

"As you wish, my lord." She patted his arm and made a valiant attempt to look as though she were a brainless twit as they neared the stables. "Of course, if a man doesn't bring his mistress home, he needn't worry that she'll embarrass him in front of his servants with inappropriate questions."

"I shall strive to remember that. Now here's my

champion in the paddock. He's called Indigo for the bluish cast to his coat."

Standing in the shadows, the stallion appeared thoroughly black to Delphine, but she supposed the horse might actually have a bluish tint in bright sunlight. "He is a beauty. Is he fast?"

"Like the wind."

Indigo recognized Michael, tossed his mane, and came toward them. "He expects a treat, and I've none for him today."

Not unlike his owner, the stallion had a powerful, frightening strength, and Delphine hung back. "My mother has a book containing the most fascinating etchings of a woman and a stallion. Is it really possible to—"

Michael took her arm to guide her away from the paddock and back toward the house. "A clever artist might draw any number of scandalous poses, but that does not mean that they are actually possible. Nor will I even attempt to coax Indigo into indulging your fantasies."

"Oh, it's not my fantasy, my lord. I would prefer your cock to a stallion's any day, or night. But I can't help but be curious."

"And I can't help but wonder if there is anything to be left to your imagination."

"Well, of course, there are a great many things I've not actually observed."

"That is more than enough for the time being, Delphine. Now I'm afraid it's too late to show you the Dower house. You'll have to stay in the main house tonight."

Delphine gazed up at him through her lashes. "You

must have a candlestick you can spare. That's all I'll need to find my way."

"I can provide you with dozens, but it's such a pretty house, I wanted you to be able to appreciate it in the daylight."

"It's not that dark yet. Come and show me now. Is it far?"

"No, it's just through the garden, but—"

Delphine took his hand to tug him along. "Oh, Michael, I'm not someone you must impress. I already believe in you. Let's just see what we can see."

He drew her to an abrupt halt. "What did you say?"

She was surprised by the question. "I said I believed in you. Look how well we did on the island with little more than our wits a few fishing poles."

He brought her hand to his lips. "Thank you for that vote of confidence, but I wish I knew who you really were. One minute you're peeling away my clothes or saying the most shocking things. Then, as you did just now, you can affect such a beguiling innocence."

"Is that too great a contradiction?" Softened by the twilight, his earnest expression was so dear, she was tempted to fall to her knees and swear she was neither as wicked nor as beguiling a creature as he supposed. Such an ill-advised confession would only serve to confuse him all the more, so she reached up to kiss him.

He responded warmly, and distracted as she had hoped, he took her hand and led her through the garden. "I believe this was actually a well-tended English garden at one time, with expertly trimmed hedges, but I prefer the Jamaican flowers and have let it go wild."

Delphine had expected him to confine her to a single room, but here they were, traipsing through a veritable jungle, and the only place she had ever felt as free was on the island. She had not expected to like anything about his home except him, and it was bewildering to be enjoying herself so greatly.

"The dower house is a miniature of my residence, but with less than half the rooms. I believe my grandmother lived here a few years, but my mother never did."

Delphine yanked her skirts away from a trailing rose bush. "What was she like?"

"Like you," Michael responded without thinking, but it shocked him to realize how true that was. "She wasn't a blonde, but she was very bright, and if she wasn't in my father's arms, she was pursuing some argument with him that might last over the course of a week. It was all good-natured fun, never angry or violent."

Delphine ducked with him to pass beneath an arch supporting a tangle of orchids. "How lucky you were to have such charming parents."

"Lucky? I suppose. That's the dower house just ahead. It looks as though Percy lit candles so you'd feel welcome."

Delphine and her mother shared a large apartment, but she had not expected the dower house to be more than twice that size. The walls of the parlor were a pale peach that while inviting in the late afternoon, would surely be lovely at dawn. The furniture was covered in silk and damask, and all of it delicate as though a man might never cross the threshold.

She had refused to live there, and quite adamantly too, but she had not expected anything as inviting as this. The rooms were spacious, the ceilings high, and while she could not stay, she could not view it as a prison.

"What is the custom, that an earl's widow would move in here, and the new earl and his countess would take up residence in the main house?"

"Yes, it is unfortunate that most women bury their husbands, and heirs being as contentious as they sometimes are, a recent widow needs the assurance of a comfortable home."

"Yes, I imagine she would." Delphine leaned down to inhale the fragrance of a bouquet of yellow roses placed near the door, and Michael slid his arms around her waist and leaned down to nibble her ear.

"Come, let's go back to my house and make our preparations for dinner there."

It had been a long trip, and she was anxious to freshen up, but having no change of clothing worried her. "Are there any of your grandmother's clothes here?"

"No, I'm afraid not. From what my mother said, she was barely five feet tall, so even if there were, they wouldn't fit you. I'm sorry not to have given more thought to making you comfortable here."

"If you were really concerned about my comfort, you would not insist that I be here," Delphine offered smoothly. "But we can discuss that again after we dine."

Michael snuffed the candles, then placed his arm around her waist as he escorted her home along the stone path. They parted as they reached the front door.

"I didn't think to hire a lady's maid either," he confessed. "But I'll have the housekeeper select one of the chambermaids to assist you."

He showed her to his mother's room before going

down the hall to enter his own rather than using the connecting door. Before Delphine could even sit down, a maid arrived. She was a tall, dark-eyed girl, in a prim black uniform with a sparkling white apron and cap.

"My name's Lucy, Miss Antoine, and I'll fetch whatever you need." She bobbed in an awkward curtsy, and then looked around the beautifully appointed room. "Hasn't nobody slept here in years, miss, but you'll find the feather bed right comfortable."

"I'm sure I will, but didn't Michael's—Lord Clairbourne's wife use this room?"

"Oh no, miss. She never left England. They were wed in Devon, and she died there. Broke the master's heart. Now will you be wanting a bath?"

"Yes, that would be wonderful."

While she waited for Lucy to return with the tub and hot water, she wandered the lovely room filled with beautifully carved rosewood furniture and an abundance of feminine touches. She sampled the perfume in small crystal bottles on the vanity and was delighted to find a comb and brush as well. Delphine laughed when she looked in the mirror and saw a twig from the garden caught in a curl.

When Michael loved Jamaica so, she didn't understand why he had not brought his wife home, but she knew better than to ask Lucy more questions that might swiftly reach his ears. He had forbidden her to even mention his wife, so that avenue was closed as well.

He had not offered any of his mother's clothing, but the wardrobe was bare, and no lingerie or any other belongings filled the drawers. The room had obviously been cleaned and prepared for the countess who had never arrived, and it saddened her to think of it remaining empty.

Michael rapped on the door while she was still styling her hair, and she opened it only a crack. "Really, my lord, it wouldn't be at all proper for me to invite you in."

Because she had no elegant gowns he had bathed, shaved, and donned a fresh shirt but worn the same coat, waistcoat and trousers he had worn earlier. "Nor did I expect it, but I feared you might be sitting here waiting for an escort to dinner."

"Give me a moment, please."

Michael nodded, but he paced up and down the long hallway as he waited. She did not keep him waiting long, but once they were seated at the long, beautifully appointed table, all he could think of was how she had teased him about making love during a dinner party. They began with a delicious clear soup, but with those erotic images in his mind, it was all he could do to sip it without drooling.

He shifted positions so often, Delphine at first wondered what was the matter, but then with sudden insight, she knew. "If we wait until your servants have all gone to bed," she suggested in a tantalizing whisper, "we might make much better use of this fine table."

"We could, but you've insisted that I show more restraint than I actually possess."

She was seated on his right, and reached out to catch his hand. "Perhaps it is enough that you'll think of it."

Two footmen came forward to remove their bowls, and Michael remained quiet until they had been served the fish course. Compared to those they had roasted on the island, it was too bland to bother eating, and he lay his fork across his plate.

"I want you to make a list of everything you need. Don't omit even the smallest item. We'll buy them all when we return to Kingston, and then you'll have all you require here."

"All I require is the freedom to leave, my lord. That should save you a good deal of money."

"Money does not concern me." He watched her take a small bite of fish, and just watching her slip the fork between her lips made him ache with desire. "Is it so awful being here with me?"

She blotted her mouth on the monogrammed napkin and sat back. It was impossible to ignore the pain in his voice, and she could barely disguise her own. "Not at all, but this is your family's home, and I don't belong here."

"I believe that you do."

The footmen again cleared their plates and then reappeared with rare cuts of roast beef surrounded by carrots and potatoes.

The meat was well-seasoned and tender, but Delphine took only a few bites. "You must have close friends other than Guy here."

"Yes, there are many men who prefer the climate and less stilted ways of Jamaica to London, and not all leave their families behind as Guy does."

"I'm glad to learn you have friends here, but please consider for a moment how few would accept your invitations once they learn your mistress would serve as your hostess. Nor would they continue to include you in their parties knowing that I would accompany you. Don't claim it wouldn't matter, because it would."

Having lost his appetite, Michael sat back, then waved off the footman who assumed he had finished. Delphine had spoken very softly, so he doubted the footmen had overheard, but he cared not at all what his servants thought.

"One of the things I love best about Jamaica," he assured her, "is that I'm not expected to participate in a tiresome round of entertainments. If I receive no invitations, I'll be relieved, not insulted."

"And just where do you expect to find a husband for the daughter I might give you, or a wife for a son? Would you send them off to America rather than take them to London for the season, where they'd receive no invitations at all?"

"Must we consider something that may or may not happen nearly twenty years hence?"

"Yes, because children are far too important to bring into the world without any hope of a secure and happy future. My mother raised me to be a demimonde, but I doubt you would wish your daughter, Lady, whatever you might name her, to be similarly educated."

Michael did signal the footmen then, who removed their plates and returned with game hens roasted to succulent perfection. An inviting assortment of side dishes now littered the table unnoticed, but he cut a slice of the flavorful fowl and chewed slowly while he tried to find answers for the excellent questions Delphine had posed.

At length he was forced to accept her view: he had simply not considered anything more than his own pleasure. Insulted by his own oversight, he took a sip of wine and noticed she had not tasted a drop of her own.

"Let's enjoy this marvelous food and discuss more important topics later. I am truly sorry that I allowed you to leave home without so much as a small bag of lingerie."

Delphine would have preferred to have pursued the problem of how he intended to present his bastards to the world, but clearly she had made him consider the question, and that would have to do for the time being. She smiled sweetly and leaned close.

"Please don't worry over my comfort. Lucy found a new toothbrush, and I laundered my lingerie when I bathed, so it will be fresh on the morrow. As for tonight, I doubt that anyone will notice I'm not wearing any."

Michael gasped and nearly choked on his last swallow of wine. That he might slide his hand up her calf and not find silk stockings and lace-trimmed pantalettes but instead smooth, warm flesh was enough to inspire him to carry her upstairs to his room without bothering with the rest of their meal.

He had to force himself to sit back and wipe his mouth on his napkin. "I don't know whether to compliment Françoise or you for your remarkable candor, but I do wish you had waited until later to confide such an intriguing detail."

Delphine licked her lips. "It is a lovely night. Perhaps we could spend a while in the garden before I retire to the dower house."

Michael nodded, but he feared the night would not be nearly dark enough to prevent every servant in the house from peering from the windows in hopes of seeing a good deal more than a couple strolling the overgrown paths in the moonlight.

He ran his finger around his collar and wished for the freedom to go without clothing they had enjoyed on the island. "My chef makes the most delicious desserts with fresh fruit and cream, but I don't believe he ever uses mangoes."

Delphine finally took a sip of wine and let it trickle down her throat. "A terrible oversight, my lord, I hope you'll plant some here."

"Oh yes, you may be assured that I will." But that night, he was intent upon planting something far more intimate within her.

Chapter 15

*Spiraling desire
Smooth, soundless harmony
Pale orchids thrive*

When dessert was served, Michael stared as Delphine licked a dollop of cream from her spoon and nearly flung her down on the table right there. He had never met a woman who teased with such provocative gestures, but then, as she had once sworn, she did not merely tantalize. She delighted in satisfying him, as well.

Though he longed to lick sweet cream from her nipples, his berry tart remained uneaten. He was closer to shocking his servants with a scandalous display of raw emotion than he cared to admit, and he reached for the bowl of whipped cream his chef had thoughtfully included should they care for more.

"Let's take this with us," he urged as he left his seat.

Delphine appeared startled, but she set her spoon gently upon the gilt-edged dessert plate and allowed him to assist her from her chair.

"Cream in the moonlight," she cooed sweetly. "I can hardly wait."

As they walked the length of the dining table, he leaned in to whisper, "I plan to nibble on you."

She answered in a voice meant to carry. "Night blooming flowers? How charming."

He led the way to the front door, then handed her the cream-filled silver bowl and grabbed a candelabra to light their way. "There's a small garden beside the dower house that I neglected to show you earlier. No one will see us there."

His servants were probably laughing at their unseemly haste, but he did not care in the least. Holding the candles out to illuminate the path, he sped along the carefully set stones then had to wait for Delphine to catch up. "I don't mean to rush you, but . . ."

"I'm flattered," she replied. "How pretty the stars are tonight. Could we stop a moment to appreciate them?"

Certain she meant only to torture him, he took her elbow. "There will be other nights just as clear. We'll name each constellation then, if you so desire."

She responded with a sultry laugh. "You're all I desire, my lord, now or any other night. Of course, I did wish to discuss how you planned to raise our child, should we have one."

"Tomorrow," he swore and hurried her along.

He took her through the dower house, left the candelabra on a table near the side window, and swept her out the door opening onto the garden. He then took the bowl of cream from her hands, set it on the wooden bench and pulled her into his arms for a hungry kiss that tasted of wild raspberries and a still wilder surrender.

She had asked troubling questions for which he had no clever answers, but they could be found later, when his mind was clear. For now, all he needed was the lovely young woman in his arms, and she clung to him as though nothing would please her more. Michael was breathless when at last he drew away.

"How could you have even considered entering a convent?"

How indeed? she mused silently, but she saw love as a painful trap as well as a priceless treasure. She traced his lips with her fingertip rather than explain.

"I didn't think you brought me here to talk, but you mustn't rumple my dress when it's all I have to wear." She pressed her hands lightly against his chest. "Give me a moment to discard it."

Ready to strip her bare himself, he stood back, but when she drew the ribbons through her fingers with a insouciant grace, he nearly growled a warning, "That gown can be replaced."

"No, it's one of my favorites." She unfastened the ties beneath her bosom, then took hold of his arm to step out of the pretty pink garment. "I won't be a moment," she promised.

He clenched his fists as she carried the dress into the dower house. He turned away to gather his wits, but when she called his name, he glanced over his shoulder and found she had the bowl of cream in her hand. Certain she had his full attention, she splashed a spoonful on her right breast.

"Is this what you wanted?" she asked.

"Oh, yes." He coaxed her down on the bench, knelt between her legs to fan the cream over her breast, then licked it off. The night was as warm as her skin, and the cool cream glowed in the moonlight.

Delphine slid her hands through his hair, and as he smeared cream over her ringed nipple, she arched into his caress. His mouth was warm, and he seemed content to suck at her breasts while she grew wet with longing for more. She angled her hips toward him, and he responded by pressing the heel of his hand against her mound.

He teased her nipples with playful bites, pulled them through his teeth, then sucked tenderly. He increased the pressure of his hand in a slow oval against her triangle of pale curls until, trembling with the first sweet tingles of release, she clamped her hands around his wrist to hold him still. He rolled her nipples between his lips, drawing out the hardened buds, and she ground her hips against his hand as she came.

Michael felt the thrill shoot through her, then broke away to stand and loosen his trousers. He grasped his cock, and slid his hand along the shaft in an all too familiar rhythm, but she hooked an arm around his thigh and leaned back to guide him between her breasts. The bench was at the appropriate height for such a seductive alignment. He fought to make his strokes long and yet not forceful enough to bruise her.

She teased his balls, then slid her fingers behind their furry sack to hold back the inevitable rush. When he could no longer bear it, she released him, and he gushed his own masculine cream over her breasts then grabbed for the back of the bench to remain standing.

Delphine caressed his bare hip and spread kisses along the crease between his thigh and torso. She reeked of sex, and yet she could still smell his sandalwood soap and the sweet scent of jasmine in the air. When he took a step backward to adjust his clothing, she rubbed his semen into her skin in a lazy figure eight motion.

"My mother swears a man's essence keeps the breasts full and firm."

Barely able to stand, Michael sank down beside her on the bench. "You're mother is a veritable font of exotic advice."

"Yes, and all of it valuable. Now, despite this thrilling distraction, we should compare our thoughts on raising a daughter."

He caught her wrist for the second time that day. "Later. Now I want to lick up the cream you've made for me."

He eased her down on the bench and angled her right leg over the back to open her wide. He leaned over to frame her navel with soft kisses and then slid his fingers into her. He stirred the slippery wetness, then sat up and licked off his fingers one at a time.

"Whenever I'm served berries and cream, I'll taste you." He dipped his head again and traced gentle swirling patterns up her cleft and around her clitoris.

The heated rush made her legs ache clear to her toes. She caught a handful of his silky hair, and again poised on the brink of ecstasy, she inhaled deeply. Sweet desserts might bring her to mind, but for the rest of her life, every sight, scent, taste or touch would remind her of him.

When Delphine awoke, sunlight streamed across her bed and lit the bedroom's pale pink walls with a silvery glow. She yawned, and caught in the sheets, rolled over to twist free. Last night, Michael had turned her very bones to liquid fire.

After carrying her into the dower house and tucking her in bed, he had returned to his own home. It had been ridiculous for them to sleep alone after their abandoned idyll in the garden. Perhaps it had been her reputation he had intended to safeguard, but she had no fine family to disgrace, so discretion for her sake had little merit.

Had he merely wished to protect his own good name? She had enjoyed being with him on the island, and did not appreciate being treated as a shameful secret here.

With whom would his servants gossip other than each other? she mused. A servant who delighted in reporting his master's peccadilloes in the marketplace was always promptly fired, as well he should be. So Michael's retreat, even when she was too limp from his lavish attentions to offer more than a soft moan in protest, had been totally unnecessary.

She had her mother's pride, and her mother's appreciation for a comfortable life that she lived on her own terms. Guy's frequent visits were always welcomed, and he frequently arrived with small gifts or treats. The three of them often played cards, favorites like Sensation or faro. Rather than money, they played only for points in an endless tournament in which Françoise insisted she would eventually triumph.

Now Delphine felt as though she had been hidden away rather than sought out, and she was hurt. It was not the way Guy treated her mother. Yet her mother never complained when he returned to England each year. Instead, she used the time to order new gowns, to redecorate her apartment, and re-read her favorite French authors.

Then when Guy returned to Jamaica, always bearing expensive presents, Françoise greeted him warmly, and they continued their romantic liaison as though he had never been away. Delphine had expected her life to have a similar rhythm, but clearly Michael held very different views.

She had longed for the time to think, but he overwhelmed her senses so easily that serious contemplation on any subject was impossible here. Giving up the effort, she yawned sleepily, and settled down into her pillow. Ignoring the ache in her nipples, as well as her heart, she was willing to follow Michael's example and put off the argument that would surely be their last.

Michael had risen early, and ravenously hungry, he had eaten an ample breakfast of fresh baked bread with honey, sausage and eggs. He had visited the stables in an effort to maintain his usual routine, but he could not forget for an instant that Delphine was nearby. Memories of her eager mouth and skilled hands invaded his thoughts and filled him with a taunting desire.

He managed to handle the necessary correspondence, and review his accounts, but by one o'clock, he was so anxious to see Delphine that he called for Lucy to wake her.

"Please give Miss Antoine these clothes. She will surely object to dressing like a groom, but assure her that these things have never been worn."

"She's to wear men's clothing, my lord?"

"How did I confuse you, Lucy? I want to take her riding, and the gown she arrived in simply isn't suitable."

He was regarding her with an indulgent smile, but she was horrified to have misunderstood him. Not wanting to ever disappoint him, she swallowed hard. "Shouldn't I take her a bite to eat? She might not be able to sit a horse if she's faint from hunger."

"Thank you, that's an excellent idea. Take her some pastries and fruit, but be quick about it."

Lucy dashed through the kitchen for a tray, and then rushed on to the dower house. She struggled to catch her breath and knocked lightly at the door. When there was no response, she eased the door open, peered inside, and called softly. When there was still no answer, she entered and rapped lightly on the bedroom door.

"Miss Antoine? Lord Clairbourne has sent clothing for you. He's waiting to go riding."

"Where?"

"I don't know where, miss, but he seems most anxious to be on the way. He loves his horses, he does."

Delphine smiled as she rose, for she had wondered where he might be waiting, not where they were bound. On the foot of the bed there was a maroon silk dressing gown that he must have delivered during the night. The sleeves hung down over her hands and the hem trailed along the floor, but she tied the belt firmly at her waist, and went to the door.

Lucy set the silver tray on the table beside the settee before shaking out the bundle of clothing. She repeated Michael's message, handed Delphine the clothes, and began to back away.

"Will you be wanting some hot water, miss?"

"Yes, thank you, but just a moment." She held up the white shirt, which was crisp and clean as promised. The cream-colored pants were knee length, and there were even some cotton drawers, stockings and new leather boots.

"I didn't expect Michael to produce a riding habit on such short notice, but I want you to thank him for what he has sent me. Tell him I'm looking forward to our ride and will join him shortly."

"Yes, miss, I'll do that."

"One other thing, Lucy, when you bring the hot water, will you please stop by the room I used yesterday and fetch the lingerie I laundered? I'll surely need it later."

"Yes, miss," Lucy assured her, and she departed with a quick step.

Delphine took a bite from one of the plum buns and stepped out onto the garden's mossy ground. She found the jasmine and broke off a sprig to wear in her hair. The wooden bench simply provided seating now, and she picked up the silver bowl that had fallen beneath it and carried it back inside.

She opened the small desk to search for pen and ink. That found, she opened the drawers for paper, but all they contained bore the Clairbourne crest. It was too expensive to use merely to make a list, and she was disappointed not to have brought along her diary.

Not that she would have confided last night's more entertaining details, but she was accustomed to being able to jot down her thoughts whenever the whim struck. Frustrated, she closed the desk and left her musings unwritten.

Michael was pacing up and down the path linking the dower and main houses when Delphine appeared. He had found clothes that would fit a slender young man and had thought they would be suitable, but as she shuffled toward him in boots that were clearly several sizes too large, he realized his mistake.

She had rolled up the shirt sleeves, and belted the pants to secure them at her waist. Rather than fasten at the knee, the pant legs brushed her ankles. Except for the fair hair she had caught at her nape, she resembled some pitiful orphan in borrowed clothes. But when she smiled at him, none of it mattered.

"I am so sorry," he greeted her apologetically. "I really thought the clothes would be a better fit."

She slid her hands into her pants' pockets and shrugged. "While I sincerely doubt that I'll be complimented on my fashions today, I'm very comfortable. Or did I misunderstand? Are you now too embarrassed by my appearance to take me riding?"

He slid his arm around her shoulders to guide her along the path, but slowed his pace to her short shuffle. "No, I still want to go. I feared you might sleep the day away."

"My mother and I seldom rise before noon. It was only on the island that I awoke early. Perhaps you did not realize that a man usually visits his mistress in the afternoon."

He bent down to kiss her cheek. "I am most definitely not most men, Delphine."

"I didn't mean that you were. I merely remarked upon their habits."

"Well, if it's other men you wish to discuss, I'm afraid a high percentage can't afford a beautiful French mistress."

They were passing through the main garden on their way to the stables, and Delphine was forced to travel so slowly she was sorely tempted to remove the borrowed boots and walk barefoot. "Is it also your belief that most men would dearly love to have one?"

"Yes, of course," he responded with an amused chuckle. "What man wouldn't want a lovely woman who devoted herself solely to his pleasure?"

"Perhaps one who loved his wife," she murmured almost to herself.

"Yes, there are a few such fortunate couples, but the larger a man's fortune, the less likely he is to wed for love."

"I would swear the last time I mentioned bloodlines, you became furiously angry with me."

He came to an abrupt halt, but glanced away rather than fix her with a piercing stare. "Nothing that happened before I awoke on the island matters to me now."

"Of course it matters, or you'd not have become so provoked with me."

Rather than argue the point, he scooped her up into his arms and continued on the way to the stables. "Well, I'm far from provoked now." He gave her a quick kiss and promptly changed the subject.

"We grow sugar cane and produce molasses and rum. We also ship a great deal of allspice from our own docks on the river, but rather than tour the plantation, let's ride through the forest to find a secluded spot for a picnic.

"I know how much you enjoy just observing things, and I should have stopped to study the stars last night as you asked. I mean to make more time for whatever it is you'd care to do. Just mention it, and I'll agree."

Another apology. He had offered several in the course of their acquaintance, and she had been amazed and gratified by each and every one. "Thank you, but last night I understood your haste, and there will be other nights better suited to stargazing."

She had also tried to force him to accept how impossible it would be to raise her children as his heirs, but he seemed to have conveniently forgotten her frequent mention of that issue. He was incredibly appealing and couched his demands in thoughtful terms, but his insistence that she become a surrogate wife was far too objectionable a demand.

"Delphine? It isn't like you to be so quiet." He put her down beside the paddock where Indigo and a handsome dapple-grey gelding had been saddled for their ride.

"I'm afraid my thoughts had strayed to last night," she offered in a coquettish whisper. When she detected a blush beneath his deep tan, she was relieved to have distracted him so easily. She meant to discuss the issue of children with him, but not while standing in the open where all his servants and plantation workers would come running to overhear.

"Now I'm afraid I might disappoint you today," she continued. "Doesn't it take more than a single outing to learn how to ride?"

"Yes, but you'll not be expected to compete in a steeplechase on the way home."

"I should hope not!" she laughed, but both horses looked enormous to her. "Don't you have a pony I might ride?"

"Ponies are for children, Delphine, and we have none here, as yet. Come on, the gray is named Phantom for his color, and he's as gentle as a lamb."

Before Delphine could offer a protest, Michael took her hand, entered the paddock, and swung her up into Phantom's saddle. She had meant to make a sincere effort at learning to ride, but that had been before she had seen what a long way down it was to the ground. She quickly gripped the reins, laced her hands in Phantom's silvery mane and slipped her feet into the stirrups, but in oversized boots, she still didn't feel secure.

"You just promised to grant my requests," she reminded him shakily.

She had grown pale and Michael was more surprised than disappointed. "You'll swim in the Caribbean as though it were no more than a large tub, but riding a horse frightens you?"

Phantom took a step backward, and she barely managed to swallow a scream. "I've never worried about falling and breaking my neck in the sea."

"Nor should you. Here, I'll lead him around the paddock a few times. That ought to give you more confidence."

Delphine fought to focus on her lover's handsome smile rather than the vast distance between herself and the ground, but she could not recall ever enjoying anything less. When Michael brought Phantom to a halt, she hastened to apologize.

"I'm so sorry," she stressed. "Phantom may very well be as gentle as you claim, but I fear I'm just not a horsewoman. Perhaps riding is a skill better mastered as a child."

Her pinched frown was enough to convince him she would not enjoy a leisurely ride on her own. He reached up to pluck her from the saddle and set her down, but he kept his hands gently wrapped around her waist.

"Please don't give up so quickly. I think you did rather well for your first lesson. You can ride in front of me on Indigo. That way you'll feel safe, and we can still go wherever we please."

Indigo shook his head as though he were even less

thrilled about the prospect of carrying them both than Delphine. "He's a very big horse," she observed.

"He's eighteen hands and a fine stallion with a valiant heart. Does my height intimidate you?"

"Only when you're angry and yell at me," she confessed truthfully.

"Then I shall have to find a chair and sit down the next time I'm tempted to raise my voice." He doubted the spirited young woman was ever daunted by his size or tone, but he gave her a quick hug and called a groom to unsaddle Phantom.

Michael mounted Indigo with an agile leap and extended his hand. "Come on, I promise you'll enjoy the afternoon."

Delphine wiped her now sweating palms on her pants before taking his hand, albeit reluctantly, and he pulled her up in front of him. He wrapped his right arm around her waist to hold her firmly lodged between his thighs, but she still grabbed hold of Indigo's long flowing mane.

"I promise you'll not fall, Delphine, and even if you do, you'll land on me."

"Is that supposed to be a comforting thought?"

"Yes, that's how it was intended. Now let's just enjoy what's left of the afternoon." He swung by the kitchen to fetch a picnic basket that he plunked in front of her. "Hang on to this please, and I'll hang onto you."

Delphine trusted him enough to lean back against the hard-muscled wall of his chest, but she gazed up at the sky rather than look down. Indigo had a smooth gait that created a gentle rocking motion, but she still hung onto his mane as tightly as the wicker basket.

When they left the plantation paths to enter the forest, Michael leaned down to nibble her ear. "The answer is yes."

"That's wonderful I'm sure, but I fear I've forgotten the question."

"I thought you'd be wondering if it were possible to make love on horseback, which is possible, but obviously involves a greater element of risk than I'd care to take with you."

"I appreciate your concern, but I'd not even imagined it. The book my mother owns involves only the one woman and a stallion, but there must be others which illustrate how it can be done. Would I have to face you?"

"It would work best that way, but we're not even going to attempt it."

Relaxing slightly, she released her frantic grip on Indigo's mane and slid her hand along his thigh. She felt his muscles contract beneath her fingertips, and he swore softly against her hair.

"I'd hoped to behave in a more gentlemanly fashion this afternoon than I did last night. You mustn't tempt me to do otherwise."

She gave his thigh a playful slap. "Surely a gentleman would not have mentioned making love on horseback in the first place, my lord."

"True, but you make it very difficult for me to remember my manners."

He was wrapped around her so closely, the chance of a nasty fall appeared remote. Emboldened by that thought, she gripped Indigo with her knees to scoot her bottom back against his crotch. Then she twisted from side to side.

"You mean *hard* to remember, don't you?"

"Indeed," he uttered through clenched teeth. He

was glad that she had finally relaxed to the point she was able to tease him, but he had been sincere in his resolve. Still fully aroused, he could not resist the temptation to loosen her belt and slide his hand down through her soft nest of curls.

"This maneuver," he promised against her ear, "is an easy one in our current pose, and Indigo's rolling gait will make it even more enjoyable than you expect."

She tensed briefly, but his circling motion was whisper light and with no way to escape his touch, nor any wish to, she leaned into his caress. She left her hand on his thigh to maintain her balance, but now she was almost floating.

"You have very handsome legs," she murmured breathlessly. "Many men are all chest and arms and have such spindly thighs and calves, but you're beautifully proportioned."

He rubbed his cheek against hers. "Thank you, but I thought you preferred my hands."

His fingers were gliding on her own wetness now, tracing an arabesque over the tender folds. "Or my tongue," he posed.

"Yes, you do deserve compliments on both, but you also have magnificent eyes. They're a glimpse of the bluest heavens."

Flattered by her poetic compliment, he nuzzled her ear and continued caressing her toward bliss. As he increased the rhythm of his strokes, he felt the oddest sensation, as though he were pleasuring himself. His cock was pressed so firmly against her bottom that he had only to rock slightly to coax forth his own release. When at last she came in a heated rush that poured over his fingers, he barely had time to yank his handkerchief from his pocket to catch his own ejaculate.

Stunned by the power of her affect on him, he thought himself a greater fool than Guy had ever been over Françoise. When at last he could breathe deeply, he felt torn between the man he had become with her, and the one he had thought himself to be. She was a young woman of extraordinary strength, and convinced that she would never accept anything less from him, he hid his torment.

Dazed and confused, Michael used his knees to urge Indigo into a brisker pace. He held Delphine pressed against his chest and fought to ignore the inviting swell of her breasts, but his whole body itched with longing. When he spoke, his voice was hoarse with desire.

"We're almost there."

Completely spent, Delphine was grateful for the security of his embrace. She also wished she weren't wearing britches so that she could turn toward him now and roll his cock into her cleft. For the moment, what they had done, and she had felt him do to himself, was enough; but she still longed for the freedom of the island where they could have lain in the wet sand for the remainder of the afternoon.

When they reached the clearing Michael had intended as their destination, he dismounted, took the basket from Delphine, set it aside, and then swung her down from Indigo's back in a gentle arc.

"I had such honorable intentions," he teased with an engaging grin, "but you are such a joy to touch that—"

Delphine silenced him with a kiss. "Which is as it should be, and while you did refuse to make love on horseback, I believe we accomplished it nonetheless."

"Which was my whole point," he replied. "I wish . . ."

"What can you possibly have left to wish for, my lord?" She turned away from him to buckle her belt, then walked to the thick grass at the edge of the small clearing to sit down and peruse the contents of the picnic basket.

"Oh, this looks delicious—bread, cheese, fruit and wine. I find it difficult to believe that your intentions were purely honorable when you included wine."

"I've not had a pure intention since we met," he replied with forced humor. Michael finally understood why Delphine had wished to remain alone on the island to think. He needed to sort out his own thoughts and come to terms with the frightening strength of his passion for her.

He sat down across from her and ripped off a hunk of bread. "There's something deeply satisfying about bread and cheese."

"I agree," she responded. "There's something elemental, like the way a man and a woman fit together."

He agreed completely, but when her mind continually ran in one direction, he could not help but wonder if there was anything that would not remind her of a matched pair. He pulled the cork from the wine, filled one of the pewter cups, and handed it to her.

"Let's drink to that perfect fit."

She nodded and took a sip. "Oh look, there's a flock of parakeets. They're a rainbow in flight!"

He turned to follow her gaze and thought her description apt. "Yes, they are. Would you like one for a pet?"

"No, I've seen them for sale in pretty cages in Kingston, but they ought to be here, flying free."

"You value your own freedom just as highly, don't you?" he asked.

She twisted a crust to break off a bite. "You'd not ask me that if I were a man."

"We'd not be here if you were a man." He chuckled in spite of himself. "I'm sorry, but in every possible way, you're a remarkable woman."

He rushed on before he forgot everything but his appalling weakness for her. "I wanted you to see the plantation, but you were right in asking me to wait a few days to make plans so that we'll be certain what our immediate future holds. Let's postpone serious discussion on any topic until next week.

"Tonight, we'll dine together, and then I'll send you to bed alone. We'll return to Kingston in the morning, and on the journey, I'm going to insist that we both behave in a circumspect manner. I fear we ignite each other's passions too easily, and then neither of us thinks as clearly as we must."

Delphine could still feel the heat of his hands on her. When had he ever preferred reserve to passion? Something was dreadfully wrong, and he was pulling away. After all, he had blamed her for their amorous adventure on the trail. Apparently, he hadn't wanted it. Perhaps that's why he had brought her to such a remote location, so that if she behaved badly, there would be no one to see.

She could pretend a disinterest she did not feel if that's what he wanted. She would take a few bites of fruit and cheese and pretend nothing was wrong, but she doubted that she could make it all the way home before a flood of tears revealed her true feelings.

Chapter 16

Tearful illusions
Fleeting pleasures, sacred dreams
A hushed forgiveness

Michael took great pains to dress properly that evening. His coat was midnight blue, his waistcoat, shirt, and cravat snowy white. His buff-colored doeskin trousers were new, and his boots were polished to a near blinding luster. His clothing was supplied by London's finest tailors but worn with a casual disregard for the expensive fabrics and superb fit.

Satisfied he looked his best, although his garments were still somewhat loose, he went to the dower house to escort Delphine to dinner. If she was tired of wearing the same pink gown, becoming though it was, she made no mention of it. A white orchid had replaced the jasmine that had been in her hair that morning, and she looked not merely lovely, but as innocent as the flower.

He bowed and kissed her hand. "Every time I see you, you're even more beautiful."

She adjusted the new cashmere shawl on her shoulders and took his arm. "I was wearing borrowed clothing this afternoon, so such an improvement isn't difficult, but you needn't flirt with me, my lord. I'm already convinced of your charm."

"And of your own beauty?"

"True beauty involves intelligence and a lively spirit, or it would be as uninvolving as a decorative painting and soon tedious to contemplate."

When he gave no witty response, she feared she had misjudged his mood, and a quick glimpse of his downcast expression convinced her of it. "Have I offended you somehow?"

"With the truth? Never. Now I hope you'll find tonight's meal as delicious as your first here."

A footman was waiting to open the front door, and Delphine stepped through it convinced this would be the last time she would be entertained there. Michael was making a polite effort to be good company, and she intended to follow his example, but it was still a strain to play the part of a fine lady when she preferred the more familiar role of vixen.

Last night their mood had been one of sizzling anticipation. Tonight, a touching awkwardness separated them. As she was seated, she glanced down the long table and tried to imagine it crowded with guests about whom she would care absolutely nothing.

They began with a cream soup flavored with curry and topped with shaved coconut. She swallowed a taste and smiled. "This is delicious. Does your chef travel with you to England, or do you have another staff waiting to provide for your every need there?"

"He remains with me, whether it is the townhouse in London, my estate in Devon, or here."

"I have spent my whole life in one place," she remarked wistfully. "But tell me, do you leave belongings in one house that you swiftly miss in another?"

"Constantly." Michael had feared she would stare at her plate and ignore him all evening, but her questions appeared to be prompted by sincere interest. "Were it not for the services of an experienced valet, none of my clothing would match."

"He must be very fond of you." After another mouthful of soup, she rested her spoon on the plate to listen.

Michael nearly gestured with his soupspoon, but caught himself in time. "Hoskins was devoted to my father, but I fear he merely tolerates me. I agree that it's important to be well-groomed, but I don't wish to spend half the day at it as some men do."

"Which leaves Hoskins with little to do?"

"No, he shared my father's interest in botany and enjoys supervising the work in our vegetable garden. We produce an abundance here and keep everyone well-fed. I can't abide families that flaunt their wealth in public but starve their servants at home."

"Do such selfish people actually exist?"

Dismayed, her eyelashes nearly swept her brows, and had he not been fighting so hard to suppress his desire, he would have leaned over and kissed her. "I'm sorry to have mentioned such disagreeable folk if you were unaware of them."

"We've not traveled in the same circles, my lord. Indeed, I have not traveled at all."

She had always treated him kindly, even that first day, when he had been extremely rude to her. "I have faults as well," he admitted with a shrug. "But mistreating the men and women in my employ is not among them."

Delphine watched him finish the last drop of soup in his bowl. As she saw it, his greatest flaw was in always demanding his own way, but then he had been raised from infancy to expect no less. He was proud, but not vain, which was definitely an asset in such a handsome man.

"My mother complains that I spoil our servants, but when I tire of clothing that is still new, I'm happy to give it to our maid. As for our cook and housekeeper, we aren't the same size, so I give them other things, like perfume, or bonnets and gloves. Of course I buy them all nice presents on their birthdays and at Christmas. Does that seem too generous to you?"

He dipped his head as though he meant to tease her, but his words rang true. "Not at all, but then I've sworn to be generous with you."

"Yes, you have," she answered. "Fortunately for you, my needs are very few." Confused, she frowned slightly. Perhaps all he really wanted was time to consider the terms of their arrangement, rather than several days to forget they had ever met as she had feared.

"Nonsense. Beautiful women need all manner of pretty things from slippers in a new color to feathers for their hair."

"Well, a lady can't go about town barefooted, can she?"

"Of course not, and it would reflect very poorly on me if you were forced to wear anything other than the latest fashions."

She smiled as though she were amused, but when he insisted upon her living so far away from Kingston, she did not know how anyone would see her often enough to comment one way or the other.

"I loved the island," she revealed impulsively, "where a nightgown and straw hat were all that were required and grooming consisted of little more than standing beneath the cistern."

"I liked the island too. I'll either buy it from Guy, or find us another."

"Oh, I'd completely forgotten, but Guy told me that you'd described the men who brought that poor wretch there as a prisoner. He recognized the leader and spoke to him. Your theory was correct. The captive had gambled and lost more than he could afford. The others took him out to the island to frighten him into paying what he owed. I should have told you sooner."

"You had other things on your mind."

His smile now held a mischievous slant, as though he knew full well that he had been the distraction. Unfortunately, he was right again, but she refused to give him the satisfaction of saying so.

Instead, she asked him to relate the history of his family's plantation. Though he gave a remarkably entertaining account, as they were served a succession of succulent dishes, he failed to notice just how little of the elaborate meal she consumed.

That night, the dessert pastries were filled with lemon custard, but rather than again rush away, they lingered over dessert for more than an hour. Delphine was adept at posing questions that prompted a lengthy response, and Michael enjoyed illustrating his replies with amusing anecdotes.

It wasn't until she began to yawn that he realized how late the hour had grown. "I'm sorry. I'd hoped to get an early start in the morning, and we should have retired long before this."

He helped her from her chair, and escorted her to the dower house; but before he could find an appropriate way to bid her good-night that did not involve removing their clothing, she had reached up to kiss his cheek and gone inside.

It was all he could do not to follow her, but he forced himself to turn away. That evening, she had not made any of her usual provocative comments, nor delightfully intimate gestures. They had simply passed the time in engaging conversation as good friends do, and he had enjoyed every minute.

Now he could not recall a single item on the menu; but he did remember how the fond light in Delphine's eyes had shown brightly whenever she had met his gaze. He hoped it meant that she was coming around to his point of view, but hope was a pale comfort when he had to climb into bed alone.

Michael's head had barely brushed the pillow before he reached for his cock. Thoughts of Delphine had already made him hard, and he pretended that her small hands were wrapped around his shaft rather than his own. He spit on his thumb and rubbed it over the tip as though it was her tongue.

He had a vivid imagination, but it was memory as well as desire that swiftly brought him to a stunning release. He savored that heat, but without the real woman in his arms, the night would be much too long.

The next day, Michael went out to his stable to request that his carriage be made ready for the journey to Kingston, but he was swiftly informed that it was unnecessary. He balled his fists at his sides and tried not to shout, but failed.

"What do you mean, my lady's gone?"

The grooms, Jacob and Ned Cleghorn, were brothers in their teens and badly frightened that they had made a disastrous error. "She was standing right where you are, my lord," Ned declared, his voice breaking into a near squeal. "She said she was ready to leave for Kingston and there was no reason to hitch a team to the carriage for a single passenger."

"That's exactly how it was," Jacob swore. "She asked if there was a buggy and driver available."

Michael was so angry with Delphine, and with them for catering to her whims, that he could barely see. "So your father leapt at the chance to accommodate her?"

"No, my lord," Ned insisted. "He wasn't eager at all, but seeing as how she'll soon be your wife, he didn't dare refuse her."

"My wife?" Michael echoed numbly. "Did she make that claim?"

The boys shook their heads and answered in unison, "No, my lord."

Jacob took a step forward and rushed to explain, "She's the only woman you've ever brought here and so very pretty. Who else could she be?"

Michael sucked in a deep breath in a futile attempt to provide a rational response to the boys' ridiculous assumption. Fortunately, he was more angry with Delphine than with them. She always spoke with an aristocratic confidence that would send anyone rushing to do her bidding. These poor lads and their father would have been no challenge at all for her.

It had not occurred to him that she would take it upon herself to arrange transportation home. When she was so wildly unpredictable, he felt a fool for not even considering it. "How long ago did they leave?"

Ned scuffed his toe in the dirt. "First light, my lord. She was waiting for us when we came to see to the horses. Said she'd come with nothing, and had gathered it up, and was ready to go. Or something like that, if that's not her exact words."

"No, that sounds like her." After her comment about liking to sleep late, he wondered if she had bothered to sleep at all. Perhaps not; he had gotten precious little rest himself.

Indigo was swift, but with such an enormous head start, he'd not be able to overtake her on the road. He trusted the boys' father to serve as a respectful escort, but he was still furious to have lost the hours he had anticipated traveling with her.

He turned his back on the grooms and tried to decide how best to proceed. He could send a man with a letter, but it might take him a day or more to line up a coherent train of thought. He swore under his breath and turned back to the boys who were attempting to stand at attention, but shuffling their feet in a nervous dance.

"Saddle Indigo for me, please. I'm going into Kingston."

"Yes, my lord," Ned exclaimed, and he turned so quickly he slammed right into his brother and nearly knocked him down.

"Take your time, lads," Michael insisted, now that the damage was done; but he feared the ride to Kingston would not be nearly long enough to compose a civil greeting for Delphine once he had arrived.

Daniel Cleghorn was a man of few words, and because it was not his place to keep fine ladies entertained, he made no attempt to break the silence as he and Delphine traveled toward Kingston. He kept glancing toward her out of the corner of his eye, but she sat with her hands folded in her lap, apparently content to enjoy the scenery.

She was one of the prettiest young women he had ever seen. Her skin was as smooth as fresh cream, her eyes more green than blue and framed with long dark lashes, and her hair a shimmering pale gold. In his view, the master had made a wise choice in a second wife.

Of course, he had not met the first, but that poor girl had not lasted long. He and his wife had been together for twenty years, and while not all of them had been good, at least they had survived them. Of course, everyone expected fine ladies to be delicate, but it was a shame they lacked the stamina of a healthy country lass.

Delphine provided him with directions once they entered town, and then embarrassed him badly by insisting that he remain to have a meal and rest awhile before he returned home. That she had the master's kindness was another point in her favor, but he dared not ask her when the wedding would be.

Françoise had just gotten dressed when she heard her daughter's voice downstairs, and she hastened to question her. "I had no idea if I'd ever see you again. Please don't tell me you actually went to a convent, where surely they would have expelled you before nightfall."

Delphine sat down in the parlor, and rested her head against the back of her chair. "No, Michael took me home to his plantation, which is beautiful; but it's no place for me, or any mistress."

"You are right, of course, my darling. You need your own apartment. But where is Michael? Didn't he wish to speak with me today?"

Delphine told the truth rather than allow her mother to assume that Michael had sent her home alone. "I convinced him we ought to wait a week before again working on terms. Or at least I believe I did. We'll simply have to wait for him to appear to hear his side."

Françoise paced a moment and then, still perplexed, she sat down on the settee to face her daughter. "I fear we made a grave error in introducing you two."

Delphine was tired and sore from the buggy ride, but still unwilling to accept her mother's views. "We weren't politely introduced. He was stranded with me with no hope of escape. It's no wonder nothing has gone as you anticipated. I still loved visiting the island, though. Do you think Guy would take me back there?"

Françoise was astonished. "Yes, he will do anything you ask, but why would you wish to go alone?"

"It's very calm and peaceful, and I love the sea." She paused to cover a wide yawn. "But for today, I want only to take a long nap."

"You may sleep all afternoon, but first, change your gown and we'll visit Madame Deschamps to make certain that you remain in excellent health."

"No, I promised Michael I wouldn't do anything to harm the babe we may have created."

"And how will he know?" Françoise leaned forward to insist. "Surely you understand that men do not do well with the truth. They much prefer our affectionate fantasies."

"Michael is unlike other men."

Françoise laughed at that impossibility. "What, he has no cock?"

Delphine joined in her mother's laughter in spite of

herself. "Oh yes, he has a fine cock, but there's far more to him."

"True, there is his enormous wealth, and I intend for you to gain a proper share of it."

Delphine rose and kissed her mother on the cheek before starting toward the stairs. "His money does not interest me. Wake me for dinner, please."

"If money were not a vital concern of mine," Françoise remarked pointedly, "you'd have no fine bed in which to sleep. I suggest you dream of begging on the streets and awake in a better mood to plan your future."

Delphine had no reply, but she had slept little more than an hour before Michael strode through her bedroom door, released the corners of a sea-green scarf, and spilled an armful of lavender orchids across her bed.

"You have no idea how thrilled I am to actually find you here," he exclaimed with prickly sarcasm.

There was no hint of a smile lurking in his expression, and wary, Delphine sat up and looped her arms around her knees. "This is my home. Where else would I be?"

"Do you really expect me to offer suggestions you might swiftly use to avoid me?" he scoffed. "Now why did you leave the plantation alone?"

She slid her hair behind her ear to clear her view of him. Dressed in a dark green coat, fawn trousers, and a tan waistcoat, he was as strikingly handsome as ever. He also smelled slightly of horse sweat, and she feared he must have galloped Indigo all the way there. Her mother had always insisted all a woman need do was retreat, and a man would give furious pursuit. Here was clear proof.

"I meant to save you a tiresome trip to Kingston," she offered unapologetically.

"Really? I was looking forward to the journey with great anticipation. Didn't you insist only yesterday that you usually slept until noon?"

"It's true."

"Except for today." He widened his stance and clasped his hands behind his back as though he were an officer castigating slovenly troops.

Rather than rebel, she smiled invitingly. "So it would seem. I'm so sorry that you felt you had to follow me, but thank you for the beautiful orchids and this lovely silk scarf."

"You're most welcome." He pulled the chair by the window next to the bed and sat down. "Don't complain about my being in your boudoir, because we both know propriety has never concerned you."

"Nor will it ever." She plucked an orchid from the bed and twirled it by the stem.

He leaned forward slightly. "It may astonish you to learn that some women actually do precisely what's expected of them."

Delphine feigned surprise. "You don't say, but isn't that being an obedient pet rather than a flesh and blood woman?"

Too late, Michael realized how just stupid his comment had been. "My mistake," he conceded reluctantly. "For a moment, I forgot that you're a woman like no other."

He reached out to wind his fingers in her hair and pulled her close to trace the gentle bow of her lips with the tip of his tongue. He then invaded her mouth in a long, slow, deliberate assault on her senses. The orchids' sweet perfume was not nearly as tantalizing as her own sleepy fragrance, and drawing closer still, he moved to sit on the side of the bed to draw her more fully into his arms.

She melted against him, but he savored the sensation for no more than an instant before pulling away. "I'll give you five more days because I want them too. I also want your promise that you'll be here when I return."

When he stood, Delphine rolled off the other side of the bed, filled the basin on the washstand with water, and gathered up the scattered orchids to keep them fresh. "I wish you'd brought me only one flower and left the rest to bloom where they grew."

That wasn't the promise he had sought, and rapidly losing control of his temper, which he had sworn not to do, he adjusted the fit of his jacket with a fierce tug. "No caged birds, no orchids in vases, and you won't belong to me either, is that what you really mean?"

That he understood nothing was entirely her fault, and sorry to have confused him so badly, she turned toward him as she untied the ribbon at her neckline and sloughed off her nightgown.

"Lock the door," she ordered in a husky whisper. "Then we'll explore my meaning."

She retrieved the scarf from the bed and tied it in a loose triangle around her waist. "You'll not need your clothes, handsome though they may be."

Michael knew exactly what she was doing: illustrating in the most fascinating way what a man could expect from his mistress. For most men, an escape into a beautiful woman's softly lit bed chamber was enough. He was still gathering his resolve to walk out the door when she stretched out across the bed, rolled over on her back, and let her head drop down over the side.

"It isn't like you to be so shy," she coaxed. "Come here and slide your cock all the way down my throat. Or perhaps you'd care to wait five days. It will give you something to anticipate."

She arched her back, thrust her breasts toward him, and shook her hair to send it tumbling toward the floor. He just stared in wonder. She was like a multi-faceted jewel that changed colors with the shifting light. She had never struck a more debauched pose, and he refused to punish himself any further.

He crossed to the door in a single stride, turned the key in the lock, and flung his coat aside as he came back toward her. "You are wicked," he swore darkly.

"Only with you, my lord. You're the one who inspires it."

He knelt beside the bed to kiss her. It was a strange, upside-down kiss that tangled their tongues in a new and thoroughly provocative manner. He found her ringed nipple, tugged gently, then slid his hand over her stomach, and down between her legs. She opened to his caress obligingly, and rolled her hips to urge him to delve deep.

While that first kiss blurred into a dozen, she unbuttoned his waistcoat and pulled his shirt from his trousers. She cupped his sex through the fabric drawn tight by his erection and traced flowing patterns over his balls with her thumbnail.

Their kiss went on and on until, lost in her, he got to his feet, shoved his trousers out of his way, and spread the moisture seeping from the tip of his cock across her lower lip. She licked it up, then opened her mouth wide to suck him deep. She reached out to catch his hip and pulled him still closer. He swayed as the sweet torment built, then desperate for a far more intimate coupling, he pulled out.

Before Delphine could catch her breath, Michael swung her around, hooked her legs over his arms, and slid into her core. He felt her innermost muscles stretch and contract around him on each thrust. She had closed her eyes, lost in him as he was in her. Her lashes fluttered against her cheeks, and parted by rhythmic sighs, her kiss-swollen lips remained slightly open.

At the last moment, he withdrew to ejaculate over the smooth bowl of her stomach. She scooped it up to smear on her breasts while he dropped to his knees, propped her legs over his shoulders, and pierced her with his tongue. This time, she came in an explosive jerk. He had to rest a long moment with his cheek pressed to her thigh before he could focus clearly enough to stand.

Michael felt as though he had fallen into a whirl-pool, a veritable maelstrom, and been tossed to the shore half-drowned. He was so thoroughly bewitched, he did not know if he could even survive for five days without her. She lay sprawled half off the bed, her legs open and so inviting he had to force himself to look away as he pulled his clothing back into place.

"We'll begin counting the days tomorrow," he announced as he unlocked her door.

"Wait," Delphine called after him. "On the fifth day, meet me on the island rather than here."

Not trusting himself to speak, he nodded and closed her door gently behind him. His knees were still weak and his legs barely carried him downstairs to the foyer, where Guy stood waiting. Michael took one look at his friend's furious scowl and immediately understood that he would no longer be intimidated by dire threats.

Chapter 17

A resplendent love
Far beyond imagining
Life-long enchantment

Guy was disgusted with his old friend's disheveled appearance and shook his head ruefully. "Poor example though I may be, I'm all Delphine has to act as her father. Come into the parlor; you owe me a few minutes of your valuable time."

Grateful for an opportunity to rest before he left for home, Michael followed him and again chose the most substantial chair. He brushed his hair off his forehead with a quick swipe and leaned back, but his implacable expression remained unchanged.

"Go on, say whatever you like. I'm listening."

"Good, because I intend to save your life for a second time this month. Françoise and I had hoped that you and Delphine would develop an affection for one another, but the fierce attachment you've displayed is simply frightening."

Michael was of the same opinion, but he scowled rather than admit to it. He could still taste Delphine's salty sweetness on his lips, and the fact that she remained in bed upstairs was a distraction.

"You threw us together," he chided, "how dare you complain of the result?"

Guy raised a hand. "I have not even begun. Bear with me, please."

"I have for years," Michael snorted.

"And I with you," Guy insisted just as emphatically. "Though the title and estate I inherited doesn't compare with yours, I was also raised with high expectations. My parents chose my bride, and we've managed to produce children, but the marriage is a regrettable sham. I watched you walk into the same miserable trap, but now you're free to select your own bride."

Alarmed by the unexpected turn of their conversation, Michael sat forward. "I'm done with marriage."

"You may have had a wife, but you've never really been married. You may think it's acceptable to ravage Delphine in her own bed, but—"

"I may well have been the one who was ravaged, but I'll not complain."

"Don't be crude," Guy scolded. "Your father selected your bride while you were both still children. A sense of loyalty prompted you to accept his choice, but your duty's done. You can't insist that Delphine give you children without doing her the honor of making her your wife. She deserves better."

Guy rose and straightened up to his full height, which was several inches shorter than Michael's. "Go home and give marriage some serious consideration. Delphine's a treasure, and your family could certainly use some new blood."

Now sorry that he had tarried the extra minutes, Michael shoved to his feet. "The only blood you're likely to see will come gushing from your nose." For a terrifying moment, he looked as though he meant to follow through on that harsh prediction, but then, shifting away, he brushed by Guy and made his way to the door.

Françoise had been straining to hear from the dining room, and as soon as the front door closed, she hurried into the parlor. "I couldn't overhear every word, but there was no mistaking Michael's belligerent tone."

Before responding, Guy drew her into his arms and hugged her to savor his own good fortune. "Quite frankly, I expected his reaction to be far worse; the truth has a way of burrowing through a man's thoughts with the zeal of an ambitious mole. He may protest, but he can't ignore my advice."

Françoise had not trusted the truth in decades. She leaned into Guy's embrace and swore softly, "I may kill you yet."

Guy smothered his chuckle in a kiss. There was something wonderfully exciting about a Frenchwoman bent on revenge.

Michael sped away from Kingston, but he could not escape Guy's appalling advice. Marriage meant Amelia to him, and any thought of her brought nearly overwhelming pain. Before he had covered half the distance toward home, he had to swing off the road and dismount. He sat down beneath a Blue Mahoe tree, cradled his head in his hands, and left Indigo to graze unheeded.

He had pointedly ignored Delphine's mention of secrets, but whether it had merely been a lucky guess or more evidence that she was an unusually perceptive young woman, she had been right. What she did not understand, however, was how closely he guarded his secrets.

This horror had nothing to do with Delphine and what he felt for her. Still, like quicksand, it lay dark and malevolent, silently awaiting a misstep. Had he ever done anything right with Delphine, he worried, or had every exchange led them closer to an inevitable parting?

He flopped back on the grass and stared up at the sunlight sparkling through the leafy canopy overhead and wished his way were as bright and clear. Despite Delphine's stubborn insistence on favorable terms, she had never actually agreed to become his mistress, so perhaps there was no point in tearing open old wounds for her sake.

If only he knew how deeply her feelings for him ran, then the risk of facing his past would not be so great. But other than when she was furiously angry with him, he had never been able to tell her artful pretense from sincere emotion.

He would not find the answer to that quandary, and too anxious to waste another minute lounging in the forest, he got to his feet and caught Indigo's trailing reins. He might not be able to think any more clearly at home, but at least he could try.

When Delphine joined Guy and her mother for dinner, they greeted her warmly, but she caught a conspiratorial glance flying between them. "I hope you've not devised another plot against Michael," she greeted them.

"Of course not," Guy assured her. "I've learned my lesson where he's concerned, but I insist that you not make any decisions until you've spoken with him. Let him describe his feelings first. You must give him the opportunity to surprise you."

That night, Delphine was too exhausted to pursue more than a few grains of rice floating in her soup, and she nodded. "We plan to meet on the island in five days, but I'd like for you to take me there early."

Perplexed, Françoise pursed her lips slightly. "Do you really believe that's wise?" she asked.

"Yes, everything is clearer to me there."

Guy was far too sensitive a man to overlook her downcast mood. "Are you merely confused," he asked, "or would you rather not see Michael ever again? If that's the case, I'll arrange a passage to England for you. Then I'll meet Michael on the island with whatever message you'd care to leave for him."

His question was so unexpected, and yet prompted such incredible sorrow, Delphine's eyes flooded with hot tears. She brushed them away, but fought to choke back a revealing sob. How had she ever thought she could leave Michael?

"I don't want to even imagine a world without him."

Guy leaned over to pat her hand. "I didn't mean to upset you, my darling, forgive me. I've already put a plan in motion which should please everyone. But you mustn't be afraid to love Michael with all your heart. It's what he needs most desperately. You must trust me to know what's best for you both. Can you do that?"

She nodded. Guy was such a charming man, but when she did not trust her own heart not to break into pieces, she dared not rely on his romantic schemes.

Michael had dined alone for months before he met Delphine, but that night he could barely concentrate long enough to eat, let alone continue making his way through Sir Walter Scott's *Guy Mannering*. The tale was rife with adventure and romance, but impossible to follow when the whole world seemed to be pressing in on him and he had no ready defense.

Laying the novel aside, he glanced toward Delphine's place and recalled how she had made even their simple meals on the island a feast. Without her, his chef's beautifully prepared entrée was tasteless. He ate, but only to stave off the pain of hunger, and he left his wine untouched.

As the moon rose, he went out for a long walk in hopes that exercise would help him sleep, but once in bed, he was unable to relax. He punched his pillows and stacked them down the center of the bed, but they were a pitiful substitute for the shapely young woman he missed with every breath.

He lay awake long past midnight, reliving the time they had shared. Though he might still suspect her motives, he came to the stunning realization that while desire had always flavored his kiss, and concern shaped his every action, he had not once revealed how deeply he cared for her in words.

He had arrogantly told her what he expected, but never why. Reluctantly, he began to suspect the barriers he had built around his own heart might keep him from ever winning Delphine's. But what if he revealed the truth of his tragic marriage, and she still turned him away?

Dawn came before he finally understood that while he had stubbornly refused to discuss his wife, no secret, no matter how painful, was worth keeping if it cost him Delphine. Without having slept, he left his bed eager to begin making plans. Lacking her gift for poetry, he would have to rely on heartfelt emotion, and pray it would be enough.

On the agreed upon day, Michael sailed out to the island in a sloop he had purchased two days earlier. He tied up at the dock, and believing he had arrived before Delphine, he hurriedly carried two baskets of provisions into the cottage.

There were already orchids in a vase on the table, and while they could not be the same flowers he had taken her, they were as deep a lavender. Her journal lay there too, and the shawl he had given her was draped over the back of one of the chairs. Eager to find her, he shrugged off his coat and waistcoat and went back out on the sand.

Scanning the beach, he saw her way off in the distance, gathering shells along the shore. If he weren't mistaken, she was dressed in a nightgown and the ruffled hem fluttered around her ankles with every step. Her hat was perched atop her head at a jaunty angle, but the breeze still made trailing ribbons of her fair hair.

He rolled up his sleeves until the left just covered her name. Because the tattoo had been drawn on his inner arm, Guy had failed to notice it the morning he had awakened them on the beach; it was easy to imagine how flabbergasted his friend would have been had he seen it.

"Fierce attachment, indeed," Michael muttered under his breath. "Guy doesn't know the half of it."

He forced himself to focus on what he wished to say, but it was difficult when he longed take Delphine in his arms and never let her go. He counted to twenty so he would not appear ridiculously eager to see her, then ducked back into the cottage, emptied the smaller of the two baskets, and carried it out to her.

"I thought you might need something for your shells," he greeted her.

Delphine had seen his boat arrive, but deliberately slowed her return to the cottage. She had gotten up with the dawn, but had only a half-dozen shells to show for her efforts. She did have news, but even after she had swallowed hard, it was desperately difficult to impart.

"Thank you," she replied hoarsely. "Perhaps you'll help me find a few more."

"I have all day," he responded, "but first there's something I need to explain."

Delphine gazed up at him. The breeze had tangled his hair, but he was still the handsomest man she had ever seen. "Yes, so do I."

"I'm sure you do, and while I don't mean to be impolite, I insist on going first." He slid his hand down her arm and laced his fingers in hers. "Let's go back to the cottage and sit in the shade."

"As you wish." Delphine walked along beside him as she had so many times, but there was something different about him that morning. He was in a friendly mood, but uncharacteristically anxious.

Guy had begged her to encourage Michael to talk, even if it took him all day to describe what he had done while they had been apart. Her mother had insisted it was always wise to allow a man to speak for as long as he wished, but even sensible advice failed to alleviate Delphine's dread of what Michael might say.

"I bought lemonade," he remembered suddenly. "Would you care for some?"

"Yes, thank you, that would be very nice." She removed her hat and laid it on a chair, then waited at the cottage door while he opened the jug and poured two cups. She took hers and raised it in a toast. "To whatever the day brings."

He touched his cup to hers and led her to their usual places beside the fire pit. He waited for her to make herself comfortable, then sat down opposite her and took a quick drink.

He sucked in a deep breath and began before his courage deserted him. "All you know about me is what you see, or rather, what I've allowed you to see."

Delphine knew better than to interrupt, and she simply nodded to acknowledge his point. She sipped her lemonade, which was the best she had every tasted, sweet, but with a lingering tart accent. She let it slide down her throat and glanced out toward the sea.

Michael focused on the ashes of their last fire. "Amelia's father was my father's best friend, and they no doubt agreed upon a match between our families before either of us was born. I was eight years her senior, but I remember her as a beautiful child. She had huge brown eyes and hair that fell in perfect curls.

"I don't recall just when my father told me how pleased he would be if I chose Amelia for my wife, but I was too young to want a bride. That I remember clearly. As for Amelia's parents, they were very protective and made certain we were never alone for even a minute.

"She was petite, and when she came to London for her first season, she was adorable. She loved to dance and was an excellent partner. She had many admirers, but I was the one she married that autumn."

He was describing his wife in such flattering terms, and Delphine readily understood why Amelia was the only woman he would ever love. That dreary prospect made her want to clap her hands over her ears and run away, but she sat on the sand in graceful disarray and listened attentively.

Michael's voice deepened as he sifted through the facts she needed to know. "I was twenty-six and she was eighteen. I won't pretend that I was eager to wed, but I knew it was time, and while my parents were no longer living, Amelia had been their enthusiastic choice."

When he fell silent, Delphine had an excruciating wait. Then he turned his arm, and she caught a glimpse of her name. If he were still in love with his late wife, why wouldn't he be wearing Amelia's name rather hers? Surely he must have feelings for her or he would never have made such a flamboyant gesture. Elated by that tardy realization, she allowed herself a quiet burst of hope.

"We were married in the cathedral in Exeter and the party following at my estate lasted several days. But when Amelia was seated beside me after the wedding, I finally realized that while she was adept at flirting, at hiding her smile demurely behind her fan, or gazing up at a man as though she were fascinated by his every word, I'd never heard her express a single original thought."

"I hoped it was merely the excitement of the ceremony, or marriage itself, but when we were finally alone that night, I could at last appreciate how clever her parents had been in always surrounding her with charming relatives who carried the conversation while she merely smiled. She had a radiant smile that promised much, but there was nothing behind it.

"I was stunned when you mentioned true beauty involved intelligence and spirit, or it would be as uninvolving as a decorative painting. That was all Amelia was, decorative."

He caught Delphine's eye and smiled. "I'm sorry. I'm doing my best to be brief."

Hope now a bright glow in her heart, she smiled as well. "Please take all the time you need."

"No, I want this over and done." He took a long drink of lemonade. "I would rather my daughters were raised as you were rather than allow them to retain a child's innocence of men. I don't even know how to describe our wedding night, but Amelia was so terrified of being alone with me that I had to get her quite drunk before I could come close enough to kiss her.

"I had already discovered she wasn't very bright, but she was young, and I thought in time she might come to enjoy my affection. When she awoke the next morning, I doubt she could recall anything that had transpired between us. I had been very gentle, but she shrank away from me as though she'd been abused.

"Thank God I had been with women who welcomed me to their beds, or I might have believed her low opinion of my skill as a lover. Still, I harbored the foolish hope that given time, we might have, if not a stimulating marriage, at least a moderately affectionate one.

"I wanted to bring her here to Jamaica for our honeymoon, but she couldn't bear to be away from her family for the holidays, so we remained in Devon.

"She continually shied away from me, and I'd not approached her since our wedding night, but that one time, with my drunken bride, was enough for her to become pregnant. She was ecstatic at the prospect of a child, and not because she wished to become a mother, but because she assumed she would not have to submit to me again. That was the word she used, *submit*."

Michael looked up and was shocked by the tears rolling down Delphine's cheeks. That she understood how badly he had been hurt, and was hurt as well, was ample proof of her feelings for him. He quickly moved to her side of the fire pit and sat down behind her to wrap her in a fond embrace. He pulled her back against his chest and nuzzled her cheek.

"Please don't cry," he begged. "You'll only make me feel worse than I already do."

She covered his hands with her own and laid her cheek against his shoulder. "I can't help but cry, for you and for poor Amelia, who didn't know enough to appreciate what a wonderful man you are. Why do mothers, who obviously know the joys of the marriage bed, keep their daughters so insufferably ignorant?"

"To keep them chaste, of course. But I don't believe all marriage beds are joyful. Not when couples are forced to wed strangers for their bloodlines, as you described it."

"I shouldn't have said that."

"No, you were right, but the proper bloodlines often don't make for a true marriage." Holding her made revealing that wretched year easier than he had thought possible, but he still failed to stifle a poignant sigh.

"Amelia loved being pregnant. She was surrounded by attentive relatives and friends. She loved to go shopping, and brought a great many things for our son. I never entered her bedroom, and she did not even come close to mine, but when others were around, she pretended to be very proud of her handsome husband."

"But you really had no wife," Delphine whispered.

"No, I didn't. But you must realize that I had close friends, like Guy, who regarded marriage as a tiresome responsibility necessary to ensure the birth of heirs, while they felt free to love whomever they chose. I might have welcomed a mistress's attentions one day, but I was faithful to Amelia.

"I had a fine doctor attend her, because I wanted to make certain that she knew exactly what would happen in childbirth. Unfortunately, at the first twinge of pain, she became hysterical. She was convinced she was dying, which she was, but none of us believed her frantic screams.

"It hurt me too badly to listen to her, and I was the last person she wanted near, so I left her with her doctor and mother, and walked to the cliffs overlooking the sea. After a while, I made my way down to the water. The doctor had told it me the child probably wouldn't be born before nightfall, so I stayed away all afternoon."

He stopped there and hugged Delphine so tightly she could scarcely breathe. "I understand," she said softly. "When you returned, Amelia was dead."

He dried his tears on his sleeve. "They both were. The boy was stillborn, and despite the doctor's best efforts, Amelia had bled to death. Her mother, a woman I'd known my whole life, shrieked at me for abandoning them, but no one could have predicted how badly things would turn out.

"Our son was perfect. He had a thatch of black

hair, long eyelashes, all his fingers and toes. I held him all night. The next morning, I dressed him in his christening gown, and he was buried in his mother's arms.

"Our marriage had lasted less than a year, but it was the worst year of my life. I hadn't loved Amelia, but I would have loved our son, and he would have been a fine boy. It was his death that broke my heart.

"Amelia's family had taken great pride in our marriage, but they were so bitter over her death that they turned on me in an instant. Whether they started them or not, hideous rumors began to circulate about the kind of husband I'd been. At the same time, I was nearly smothered by my friends' effusive sympathy.

"I came home to Jamaica and stayed drunk until Guy refused to allow me to wallow in such sorry self-pity. Had he left me alone, I honestly believe I would have shaken off my sorrow in time, but then I'd not have met you, which would have been another great tragedy."

Delphine turned in his arms and kissed away the last of his tears. "I wish we had met sooner. I'm so sorry you were all alone with your grief."

He caught her hands and leaned back to study her expression, but rather than the pity he would have promptly rejected, he saw only a reflection of the love he felt for her. The words came easily to him now, but he had practiced.

"*Je vous aime.*"

"Oh, Michael, you've been studying French?"

She looked delighted, so he kissed her soundly and then tried again. "I've only learned two phrases, but I was hoping you'd say the same thing to me."

"Yes, I love you too. *Je vous aime beaucoup.*"

"You don't think less of me for swearing off marriage because Amelia and I were so unhappy?"

She ran her fingertips across his tattoo. "No, with my name written on your arm, it's a wise decision."

"It might have been at one time, but no longer." He kissed her again and again, until at last they lay sprawled on the edge of the ashes. "As I said, I learned two things in French, and I hope I'll say this right. *Voulez-vous m'épouser?*"

His weight kept her from leaping to her feet, but she stared up him as astonished as though he had suddenly sprouted huge feathered wings. "Marry you? Oh, Michael, you know we can't marry."

He caught her wrists and leaned down to nuzzle her throat. "Why not? It sounds like a very good idea to me. You don't want our children to be bastards who'd be shunned by polite society."

His tender kisses tickled her throat and Delphine tipped her head back in the sand. Michael had been with Amelia only once, and he had been with Delphine often, but the results had not been the same. "I'm so sorry to disappoint you, but there is no child. So you needn't offer marriage."

He sat up and pulled her into his arms. "Did I ask you about a child before I made the offer?"

"No, but—"

"Delphine, I do want to have children with you, but it's you I want most. Now when a man proposes, rather than change the subject, it's customary for a woman to provide a response, preferably a favorable one."

Overwhelmed, she threw her arms around his neck and hugged him for a long moment before drawing away. Her mother had not prepared her for this, but she could answer only one way. "I'm honored, of course, but no. I can't marry you."

She tried to stand, but he clamped his hands around her waist and moved her across his lap. "When you say you love me, no is the wrong answer. I'll not accept it."

"I do love you, and dearly, but you can't marry a—"

"Don't say it. You're no whore."

"That's not what your friends will say." She was adamant about it, but when he ducked his head, she could not resist returning his kiss. His mouth was warm and inviting, and he was the first to pull away.

"It wouldn't be enough to have you as my mistress," he swore against her lips.

She kissed him again. "No, I'll not be your mistress either."

Michael rested his forehead against hers. "But you'll love me forever."

"And then even longer," she assured him.

That the woman he adored loved him too, yet was still so impossible to keep, was almost more than he could bear. Almost. "What shall we do then?" he asked. "Shall we just swim out into the Caribbean until we drown?"

She stared at him in horror. "No! What an awful idea."

Confident he had her full attention, he kissed her again. "You're right, that would be a cowardly thing to do. It would also be a waste of the nice pony I bought for you."

"You not only studied French, you purchased a pony?"

"*Oui.* She's a ginger-colored mare with a white mane and tail and a very sweet disposition. You'll love her. I also bought the sloop you see tied at the dock. I thought as often as we'll want to come here, we ought to own a boat."

Delphine bit her lip rather than cry, but she was touched by how much he had done for her. He had been so honest with her, she could no longer postpone her own confession. "From the moment I fell in love with you, I knew I couldn't be your mistress. That's why I gave myself to you our last afternoon on the island. It was meant as good-bye."

He tilted her chin with his fingertip. "A mistress can't love her paramour?"

His blue eyes shone with a curious light, not disdain, and she struggled to explain. "No, it makes her too desperate for his affection, and he'll quickly tire of her and seek another."

He was amazed she thought his behavior would be so easily predictable, and then he knew why. He kissed her cheeks lightly. "That's your mother's opinion?"

"Yes, and one she gained rather painfully after she'd given away her heart."

"I see, so she's speaking from experience. But you mustn't confuse your life with hers. She's known only men who were dissatisfied at home and seeking an affectionate companion. That isn't our situation at all.

"It seems you were convinced you shouldn't love me, and I thought you never would. We were both wrong, but we needn't compound our mistakes."

"I agree, but you can't take a wife who lacks a fine family or even a fine reputation of her own."

"Is that your only concern, that if I marry you, it will disgrace me somehow?"

"Well, it surely would, and you don't deserve that."

"I don't deserve to live the rest of my life without

you, either. Now if it's simply a fine family you believe you need, let's invent one."

"You can't just make up a family. I do have a mother, and a father who was lost at sea." She tucked her hair behind her ear, and waited for him to accept the obvious.

She was seated so proudly on his lap, but her filmy nightgown had slipped off her shoulder to allow a glimpse of a succulent pink nipple and a bright gold ring. That he had once been shocked rather than aroused by the sight amused him now.

"You're right of course, you do have parents, but that's no reason not to create a slight variation on the truth if you're worried about disgrace."

He'd slid a hand beneath her gown, and Delphine's breath quickened as he began to tease her thighs apart. "What sort of variation did you have in mind?" she asked breathlessly.

"Your mother claims to have fled the French revolution."

"Yes, and only her tender age and a devoted gardener saved her from the guillotine." Too late she realized that in raising up slightly to respond, she had invited a more intimate caress. They were discussing such a serious topic, but accepting the inevitable, she arched her back to rub against his hand.

He shifted position slightly to loosen her gown. "England is at peace with France and people are inclined to be sympathetic to aristocratic refugees. All we need say is that your family fled the revolution with little more than their lives, and that your safety depends upon continued secrecy in the matter. What people imagine will be their own choice."

"My mother has never made any claims to royal

blood." He was rubbing her ever so gently, and a delicious warmth flooded her as she relaxed against his chest.

"Neither will we, but Delphine, you have the beauty of a princess and carry yourself like a queen. Anyone who meets you will readily accept you as a suitable wife. As for me, I will love you forever, and be proud to be your husband. Have you any other reservations that must be disposed of before I carry you inside?"

"Your children would be half-French," she cautioned.

"A quarter French actually, you mustn't forget your father." A father he doubted was either a Russian count or a seafaring Dane. But he would know who had fathered her children, and nothing else mattered to him in the slightest. "Is there anything else?"

"Men don't often love their wives," she murmured, "and I couldn't bear to share you with a mistress."

He understood everything now and eased her off his lap long enough to stand and scoop her up in his arms. "You were raised to believe a mistress had to remain aloof to retain a man's affection, and that wives were miserable, lonely creatures whom husbands never loved."

She nibbled his earlobe. "Isn't it true much of the time?"

"I've no idea because I've not studied the question as your mother has, but it isn't true with us, is it?"

He sat her down on the edge of the bed and began to ease her nightgown slowly up her long, lightly tanned legs, and then gently eased it over her head. When it went sailing toward the floor, she stretched out and closed her eyes.

"No, my darling, I believe we've created our own truth."

"Exactly, *mon chère*, now let's live it." He nearly ripped off his clothing to join her in the bed. She welcomed him with a playful giggle, and as he slid into her with a single deep thrust, he realized she had given him an indelible erotic dream, and vowed to make all their memories just as sweet.

"Delphine, did you happen to bring along that silk scarf I gave you?"

SHIRL HENKE

What happens when a beautiful lady gambler faces off against a professional card shark with more aces up his sleeve than the Missouri River has snags? A steamboat trades hands, the loser forfeits his clothes, and all hell breaks loose on the levee. But events only get wilder as the two rivals, now reluctant partners, travel upriver. Delilah Raymond soon learns that Clint Daniels is more than he appears. As the polished con man reverts to an earlier identity—Lightning Hand, the lethal Sioux warrior—the ghosts of his past threaten to tear apart their tempestuous union. Will the River Nymph take him too far for redemption, or could Delilah be his ace in the hole?

The RIVER NYMPH

AVAILABLE FEBRUARY 2008!

ISBN 13: 978-0-8439-6011-2

EMILY BRYAN

BARING IT ALL

From the moment she saw the man on her doorstep, Lady Artemisia, Duchess of Southwycke, wanted him naked. For once, she'd have the perfect model for her latest painting. But as he bared each bit of delicious golden skin from his broad chest down to his—oh, my!—art became the last thing on her mind.

Trevelyn Deveridge was looking for information, not a job. Though if a brash, beautiful widow demanded he strip, he wasn't one to say no. Especially if it meant he could get closer to finding the true identity of an enigmatic international operative with ties to her family. But as the intrigue deepened and the seduction sweetened, Trev found he'd gone well beyond his original mission of...

DISTRACTING the DUCHESS

AVAILABLE MARCH 2008!   ISBN 13: 978-0-8439-5870-6

LAURA DREWRY

GIVING THE DEVIL HIS DUDE

Shoveling sulfur and brimstone could really get a girl down.
When her dad offered freedom from the fiery depths in
exchange for one simple soul-snatching, Lucy Firr jumped
at the chance. With her considerable powers of seduction,
she threw herself at rancher Jed Caine. Yet instead of taking
her to bed, he made her muck out the pigsty.

It would take the patience of a saint to resist the likes of
Lucy Firr—and Lord knew Jed was no saint. The temptress
fired his blood like no woman he'd ever met. Why she'd
suddenly latched on to him, he had no idea. But the safest
place for her—and her virtue—was out in the barn.

She was supposed to steal his soul, yet here he was...
capturing her heart.

THE DEVIL'S DAUGHTER

AVAILABLE APRIL 2008!

ISBN 13: 978-0-8439-6048-8

To order a book or to request a catalog call:
1-800-481-9191
This book is also available at your local bookstore, or you can
check out our Web site **www.dorchesterpub.com** where you
can look up your favorite authors, read excerpts, or glance at
our discussion forum to see what people have to say about
your favorite books.